Writing Queer Performance

Writing Queer Performance

Contemporary Texts and Documents

Edited by
FINTAN WALSH

methuen | drama
LONDON • NEW YORK • OXFORD • NEW DELHI • SYDNEY

METHUEN DRAMA
Bloomsbury Publishing Plc
50 Bedford Square, London, WC1B 3DP, UK
1385 Broadway, New York, NY 10018, USA
29 Earlsfort Terrace, Dublin 2, Ireland

BLOOMSBURY, METHUEN DRAMA and the Methuen Drama logo are trademarks of Bloomsbury Publishing Plc

First published in Great Britain 2025

Cover design by Matt Thame
Cover image © Davis Hoyle

A catalogue record for this book is available from the British Library.

A catalog record for this book is available from the Library of Congress.

ISBN: HB: 978-1-3504-3150-8
PB: 978-1-3504-3149-2
ePDF: 978-1-3504-3152-2
eBook: 978-1-3504-3151-5

Series: Methuen Drama Play Collections

Typeset by RefineCatch Limited, Bungay, Suffolk
Printed and bound in Great Britain by Bell & Bain Ltd, Glasgow

To find out more about our authors and books visit www.bloomsbury.com and sign up for our newsletters.

Contents

Acknowledgements

In the course of developing this anthology, I engaged in sustained conversations with the artists represented, which required them to write and revise performance texts, retrieve documentation and photographs, solicit permissions, and recall information that had already slipped from easy recall. I'm grateful to all those included for their willingness, commitment and patience to bring this publication to print, including David Hoyle, Dickie Beau, George Heyworth, Ivor MacAskill, Le Gateau Chocolat, Liv Morris, Louise Mothersole, Ray Young, Rebecca Biscuit, Rosana Cade and Vijay Patel. Those with whom they work were also extraordinarily helpful during the process, including Jayne Compton, Lauren Church and Princess Bestman. In the early stages of developing the project, Mojisola Adebayo shared valuable insights from her experience of editing the anthology (with Lynette Goddard) *Black British Queer Plays and Practitioners: An Anthology of Afriquia Theatre* (2023). I'm thankful to Mojisola for her exchanges, including for providing me with a steer on work that deserved attention. I'm also grateful to peer reviewers for their appraisals.

Special thanks are due to Dom O'Hanlon, Commissioning Editor for Plays at Methuen Drama, for his enthusiasm for this project, which emerged during a conversation in 2022. Dom's dedication to publishing under-represented voices and forms is the reason why anthologies such as this one exist.

I first encountered the work of many of the artists included in this anthology while living in Dublin in the 2000s, through the programming of THISISPOPBABY, led by Jenny Jennings and Phillip McMahon, including David Hoyle, Dickie Beau, Bourgeois & Maurice and Le Gateau Chocolat. I remain in awe of all that Jenny and Phillip have done to develop, expand and internationalize queer performance, and nurture and support its artists, and dedicate my contribution to this anthology to them both.

Fintan Walsh, London, 2024

Introduction: Brief, Bright Life

Fintan Walsh

Queer performance is expected to live a brief, bright life and not circulate as text for reading, record or reproduction. Indeed, it rarely begins with a coherent script at all, often being developed instead via devising, co-creation and ad hoc practices, taking the form of outlines, notes and diagrams, with a script sometimes only emerging during rehearsals or following the creation of a performance. These modes of making typically prioritize performance strategies designed to fill the noisy bars, clinking cabaret venues, awkwardly repurposed social spaces and small fringe theatres in which queer performance is often presented, frequently for short runs, while also reflecting an economy of disposability that assumes that this work need not be engaged again. However, the dearth of published queer performance writing and documentation belies the varied textual forms and practices that surround its creation, while rendering it vulnerable to disappearance in the diaphanous archives of memory. This anthology intervenes these conditions of production by documenting some of the UK's most exciting queer performance via a combination of performance texts and performance documents (e.g. photographs and evidence of supporting text).[1] It does so to highlight queer performance's textual basis, to ensure its recording in print, and to enable its circulation long after the event of live performance.

In the past decade in the UK, queer performance has become a thriving form, filling bars, clubs, theatres, festivals and digital platforms. This flourishing was enabled by the generous programming of venues (e.g. Camden People's Theatre, London; HOME, Manchester; Soho Theatre, London; The Royal Vauxhall Tavern, London), festivals (e.g. VAULT Festival, London; Homotopia Festival, Liverpool; Fierce Festival, Birmingham; SPILL Festival, Ipswich; Outburst Queer Arts Festival, Belfast; Edinburgh Festival Fringe) and organizations (e.g. Live Art Development Agency, London).[2] Despite this growth, the emphasis within the form has remained on the artist as performer, despite the fact that many performers also write their own material. In one positive sense, this condition has helped nurture queer performance aesthetics and contributed to the professionalization of the form and its performers. Simultaneously, however, it also risks downplaying the literary and textual dimensions of the work, including the status of the queer performer as writer, whose work merits textual documentation in the service of continued engagement. While contemporary queer theatre and performance in the UK has been the subject of academic research (e.g. Walsh, 2023; Greer, 2019), nothing substantial has been published on its processes of creation, in particular the unique modes of writing and textual documentation that underpin it. The selection in this anthology features work representing a range of forms, themes, cultural views and generational perspectives, to offer a panoramic snapshot of the writing practices and textual modes that support contemporary queer performance in the UK.

Performers writing, writers performing

There are a number of reasons why the evolution of queer performance has prioritized the live event and the performer. First, queer performance typically aims to promote LGBTQ+ visibility and assembly in the varied spaces of its production. For Alyson Campbell and Stephen Farrier, queer performance assumes that there is 'something in excess of the logic of language', in particular the 'affective, experiential, transgressive power of performance' (2016: 13). Second, in a cultural climate that assumes queer performance to be a niche enterprise, its staging often depends on the determination of individual artists to support it from the birth of an idea through to performance, to secure a successful production. Third, queer performance is largely considered to be an ephemeral and expendable form, which primarily speaks to the moment of its production and does not necessarily merit textual or other forms of documentation for future reference. Fourth, queer performance – including written work – is often closely connected to the identity, experience and sensibility of its makers, laying the conditions by which its creators either don't want the work reproduced by others, or they can't rely on anyone else do so, rendering a published script less significant.

This anthology seeks to counter some of these expectations by featuring the performance texts of writers and performers whose work has never been published before, with the exception of Sh!t Theatre.[3] While certainly not an exhaustive selection, it includes texts and documents that cover a range of forms, approaches, themes and cultural perspectives. While my decision to publish this anthology is underpinned by a wish to afford queer performance writing due recognition and dissemination, it has also been informed by more personal reasons of often struggling to access materials to research and share with students. Many of us who research and teach queer performance will have had the experience of trying to cobble together an impression of a live performance from reviews or grainy YouTube clips, sometimes seeking out a performer's contact information to request a draft script. The anthology not only serves, therefore, to give due status to the writing that surrounds queer performance, but to enable its wide circulation for future research, teaching, reading and reference.

There are risks, of course, in elevating the status of the text within queer performance. The most obvious one is that it may afford an over-determined value to the written document, which might downplay the unique aesthetic features of queer performance, or expose artists to a literary critique of a 'well-made play' that doesn't acknowledge the nuanced and complex contexts of queer performance making, production and reception. A text can never fully capture the electricity that surges through a live performance encounter, which will differ every night, and often depart from a script. Additionally, live performance gives artists the freedom to say and do things that can evade the kind of scrutiny reserved for the written word. In Sh!t Theatre's *DollyWould*, for example, this is apparent in the script's redaction of text to circumvent the risk of defaming its subject, which would be heightened by print publication, and to enjoy the protections afforded to caricature and parody under UK copyright law.[4] But this anthology proceeds from the conviction that the benefits of elevating performance texts outweigh the risks of their erasure.

Writing/Making

While endeavouring to amplify queer performance writing with this anthology, I think of the works gathered here as performance texts rather than play scripts. While plays are typically written by playwrights to be performed by others, over and over again, performance texts are more akin to templates or scores, often to be interpreted, adapted and performed by those who write them. While a play is often quite fixed by the night of its production, or via a published script, performance texts are agile, elastic forms designed to guide or document a performance. The inclusion of additional textual and visual documents with each performance text in this anthology evidences the broader conceptualization of writing and text that queer performance requires.

In capturing the multiplicity of roles that queer artists typically perform, they are frequently referred to by the catch-all term 'performance-makers'. In *Theatre-Making: Interplay Between Text and Performance in the 21st Century*, Duška Radosavljević examines the history of the shifting hierarchies of text and performance in theatre production. While playwrighting tends to locate the authority of a production in a single author, including when it comes to new play productions, Radosavljević tracks how the evolution of the term 'theatre-making' 'implies a different model of the division of labour to the previously established ones which feature clearly delineated playwrights, directors, designers, producers and actors' (2013: 23). In devised theatre, as opposed to text-led theatre, Radosavljević argues, 'the creative process seems to be more important than the formal division of labour itself' (2013: 23).

Radosavljević's study of theatre-making illuminates how the decentralization of the text in performance produces a different system of roles and hierarchies, which emphasizes collaborative process. But it also suggests that this shift is not just the result of ethical, aesthetic or methodological factors, but potentially also 'perpetuated by political and economic reasons' (2013: 86). Similarly, queer performance is often developed by collaborative methods, rather than a single playwright's pre-prepared text, which reflects the sociality of queer cultural production, as well as the economic necessity of makers working together to put on a show, rather than necessarily relying on play commissioning to support it from the outset, or an independent director to lead a script to production. One of the ways we see this show up in the work represented in this collection is that performance is often developed by a variety of performance making practices, with writers also often serving as performers, directors, producers and designers. In this, the work reflects John Freeman's observation in *New Performance/New Writing* that 'No clear distinctions between performance and theatre, or performance writing and performance composition exist' (2007: 8).

The status of queer performance writing reflects some of the broader changes to and supports for writing in the UK in the past three decades, and in particular in England. As outlined in the British Theatre Consortium's report Writ Large: New Writing on the English Stage, in the 1990s the term 'new writing' was used to describe the dramatic growth of 'individually-written works, predominantly straight plays', with devised work and physical theatre considered 'a minority component' (2009: 8). In 2000, the Arts Council of England published The Boyden Report (2000), which claimed that traditional text-based theatre was in decline, advocating for more collaborative means of making. Subsequent reports embedded this emphasis, with The Next Stage: Towards a National Policy for Theatre in England (2000) calling for an embrace of 'the creative and commercial potential of collaborative practice' (7), and The Arts Council of England's National Policy for Theatre in England (2000) promoting experimentation (3) and a 'culture of innovation' that favoured new ways of working and collaborative practice (5). These policy recommendations were seen by many playwrights as privileging devised, performance-based work over individually-written new plays (Writ Large, 2009: 4). Despite this, the report claimed that there was no 'evidence for a substantial shift in taste towards devised theatre or work in which the writer is not the initiating artist', while recommending that 'new writing be reinstated as a policy priority.

The 2009 Arts Council England report, New Writing in Theatre 2003–2008: An assessment of new writing within smaller scale theatre in England, acknowledged fears that sections of the theatre industry were 'less favourable to the writer-centred approach' which could damage 'the emergence of good new writers who write a "traditional" play' (2009: 9). The same year, the Arts Council of England's Theatre Assessment reported a widespread view among practitioners that while there had been a growth in development of writers there had been a reduction in the amount of work commissioned and produced (2009: 4), and fears that the move towards collaboration marginalized the writer (2009: 76).

Contemporary queer performance reveals itself to be caught up in the tensions and risks identified by these early reports. While often deemed to be experimental and collaborative, one of the effects of this focus has been that text is often underplayed, under-supported and undervalued. While the UK boasts many play development opportunities, there are more means for performers and companies to stage performance than for a writer to have a new play produced. This is not to say that queer performers who write all harbour desires to be seen as playwrights who might have their work performed by others, but it does suggest that the structural conditions make it more likely for a performance to take place than for a playwright to have a play produced, which can have the effect of consolidating the queer performance writer as necessarily a performer, and sometimes a director, designer and producer too.

Despite the relative dearth of published queer performance texts, in recent years queer plays have enjoyed wider circulation. In their seminal anthology, *Black British Queer Plays and Practitioners: An Anthology of Afriquia Theatre*, Mojisola Adebayo and Lynette Goddard use the term 'afriquia theatre' to describe 'the oneness of being both Black and queer and the inherent Africanness of queerness, or, rather, quia'ness' (2023: 1). While focusing on plays, the editors highlight the importance of 'the ephemeral work of Black queer artists who have made significant contributions to the performance scene' (2023: 2), including those artists whose writings for performance have never been documented and published.

In a sense, this anthology builds on Adebayo's and Goddard's collection, by publishing queer performance texts rather than plays – what the editors might consider to otherwise have been ephemera. In addition, it emerges from a collection of plays and performances that I published in 2010, *Queer Notions: New Plays and Performances from Ireland*, which similarly sought to document queer performance in Irish theatre. In writing the introduction to that anthology, I noted the importance of international artists, and in particular UK artists, in invigorating Ireland's queer performance culture.

It was through the programming of THISISPOPBABY in Ireland that I first saw the work of Bourgeois & Maurice, David Hoyle, Dickie Beau and Le Gateau Chocolat.

Queer textual forms

All of the performance texts gathered in this anthology include elements of biographical writing, and often autobiographical writing, filtered through narrative, musical and lyrical intertexts, and social and cultural history. Many of the entries are solo works, written and performed by the same artist, and in some cases duets. Sometimes the work takes the form of sharing personal experience to witness, and sometimes it takes the form of appealing to figures in history to inspire and guide, drawing on archival evidence and other cultural sources. A recurrent feature of this work is that artists turn to queer muses and icons to tell more personal stories. In this, the performance texts reveal the importance of personal experience and relationships to queer performance, and of the necessity of appealing to cultural history and archival sources to stimulate and sustain queer cultural production.

While writing underpins the performances represented in this anthology, the works themselves are striking for their reliance on highly visual, sonic and often musical means of presentation, with some reliant on audience interaction (e.g. *Pleasure Seekers* and *Ten Commandments*). The forms are indebted to monologue drama, autobiographical performance, cabaret, musical theatre, comedy and live art, with the tone veering across camp, contemplative, nostalgic, mournful and hopeful registers. While these forms and aesthetics are apparent in the performance texts, it is the live performance that gives the tone and impact its full expression, which text doesn't capture in the same way.

While presented chronologically by year of first production, the layered histories underpinning each work resist claims to a clear progression of themes or forms throughout the time period in question. However, some of the works map important social and political issues affecting queer culture and recent UK social, political and cultural history. In *Black*, mental health is a central preoccupation, which reappears in *Re-Member Me*'s concern with stigma and homophobia, and in *The Making of Pinocchio*'s reflection on the impact of transition on a relationship. The experience of queers of colour and those of minority heritage backgrounds appears in *Black*, *Pull the Trigger* and *NIGHTCLUBBING*, with the latter two being produced during the Mediterranean migrant crisis, which led to then Prime Minister David Cameron describe those crossing the sea as a 'swarm'.[5] The UK's hostile environment towards transgender people in the past decade forms the backdrop to *The Making of Pinocchio*, although it sidesteps direct engagement by offering us a deeply personal account, refracted through metaphor. The legacy of economic austerity since the financial crash of 2008 until the Covid-19 pandemic of 2019, in light of environmental destruction, supplies the context for David Hoyle's *Ten Commandments*, despite being addressed in often comic terms. Indeed, there is plenty of humour and joy to sustain audiences and readers in the anthology, perhaps best reflected in the mischievous adventures of *DollyWould* and *Pleasure Seekers*.

In *Black*, Le Gateau Chocolat (George Ikediashi) offers an intimate portrait of his life and personal history, exploring issues of being Black, depression, body-image and the suicide of friends. Le Gateau Chocolat is a performer and maker of Nigerian heritage whose work spans drag, cabaret, opera, musical theatre, children's theatre and live art. His previous productions work includes *Le Gateau Chocolat* (2011), *I Chocolat* (2012) and *In Drag* (2013), with *Black* commissioned by Homotopia in 2013. Le Gateau Chocolat is celebrated for his striking baritone voice, which has been heard at the Royal Albert Hall, the Barbican Centre and Sydney Opera House.

Black is a solo performance that includes personal monologues intercut with animated projections and music from Nina Simone, Whitney Houston, Purcell and Wagner, among others, delivered with orchestral accompaniment. In so doing, *Black* not only provides a window into experiences rarely seen in contemporary theatre and performance, but in melding memoir, lyrics, image and music, it offers us an expanded sense of the textual languages of queer performance.

Pull the Trigger (2016), by Vijay Patel, recounts the performer's experiences of working in his family's corner shop. Patel recalls their experiences as a queer child with affection, and persistent curiosity around what it means to be 'a good Indian son'. Simultaneously, *Pull the Trigger* reflects on Patel's family's history of migration, and their experiences of making a home in the UK. In this, the piece builds on their previous live art/theatre project *The Weighting Game* (2014), which explored cultural expectations around arranged marriages and sexuality.

Pull the Trigger takes the form of a solo performance, embellished with music, that seeks to amplify the experience of queer of colour, working class and migrant communities in the UK, to give voice to under-represented stories within contemporary theatre and performance and queer culture. Here, the shop of Patel's youth becomes the primary site of queer inquiry, which is given new life in its theatrical rendering.

In *Re-Member Me* (2017), Dickie Beau (Richard Boyce) explores queer culture's relationship to *Hamlet*, uncovering the queer male actors in history who played the title role.[6] Beau's performance departs from the realization that playing Hamlet has served to legitimize actors as serious, leading men, but how this has also involved the concealment of the queerness of the actors, and the queerness of Hamlet, which his performance strives to redress. At the heart of the work is the uncovering of Ian Charleson's performance as Hamlet in the National Theatre in 1989, a part he played while dying of AIDS. Beau reanimates this forgotten performance, and invites other queer Hamlets to step forward like the characters in *A Chorus Line*, alluded to in the text, to take their place in theatre history.

Beau's solo work typically involves using lip-synching and playback techniques to mine historical figures and myths, stitching them together in performance, as in *Blackouts: Twilights of the Idols* (2011), *Lost in Trans* (2013), *Camera Lucida* (2014) and *iSHOWMANISM!* (2022). *Re-Member Me* is assembled from interviews and archival materials, which he presents on stage using scripted text, audio, digital screens, and his precise lip-synching skills. The production premiered at the Almeida Theatre, London, in 2017, as the UK marked the fiftieth anniversary of the Sexual Offences Act 1967, which partially decriminalized sexual acts between men, initially programmed to take place right before Robert Icke's production of *Hamlet* on the same stage, starring Andrew Scott. The performance text included in this anthology captures the textual strategies of collage, stitching and echo which characterize Beau's work.

Sh!t Theatre (Rebecca Biscuit and Louise Mothersole) make politically-engaged shows using a combination of documentary, song, comedy and multimedia. The duo refuses to hide its DIY aesthetic, with the pair typically undertaking all the production roles. Many of Sh!t's work takes the form of an investigation into a subject or person of fascination, which is shared with the audience on stage via documentary evidence (recorded footage, photographs) intercut with tales from international travel and personal experience. Such is the case with *Evita Too* (2022), in which they pursue Isabel Perón, the forgotten third wife of the former Argentinean President, Juan Perón, and *Drink Rum With Expats* (2019), in which they investigate British expats in Malta following the 2016 Brexit referendum.

DollyWould (2017) was created using similar making and performance strategies. In it, the pair recount their obsessive love for Dolly Parton, which led them to travel to her theme park, Dollywood, in Tennessee, an adventure that is warmly and wittily relayed on stage. Perhaps less overtly political than some of their other works, including those previously mentioned, the piece is an intricate dissection of one of queer pop culture's most celebrated icons.

In *NIGHTCLUBBING* (2018) Ray Young unites text, performance, visuals, music and costume via an Afrofuturist aesthetic to celebrate their queer female cast and the legacy of Grace Jones. *NIGHTCLUBBING* looks to Grace Jones's 1981 album of the same title for inspiration, to steel three female-presenting women on stage shown to be excluded from entering a nightclub in the present day. Faced with racist screening, Jones's soundtrack inspires the figures into 'claiming space black'.

Young is a transdisciplinary artist who tests performance and literary conventions to address issues around queerness, race, neurodiversity and our relationship with the environment. Their previous work, *OUT* (2017), is a duet featuring two bodies onstage to challenge homophobia and transphobia, while their more recent immersive sound productions, including *BODIES* (2022) and *THIRST TRAP*, invite us to explore our relationship to water and the climate respectively.

Bourgeois & Maurice (George Heyworth and Liv Morris) are best known as cabaret artists, distinctive for their acid, satirical lyrics and energetic performance style. Notionally alien siblings, in addition to appearing on the cabaret circuit, they have created ten full productions, including *Middle of the Road* with David Hoyle in 2015, which addressed the death of queerness under the rise of the status quo, and the musical *Insane Animals* in 2017, which explored human survival in the face of the threat of environmental destruction.

In *Pleasure Seekers* (2022), the duo question their relationship to pleasure in all its forms, through their unique combination of wry repartee, song and exuberant performance. The premise of the show is that the performers doubt their self-esteem being so tied up in their cabaret act, so they explore other forms of pleasure, from hedonistic chemsex parties, to shopping on Amazon, to violently breaking a piñata on stage. Rippling through this performance is a critique of commodity culture as well as a celebration of pleasure over cynicism, and performance's unique capacity to deliver it to its audiences.

In *The Making of Pinocchio* (2022), Scotland-based artists and partners Rosana Cade and Ivor MacAskill explore their experience of Ivor's gender transition. Drawing on theatrical and cinematic languages, using text, performance, puppetry, sound, digital screens and scaled effects, the performance uses the story of the wooden puppet Pinocchio, who wanted to be a *real* boy, to explore MacAskill's transition and its impact on him and his relationship with Cade.

The Making of Pinocchio bears the imprints of Cade's previous work as a performer invested in exploring intimacy in performance, and MacAskill's experience of making theatre for children. In *Sister* (2015), Cade appeared on stage with their sister, who had previously engaged in sex work, to explore their relationship, while in the one-to-one project *Walking: Holding* (2011), Cade held hands with an audience member to take a conversational walk through a public space. With collaborator Fiona Manson, MacAskill has made several works for young children that have toured internationally, including the award-winning Polar Bears trilogy, first created in 2010.

David Hoyle is a pioneer of queer performance in the UK, celebrated for breaking the boundaries between live and visual art, performance, theatre and cabaret for over four decades. A regular presence in the Royal Vauxhall Tavern, London, Hoyle's work has toured the UK and internationally, with a major career retrospective called 'Please Feel Free to Ignore My Work' held at Aviva Studios in Manchester in 2024.

In *Ten Commandments* (2022), Hoyle speaks from a pulpit to critique the dystopian present, while urging his audience to imagine a better world. Hoyle does so by issuing new commandments to live by, which signpost a future free from poverty, nuclear weapons, landfill and burning forests. Social immiseration, political corruption and cultural marginalization, which are regular points of critique for Hoyle, all feature in this work, chased by a rallying cry to build a better future from the ashes of the present. Combining lecture, comedy, visual projections, song and audience interaction, Hoyle's performance positions his audience as a congregation, gathered to benefit from his wisdom.

Conclusion

While this anthology demonstrates how queer performance is a rich and varied form, it also reminds us of how vulnerable it is to disappearance. Like many art forms, its health is challenged by a lack of opportunities, funding cuts, festival and venue closures, which have only deteriorated under the Conversative Government since the Covid-19 pandemic. But it is additionally fragile because of its uneven documentation, which makes it easy to forget or ignore. I hope that this anthology serves to champion queer performance, while encouraging us to recognize and remember its textual underpinnings and traces, in order to ensure that queer artists and their eclectic approaches are adequately documented, disseminated and archived. Queer performance may well have a brief, bright life, which is part of its distinctive allure, but its form and impact deserve to be remembered long after its live production.

Notes

1 While in most cases the performance documents follow the performance texts, in *DollyWould* they are interspersed throughout the text, as they appeared in the production and the original publication of the play.

2 While it is true to say that queer performance flourished in the decade in question, recent cuts and closures also put it at risk. For example, Live Art Development Agency, which supports queer performance and live art, lost its portfolio funding in 2023 (before being

reinstated), and VAULT Festival, which nurtured new queer theatre and performance, closed in 2024 after funding for a new venue fell through.

3 *DollyWould* was previously published by Oberon Books in 2018.
4 See Exceptions to copyright: Guidance for creators and copyright owners (2014), https://assets.publishing.service.gov.uk/media/5a7f4cf640f0b62305b864e6/Exceptions_to_copyright_-_Guidance_for_creators_and_copyright_owners.pdf
5 Speaking about the migration crisis in an interview for ITV aired on 30 July 2015, then UK Prime Minister David Cameron spoke of 'a swarm of people coming across the Mediterranean', aligning migrants and refugees with pests.
6 For more on *Re-Member Me*, see Fintan Walsh, *Performing the Queer Past: Public Possessions* (London: Methuen Drama, 2023), pp. 31–57.

References

Adebayo, Mojisola and Lynette Goddard (2023), 'Introduction and Survey of Afriquia Plays', in *Black British Queer Plays and Practitioners: An Anthology of Afriquia Theatre*, eds Mojisola Adebayo and Lynette Goddard, London: Methuen Drama, 1–20.

Arts Council England (2000), The Next Stage: Towards a National Policy for Theatre in England.

Arts Council England (2000), The Arts Council of England's National Policy for Theatre in England.

Arts Council England, Theatre Assessment (2009), https://www.artscouncil.org.uk/sites/default/files/download-file/Theatre_Assessement_2009.pdf (accessed 1 March 2024).

Campbell, Alyson and Stephen Farrier (2016), 'Introduction: Queer Dramaturgies', in *Queer Dramaturgies, International Perspectives on Where Performance Leads Queer*, eds Alyson Campbell and Stephen Farrier, Basingstoke: Palgrave Macmillan, 1–26.

Dunton, Emma, Roger Nelson and Hetty Shand (commissioned by Arts Council England) (2009), New Writing in Theatre 2003–2008: An assessment of new writing within smaller scale theatre in England, https://www.artscouncil.org.uk/sites/default/files/download-file/New_writing_theatre_2003-8.pdf (accessed 1 March 2024).

Freeman, John (2007), New *Performance/New Writing*, Basingstoke: Palgrave Macmillan.

Intellectual Property Office (2014), Exceptions to copyright: Guidance for creators and copyright owners, https://assets.publishing.service.gov.uk/media/5a7f4cf640f0b62305b864e6/Exceptions_to_copyright_-_Guidance_for_creators_and_copyright_owners.pdf (accessed 1 March 2024).

Greer, Stephen (2019), *Queer Exceptions: Solo Performance in Neoliberal Times*, Manchester: Manchester University Press.

Peter Boyden Associates (2000), Roles and Functions of the English Regional Producing Theatres [The Boyden Report].

Radosavljević, Duška (2013), *Theatre-Making: Interplay Between Text and Performance in the 21st Century*, Basingstoke: Palgrave Macmillan.

Sh!t Theatre (2018), *DollyWould*, London: Oberon Books.

Writ Large: New Writing on the English Stage 2003–2009 (July 2009), https://static1.squarespace.com/static/513c543ce4b0abff73bc0a82/t/5734fad5b6aa60fb98eae247/1463089890119/Writ+Large+-+New+Writing+on+the+English+Stage.pdf

Walsh, Fintan (2010), 'Introduction: The Flaming Archive', in *Notions: New Plays and Performances from Ireland*, ed. Fintan Walsh, Cork: Cork University Press, 1–16.

Walsh, Fintan (2023), *Performing the Queer Past: Public Possessions*, London: Methuen Drama.

Black

Written and performed by Le Gateau Chocolat (George Ikediashi)

Credits

Director and Co-writer: Ed Burnside
Orchestration, arrangement and musical direction: Julian Kelly
Digital animations: Mark Charlton
Narrator: Ed Burnside
Set and Costume Designer: Ryan Dawson Laight
Lighting Designer: Joshua Carr
Sound Designer: Tom Aspley

Premiere: Homotopia, Unity Theatre, Liverpool, 14 November 2013.

Note on staging

A bed occupies centre stage. Above it hangs a screen onto which animations of Little Black are projected during the narrator's voice over. Surrounding the bed is a small orchestra that plays throughout the performance. In between songs, **Le Gateau Chocolat***, as Little Black, changes costumes.* **Le Gateau Chocolat***'s voice overs are delivered in a conversational style having been recorded in interview.*

The lights go up on **Le Gateau Chocolat** *centre stage wearing a black taffeta gown with an oversized beaded collar.*

Sings: 'Dich, teure Halle' from Tannhäuser *by Richard Wagner.*

Leaves stage.

Narrator (*voice over*) This is the story of Little Black.

This is Little Black.
Little Black lived in a place far away over the sea in Africa.
That magical place is called Lagos.
Little Black and his sister lived in Lagos in a big house with lots of aunties and friends.

Little Black loved his sister, mummy, aunties and friends very much and he felt his happiness deep inside him. It burned away like the big bright Nigerian sunshine.

All the time, Little Black had a dream: he wanted to be a star but not a pop star or even a movie star. He wanted to be the next star of the Opera House: a great soprano diva with a beautiful taffeta gown and a string of sumptuous jewels around his neck.

Everyday, Little Black dreamed of what life would be like: adored by audiences, dinners in beautiful salons, trunks and wardrobes spilling with lavish furs. This dream made Little Black's happiness grow and everywhere he went people loved to play with the happy little cuddly boy.

One day, Little Black decided to go swimming. He imagined he was an Olympic synchronized swimmer like the ones he had seen on the television . . .
Representing Nigeria . . . LITTLE BLACK.

Le Gateau Chocolat *comes back on stage wearing a full-body 1950s style orange and red swimsuit, with a black leotard underneath, which he eventually exposes, and improvises a dance to 'Fing' eine diese Faust' from Wagner's* The Ring. *At the end, he peels down the bathing suit to reveal a black leotard to sing the next song.*

Sings: 'Strange Fruit' by Abel Meeropol. Arrangement by Julian Kelly.

Le Gateau Chocolat (*voice over*) I used to go swimming in my sister's bathing suit which was a two-piece, by the way. Ha. Bikini top and little pants. And, um, I was told by the lifeguard at the pool that if I ever wanted to come swimming there again, I couldn't wear that. Um . . . I also felt that it was an amalgamation . . . it was a compilation of different people going up to the lifeguard – maybe parents and other people going that it was inappropriate. I felt like he didn't just say it with his voice, I felt like it was the voice of everyone who was at the pool that day.

Sings: 'My Man's Gone Now' from Porgy and Bess *by George and Ira Gershwin and DuBose Heyward, now wearing a brown moleskin coat with a headscarf.*

Narrator (*voice over*) Poor Little Black!

The nasty man at the swimming pool had made him feel ashamed and his dream floated away from him as quickly and as naturally as it had formed.

Little Black's happiness that had once burnt inside him was not there anymore. Instead it sat outside of him: still in a place where he could see it but not warming the inside of him as it once had been.

Poor Little Black! What should he do? Who could he speak to?
The nasty man at the swimming pool had scared Little Black.
So, Little Black started to eat his favourite foods.

The sweet tasting food that his mummy cooked was so delicious and sometimes he forgot about his dream and felt happy.
What did this do to Little Black?

It made him grow and grow and suddenly Little Black wasn't so little anymore . . .

Narrator (*voice over*) *Projected on screen:* Tips for the fat #1: Disguise

As the voice speaks, **Le Gateau Chocolat** *comically plays with a cushion, mimicking the advice of the narrator, while wearing a black leotard.*

Relaxing at home. When good friends, colleagues and visitors call to disguise unsightly plumpness, make sure you have a cushion to hand. Place about the body. Accessorize and experiment with different sizes, angles and patterns. Smaller dogs, kittens or another small animal can also be used . . . No matter how hungry you are though, don't eat it.

Narrator (*voice over*) Little Black is now at school. He is growing up and growing out. Little Black likes school. He gets to play with his friends in the playground and he's very good at his school work.

He still dreams about his life in the Opera House but the dream felt hazy like a memory from the distant past or belonging to someone else.

Some of the boys do see Little Black's dream though.
They don't like it! They want to take Little Black's dream and change it.

Poor Little Black tries to hide his dream so that they couldn't see it but one of them can see it very clearly indeed and he tries to take it away from Little Black by hitting him, beating him.

Poor Little Black just lies on his bed and lets the boy beat him and take his dream away.

Sings: 'Black Is The Colour of My True Love's Hair' by Emile Latimer. Arrangement by Julian Kelly.

Narrator *Projected on screen:* Tips for the fat #2: Shopping

As the voice speaks, **Le Gateau Chocolat** *demonstrates how to style a small jacket to the instructions.*

When out shopping for a new outfit for a funeral or other special occasions. Recalibrate your understanding of the phrase 'it fits'. Remember, once the garments are in the sleeves, the garment fits. Be careful to maintain elegance and poise at all times

Le Gateau Chocolat (*voice over*) When you cross over from being er . . . the chubby cuddly four-year-old to just being fat, I think my dad was waiting for that to take over and, as soon as it did, he was like 'you have to do something about your weight' – but no mind of supporting. Always kind of judging. And then . . . and this is what I mean about not being naturally a dad – maybe in his warped understanding him buying things that wouldn't fit was an incentive for us to kinda get into them but they were just heartbreaking . . . they were just . . . you know . . . (*mutters*) that's too . . . that's too tight.

Sings: 'Sleep' by Ivor Gurney.

Bulb buzz. **Le Gateau Chocolat** *gets out of bed. Down light.*

Sings: 'I Wanna Dance With Somebody' by George Merrill and Shannon Rubicam. Arrangement by Julian Kelly.

Narrator (*voice over*) Little Black is all grown up now.

He's a big boy with a deep voice and it's time for him to make a journey: a long journey across the great plains of the Northern Sahara, over the snowcapped peaks of the Atlas Mountains, flying on an eagle's back faster and faster over the calm waters of the Mediterranean, scaling mountains and passing continents until he reached a place called England.

Here he is in England: Little Black is trying out a new dream: a dream that his daddy has given him: to be a rich lawyer. For some reason, this dream doesn't keep him warm like the old one. This one is heavy and doesn't belong to Little Black but he carries it around with him.

It gets heavier and heavier until eventually the cord that is holding it around him snaps and the dream is lost forever.

Poor Little Black is floating through the sky with no dream to anchor him.

Eventually he floats down into a strange place: an office full of people and telephones. There are no red velvet seats, no sumptuous gowns here, just the whirring of an office fan and the smell of instant coffee and lavender air freshener.

Sings: 'N.H.S. Direct' by Orlando Gough (commissioned for the show).

The call centre.
The twilight zone.
Reads Heat *magazine.*

The child isn't his . . . her heart-ache . . .
Her mother speaks out . . .
Hallo, NHS Direct, how can I help?

Yes, yes . . . yes, yes, you got your ears pierced.
That's nice.
Yes, yes . . . yes, yes . . .
No, sir, it's unlikely that you have H.
I really can't be sure but it's unlikely, unlikely, unlikely that you have HIV.
Hallo, NHS Direct, how can I help?
Yes, yes, you're five months pregnant. Congratulations!
Yes, yes . . . yes, yes . . .
Yes, madam, you can still use . . . your hair straight'ners.
Yes, madam, you can still use . . . your hair straight'ners.
I'm really really sure that, really really sure that you can still use your hair straight'ners.
No! No! No! No! No!
I've got a law degree! I can sing! Get me out of here!

Picks up a copy of Hello *magazine.*

Cupcakes versus Botox . . . a five-day detox . . . Shellac your hair . . .
Hallo, NHS Direct, how can I help?

Yes, yes . . . you took a taxi . . . yes . . .
The driver sped up over the bumps . . . yes.
Your insides were all shaken . . .
No madam, it's unlikely . . . I expect you've still got your womb.
Really, really, really sure that really really sure that really sure that you've still got your womb.
No! No! No! No! No!
I've got a law degree! I can sing! Get me out of here!

A copy of Grazia *magazine is at hand. (But it brings little solace.)*

Fairytale wedding . . . a honeymoon in paradise . . .
Five star resort
Hallo, NHS Direct, how can I help?
Yes, yes, you must get in touch with your dentist . . .
He will make you a new set
When did the pain start?
Oh . . . they didn't fit
Oh oh oh oh oh oh oh oh
superglue? Oh no . . .
Oh oh oh oh oh oh oh oh, superglue . . .
Hallo, NHS Direct, how can I help?
Yes, yes, yes, no!
Madam, Nitromors will not get rid of stretchmarks!
No! No! No! No! No!
I've got a law degree I can sing! Get me out of here!
Get me out of here – Get me out of here – Get me out of here
Hallo.

Narrator (*voice over*) Little Black is very sad. His happiness has faded away and all he can do is lie in his bed. Lost and tired but unable to sleep. His dream has disappeared.
Vanished, leaving not even a faint trace behind. . . .

Le Gateau Chocolat (*voice over*) You contemplate the idea of what it would be like to not have to cope with any of this anymore. This self-hatred and want to deal with the weight issues or being stared at or pointed at . . . or always having to . . . kind of scaffold yourself because you want to go out and get on the train without having to deal with what people expect you to look like or dress like, or because you're Black and bearded how you should be . . . and, you know, why are your nails painted or why are the shades you're wearing looking like . . . you know . . . what a life . . . well, what it would be like if you didn't have to deal with any of that and um . . . I think you contemplate what that is, or what that could be, and then for the very first time . . . the very idea of not having to deal with any of those things leads you down the path of ending it, suicide, actually contemplating . . . contemplating not have to deal with any of this stuff anymore.

Sings: 'Dido's Lament' from Dido and Aeneas *by Henry Purcell.*

Le Gateau Chocolat (*speaks*) So how does the story end? In a world where Little Black is condemned to being a black sheep, does he end his life or decide to go on? I'm still here. I accept that the darkness will forever be a part of my life now. The depression never goes away, not entirely. I've tiptoed right to the very edge, being consumed by being fat, by being gay, by being Nigerian and not out to my parents, by being Black . . . in the last two years, two friends have committed suicide and, in so doing, affirming it as a real choice but also inspiring this piece. I now understand that there is no prescribed path to the light . . . just the decision to journey forward, or at least in some direction. I accept. I forgive and I live in hope.

Sings: 'Make our Garden Grow' from Candide *by Leonard Bernstein.*

Ends

Performance Documents

1 Le Gateau Chocolat sits in front of the projected animations of Little Black, Unity Theatre, Liverpool, 2013. Courtesy of Le Gateau Chocolat.

2 Le Gateau Chocolat performs 'My Man's Gone Now,' Unity Theatre, Liverpool, 2013. Courtesy of Le Gateau Chocolat.

3 Animation of Little Black projected on a screen. Animation by Mark Charlton. Courtesy of Le Gateau Chocolat.

4 Animation of Little Black projected on a screen. Animation by Mark Charlton. Courtesy of Le Gateau Chocolat.

5 Sheet music for 'N.H.S. Direct' by Orlando Gough. Courtesy of Le Gateau Chocolat.

2
28
rejects the call
V. I real-ly can't be sure but it's un - like - ly, un - like - ly, un - like - ly that you have H. I. V.
33
ring ring
Hal - lo, N. H. S. Di - rect, how can I help? Yes, yes... yes, you're five months
39
preg - nant. Con-gra-tu - la-tions! Yes, yes... yes, yes... Yes, ma-dam, you can
44
still use_ your hair straight-'ners. I'm real-ly real-ly real-ly sure that, real-ly sure that, real-ly sure that you can use your
49
rejects the call
(fall off note)
hair straight-'ners. No! No! No! No! No! I've got a law de- gree! I can sing! Get me out of here!

5 *Continued*

3
55
George picks up a copy
of Hallo magazine
tr
mf
sfz
mp
p
mp
60
mp
cup - cakes ver-sus bo - tox... a five day de - tox... shel-lac your hair....
ring ring
mf
Hal - lo,
f
65
N. H. S. Di - rect, how can I help?
mp
mf
Yes, yes... you took a ta - xi... yes... The dri - ver sped up o - ver the
70
bumps... yes... Your in - sides were all sha - ken....
sfz
f
mf
No, ma - dam, it's un -
74
like - ly.... I ex - pect you've still_ got your womb. Real - ly real - ly real - ly sure that real - ly sure that real - ly sure that you've still got your

5 *Continued*

4
rejects the call
womb. No! No! No! No! No! I've got a law de - gree! I can sing! Get me out of here!
A copy of Grazia magazine is at hand. (But it brings little solace.)
fai - ry tale wed - ding... a ho-ney moon in pa - ra - dise...
ring ring
five star re- sort... Hal - lo, N. H. S. Di - rect, how can I help? Yes, yes...
Yes, yes... you must get in touch with your den- tist... He will make you a new set...
(to himself)
When did the pain start? Oh... they did-n't fit... Oh oh oh oh oh oh oh oh,

5 *Continued*

(to the caller)
(to himself)
(to himself)
su - per- glue?
Oh no...
Oh oh oh oh oh oh oh oh,
su - per- glue....
ring ring
Hal - lo,
N. H. S. Di - rect, how can I help?
Yes, yes...
yes... no!
Ma - dam,
Nit - ro - mors will not get rid of stretch - marks!
rejects the call
No! No! No! No!
No!
I've got a law de - gree!
I can sing!
Get me out of here!
Get me out of here Get me out of here Get me out of here
falling apart
ring ring
barks into the phone
rejects the call.
Hal - lo.

5 *Continued*

Pull the Trigger

Written and performed by Vijay Patel

A show about being a queer performer and an Indian shopkeeper.

Credits

Written and performed by: Vijay Patel
Dramaturgy: Annie Siddons, Ray Gammon, Suzanna Hurst, Ray Young and Phoebe Patey-Ferguson
Producer: Tilly Bungard
Lighting Designer: Jo Palmer
Sound Designer: Nicol Parkinson
Tech Operator: Livvy Lynch
Trailer: Claire Nolan
Recorded audio: Rajat Patel

Premiere: 28 October 2016, SPILL Festival, Ipswich.

Thank you to our funders/commissioners: Arts Council England National Lottery funding, Theatre in the Mill, Camden People's Theatre, Colchester Arts Centre, Norwich Arts Centre and SPILL National Platform 2016.

Stage is dimly lit. Audience enters.

Towers of cardboard crisp boxes are set up around the stage, resembling the aesthetic of a family run Indian corner shop. A DAB radio is seen centre stage on top of a crisp box. There is low-level Hindi music ('Mere Hathon Mein' and 'Mehndi Laga Ke Rakhna') playing through the radio.

Once the audience are seated, a recorded audio of **Vijay***'s dad is heard (via the PA speakers) talking about his lived experience of the Ugandan-Asian expulsion of 1972. The words are raw and unedited accounts from* **Vijay***'s dad.*

The audio text reads:

We came from Uganda in 1972: five sons, a mum and dad. We were stateless people, we didn't have any money at all, we were basically kicked out with what we had on, the clothes on our back, in September 1972. We arrived here, stayed at some of my dad's friends. Within a few weeks, my dad decided to go and visit a bank manager and he just walked in and said, 'I want a loan to buy a shop and I'll pay you back.' The bank manager was quite astounded to find that somebody had come in without any kind of collateral and wanted a loan. My dad explained his situation, that he was also a business man in Africa and he knew how to run a business. The bank manager agreed. Within weeks, my dad bought a business with 100 per cent loan with a lot of extra margin for the bank, but he didn't mind, as long as he was able to look after his own family and live upstairs in the shop. So we had a home, we had a business and we were working.

So we all had to work together, from morning to night, and go to school. There was a lot of racism back then, the people didn't like it, just like now with other communities, we had a lot of racism. We managed to combat that by just keeping to ourselves and just working, and educating ourselves, and to get better and to get back to where we were back in Africa, pretty rich and a pretty well-to-do community. Just like now, in many cases with Syrians who have lost everything, lots of people around the world facing the same sort of problems, we can sympathize with that.

We quickly grasped the knowledge of English; basically, we went to school, tried to do as best as we can at school, go home and straight into the shop –

Lighting changes to general wash, **Vijay** *enters on stage and starts to set up the 'shop' with stock, moving towers of crisp boxes into place.*

– to relieve my mum and dad who had been working since morning, fill up the shop and be in the shop till late. Our competition was the local Sainsbury's, which shut quite early in those days. Sainsbury's used to shut at 17.30, and then basically, from 17.30 if you kept your business open till 20.00 or 21.00, it was all your business. We had no competition, all the little shopkeepers were thriving. They had their time to do business, so we, as local shopkeepers, all the Asians did quite well, 'cause there was a niche market where people wanted it when they come back from work. They wanted milk, eggs, bread, whatever, and we were there to supply it, we were the only ones there open, we were the ones who wanted to work hard. Seven days a week, we never closed. Very hard, we also had to study in the shop, there was no other time for us, but the shop itself was an education, people came in from all backgrounds, we learnt from them and we thrived.

Audio of **Vijay***'s dad ends, the radio onstage instantly plays another Hindi track ('Ho Gaya Hai Tujkho To Pyar Sajna').* **Vijay** *notices a cardboard crisp box which has a pricing gun inside, he takes it out, shows it to the audience and then he starts lip-synching.*

While lip-synching, **Vijay** *moves upstage left, across the back and comes back to downstage right.* **Vijay** *then takes a microphone out of a Barbie doll box, which is placed inside another crisp box nearest to his position.*

Vijay *reads below 'Good Indian Son' text on the microphone. He reads it in an Indian accent.*

Vijay The good Indian son is respectful.
The good Indian son is obedient.
The good Indian son does what is asked of him.
The good Indian son is straight, married, with kids.
The good Indian son does his homework and does additional Maths, Science and English.
The good Indian son is selfless for the family.
The good Indian son is respectful.
The good Indian son cleans the house.
The good Indian son looks after his grandma.
The good Indian son does the gardening.
I need to be careful how I put this.
The good Indian son isn't disrespectful.
The good Indian son is a shopkeeper.
The good Indian son will take over the shop when he comes of age.

Radio static is heard as if not quite tuned to a radio station. The track starts to blend into the Band Aid II 1989 version of 'Do They Know It's Christmas?'

Once the radio static clears and the track is heard clearly, **Vijay** *starts another task of pricing up Christmas cards and laying them across the front of the stage.* **Vijay** *performs this in a mundane way, depicting the labour of migrant shopkeeping and re-enacting that work ethic.*

This task lasts until **Vijay** *pulls out a vintage Britney Spears Barbie doll from within the box full of Christmas cards.* **Vijay** *pulls out the doll to have a closer look at it.*

*At this point, the radio static is heard again which plays another Hindi track ('Chudiyan Khanak Gayeen' (*Lamhe *'91)).*

Vijay *places the Britney doll down, next to the radio on stage. He begins to clear up Christmas cards.*

Vijay Christmas was a season that we would work in my dad's shop. It was ALWAYS on my school holidays. I was missing out on very important gossiping about Britney's new cassette (*I know, I was just within that era*). But, instead it was 4 am starts, which as a kid, just felt like work. Cold, hard, brutal work. I was five and wishing I had found a Britney Spears doll hidden within forty years of stock. A boy can dream. At least I had some vital skills in shop keeping, one day I could be an independent ethnic sensation of glamour and cardboard crisp boxes and pricing guns. I'm working on that one.

He then gives the Britney doll to an audience member to look after.

I need to check the stationery. I think we're out of blue biros. Are we out of blue biros?

He walks to where the 'stationery' area is, this is depicted by a tower of crisp boxes centre stage. He reads the below text as he starts to check each item of 'stationery'; these are recalled in his head and the items are not visible on stage.

Vijay Black biro, Blue biro, Red biro
Black marker, Green marker, Red marker, Blue marker

Vijay (*to audience*) This is the stationery by the way.

Turning his back to check the stationery.
Rubber,
Mail bag, International Mail Bag,
Brown envelopes A4, White envelopes, Big envelopes (white and brown),
Big roll of bubble wrap, Scissors.

Vijay *repeats the stationery text three times.*

After the third time the stationery text is repeated, the radio static comes in again interrupting Hindi music. A recorded piece of text from the 1985 film My Beautiful Laundrette *plays through the radio.*

The audio text reads:

In this damn country, which we hate and love, you can get anything you want. It's all spread out and available, that's why I believe in England. Only you have to know how to squeeze the tits of the system.

Vijay Squeeze the tits!?

*Another Hindi track ('Tu Mere Samne' (*Darr, '94*)) then plays on the radio.* **Vijay** *stands up and does a hand gesture as if squeezing tits, in time with the introduction of the track.*

Vijay *speaks over the track*

Squeeze tits? Am I meant to squeeze tits?

Whose tits? The customer's tits? Britney's tits? The crisp boxes' tits? Margaret Thatcher's tits? Theresa May's tits?

Which family squeezed tits? Am I going to benefit in my life from squeezing tits? Do I have to squeeze some tits? Not if I don't want to. It's not appropriate for me now or any other time to squeeze tits. How do I squeeze tits? Tits? Blue tits?

Vijay *freestyles repeating the word 'tits' in different ways.*

Vijay (*interrupting 'tits' repetition*) SHIT! I FORGOT TO BRING IN THE NEWSPAPERS.

He exits and re-enters with a bundle of newspapers.

He starts laying out the newspapers and reads the titles/amounts of each one, this is dependent on the order of the newspapers but one example of the text reads:

Vijay 5 × *Sun*
4 × *Daily Mail*
5 × *Daily Mirror*
4 × *Daily Star*
3 × *Telegraph*

He goes through each title of the newspapers until he reaches Attitude *magazine. He looks at it and opens the back page as if this is his first queer discovery.*

The radio static plays again transitioning into the opening of Britney Spears' track 'Gimme More' (first 18 seconds of audio).

Vijay *flicks through the pages of the magazine as the track plays, he lip-synchs some of the words 'I see you, I just wanna dance with you' and does the little Britney giggle in the audio.*

A bell sound is heard resembling a customer who has just walked into the shop.

Radio static plays again and transitions into another Hindi track 'Ab Chahe Maa Roothe'.

Vijay *hides* Attitude *magazine quickly behind his back and heads towards the cash register (which is not visible but is around the cardboard crisp boxes placed up stage centre). He hides* Attitude *magazine under the counter (which is resembled by the crisp boxes up stage).*

Vijay *clears his throat as if he's been caught and starts talking in an overdramatic masculine voice:*

Vijay Oh, you alright, mate? Yeh I'm good, mate. The missus OK, mate, yeh? Mate you want your twenty B&H as usual, mate? Standard, mate! Nice one, mate! See ya, broooooooooooo!

A shop bell is heard again to show the person leaving.

Vijay *drops the overdramatic masculine voice after the shop bell is heard.*

Vijay I've never said 'mate' as much as when I'm in the shop. It's not deliberate but I can't help but put on a character when I'm there. I've got to fit in when I'm in the shop, no one wants to hear the shit I get up to.

A rumbling noise plays over the PA system, getting louder to drown out the sounds of the radio which is still playing Hindi music. The rumbling noise resembles the noise of the fan on a drinks fridge.

Vijay I need to check the fridge . . .

Vijay *moves downstage left where a tower of cardboard crisp boxes resembles the fridge in his dad's shop.*

He recalls and checks the drinks as they are stocked in the fridge.

Vijay Coke, Coke, Coke,
Diet Coke, Diet Coke, Diet Coke,
Coke Cherry Zero Sugar, Coke Zero
Oasis Summer Fruits, Oasis Citrus Punch.

The radio static then interrupts the Hindi music once again, this time transitioning into playing the introduction of Britney Spears' 'Breathe on Me' (first 20 seconds of audio).

Vijay *does a fun dance while listing drinks in the above text.*

A shop bell is heard again, resembling another person who has entered the shop.

Radio static is heard again, transitioning into another Hindi track 'Zara Sa Jhoom Loon Main'.

Vijay (*talking in the same overdramatic masculine voice as before*) Uh you alright, mate?

Vijay *turns back to the drink stock-take.*

Vijay Oasis Summer Fruits
Volvic a Touch of Fruit Orange and Peach,
Diet Coke, Diet Coke, Diet Coke, Are we out of Diet Coke?

Vijay *appears more on edge this time as it's the second time he has been caught out.*

Vijay (*turning his back to the customer who has just walked in*) Mate, I was just checking the drinks and pricing them up. Everything OK, mate? Yeh, mate, all good all good. Mate, you just have a look around. I'll be with ya in two yeah, mate, sweet, mate.

A shop bell plays again to resemble the person leaving.

Vijay *notices the* Attitude *magazine that he placed behind the cash register area earlier. As he picks it up, the radio static comes in again which transitions into Britney Spears's 'Gimme More' (first 40 seconds of the track).*

Vijay *dances with the magazine, this time flicking through the magazine vigorously and prancing about the shop taking in all the eye candy.*

The shop bell is heard again which plays as the track ends and the radio static kicks in, the radio transitions to another Hindi track 'Mere Khwabon Mein'. Another person has entered the shop, interrupting **Vijay***'s gazing at the magazine.*

Vijay Uhhh you alright, mate, uhhh I was just, errrr, checking . . .

Goes to the fridge area to disguise his awkwardness.

Vijay (*continues, slightly frantic and embarrassed*) Coke Coke Coke
Diet Coke Diet Coke Diet Coke
Coke Cherry Zero Sugar Coke Zero
Oasis Citrus Punch Oasis Summer Fruits
Volvic a Touch of Fruit Orange and Peach
Diet Coke. Diet Coke. Diet Coke. Are we out of Diet Coke?
I'll get some more in, mate. Tuesday, mate.

A recorded audio of **Vijay***'s dad plays over the PA speakers over the sound of the radio, which is still playing Hindi music. Similar to the previous audio text, the words are raw and unedited accounts from* **Vijay***'s dad.*

Vijay *is building up all the cardboard crisp boxes into two towers stage left.*

The audio text reads:

My regrets are that I didn't have a childhood. I now think back and contemplate life in this country and think what was it all about? It's not about money, we didn't have a life, we gave up our life for the family, so that the family could establish themselves. My dad was adamant that he would never ever take anything from this country, in terms of housing or any kind of help whatsoever. We didn't ask for help, we were on our own and that's what we wanted. We would manage ourselves, and we did it, but we had to work very hard. In that, my regret is that we suffered as children. We didn't have any childhood, we didn't have any life whatsoever.

To this day, even now, I still feel I'm burdened. I don't have any life, I don't have any free time, I never have any time off at all unless my son gives me a day or so occasionally. Other than that, we worked seven days a week, seven days, every day, Monday to Sunday, whether it was bank holiday, Christmas Day, Boxing Day, any day we worked, serving the community, serving the people. That's the regret. I often used to stand there sometimes on a very hot day, looking out of the shop window from within, people passing by on a hot sunny day laughing and joking. I was hoping that I should be out there but, no, I had to serve customers instead, and pick up my book and study. But, I did study, I did well, the cost is very hard to bear.

An interview audio of Britney Spears talking about her song 'Breathe on Me' plays through the radio. **Vijay** *stops to listen but then continues with his pricing action.*

Interview text reads:

Interviewer You really think that's what it's talking about?

Britney It does! That's what it says, it says 'Breathe On Me'! That's it!

Interviewer I know what it says but one of us wasn't born yesterday, do you really think that's all it's talking about?

Britney Well I think it's supposed to get you in the mood, you know like how a song gets you in the mood to feel a certain tension or a certain vibe.

Cut-away Commentary And the girl who always played it close to the line on how much skin she showed, posed like this – (**Vijay** *does a pose with the pricing gun*) – for *Esquire* magazine. Consider the line officially crossed.

Interviewer What happened to your clothes?

Vijay *looks at his own clothes.*

Britney Well I own clothes now.

Interviewer I know, but what's this about? No kidding, what is it about?

Britney What is it about?

Interviewer Yeah!

Britney It's about doing a beautiful picture and . . .

Interviewer (*cuts off* **Britney**) Is it about shocking people?

Britney You know I feel comfortable in my skin, I think it's an OK thing to, erm, express yourself, express yourself, express yourself, express yourself . . .

The words 'express yourself' repeat in the audio. **Vijay** *is doing a task where he takes Haribo sweets, prices them then puts them into another box. This task lasts for a while until* **Vijay** *discovers a lipstick placed within the crisp box containing the Haribo sweets.*

Once he has discovered the lipstick, the radio static comes back in to interrupt the Hindi track with another Britney Spears 'Breathe on Me' segment (1 min of the track).

While this is playing **Vijay** *does a dance, stares at lipstick and puts it on in a grotesque way like someone who has never put on lipstick before, or someone who just wants to 'get it on' quickly.*

As **Vijay** *smothers the lipstick all over his face, a shop bell is heard once again, showing another person who has entered the shop.*

Vijay We're closed!

There is silence. No Hindi music is playing through the radio for the first time.

Vijay *turns to the audience, wipes his lipstick and takes a microphone from the crisp box down stage right.*

He takes a letter out of pocket and delivers it to the person who he had previously asked to look after the Britney Spears doll.

Vijay Although I feel more and more like I'm going to perform on a stage like you, it's not easy. I still have to cover my dad's shop, but this time, on my own. I know how to do everything on my own but I feel more responsibility, to my family, to myself, to my life choices. The time it takes me to do everything for my family means I find less and less time for what I need to do. Or is it just what I want to do? And I feel guilty about saying that, because, there doesn't need to be one or the other but I just don't feel like I was using my time well. I want to be doing what my friends are doing. Britney, you're all kinds of fab but I think about all the reasons why I could never be like you and a shopkeeper, I just need to make a choice. FUCK SAKE VIJAY, MAKE A FUCKING CHOICE. Every moment I spend in the shop I play your music, but it's not enough to keep my dreams alive.

I often dream of the power of queerness
I often dream of not feeling I have to hide
I often dream of holding hands with Justin Timberlake
I often dream of listening to your whole album interrupted, uncensored.
I often dream of buy one get one free offers
I often dream of the power of Britney to queer folk, gay men and the undecided.
I often dream of sell out tours and interviews with Ellen Degeneres
I often dream of the phone calls to suppliers when the newspapers are late
I often dream of belting out 'Born to Make You Happy' by Britney Spears with a hairbrush in hand and pigtails
I often dream of what a radical Indian son looks like
I often dream of what my shows would have looked like
I often dream of not giving up
I often dream that double lives are not real and many people don't also have to live them for self-imposed shame
I often dream.

Vijay *stops reading from the letter and directs the last line to the audience.*

It feels distant.

He takes the doll from the audience member and thanks them.

Vijay (*to audience*) I was twenty and my favourite artist was Britney Spears. I fell in love. I came out.

I need to pack up and tie the newspapers.

Vijay *starts to pack the newspapers away for the day. He names each title of the newspapers, while counting how many there are.*

He finds the Attitude *magazine one last time amongst the newspapers.*

The radio static comes in again and plays a very jarring version of Britney Spears 'Gimme More', which is almost drowned out by the static.

He reads it and fantasizes over the men on each page. He goes one step further by doing a really raunchy dance and ending up on the floor on all fours absolutely engrossed. His lipstick is still smudged and he is living out a queer fantasy.

This continues until a repeated audio of his dad plays over the PA speakers.

The line that is repeated is 'To this day, even now, I still feel I'm burdened. I don't have any life, I don't have any free time, unless my son gives me a day or so, occasionally.'

Vijay *quickly places the* Attitude *magazine in with the bundle of newspapers. He ties the newspaper bundle up with string and makes knots around his wrist.*

Vijay *then stands up with newspaper bundle attached to his wrist, a Hindi song plays though the radio 'Ghar Aaja Pardesi'.*

Vijay *moves around the stage then heads towards the microphone box with the weight of the stack of newspapers taking a toll on his wrist.*

He then takes the microphone from the box and speaks into it.

Vijay (*speaking in an Indian accent*) The good Indian son is respectful.
The good Indian son is obedient.
The good Indian son does what is asked of him.
The good Indian son is straight, married, with kids.
The good Indian son does his homework and does additional Maths, Science and English.
The good Indian son is selfless for the family.
The good Indian son is respectful.
The good Indian son cleans the house.
The good Indian son looks after his grandma.
The good Indian son does the gardening.
I need to be careful how I put this.
The good Indian son isn't disrespectful.
The good Indian son is a shopkeeper.
The good Indian son will take over the shop when he comes of age.
The good Indian son isn't disrespectful.

He drops the Indian accent.

AM I a good Indian son?

Maybe I'm a bad Indian son, sometimes I feel the guilt like a bad Indian son. For unfulfilling duties, for not keeping the sweets in line and replenished. I'm always conscious of what I wear when I'm working in the shop and what is appropriately dressed to work there. And no one has ever said that's wrong to my face – to be out as queer, to love Britney, to wear lipstick. It's just the thoughts I sometimes feel about wanting a life that is my own and not having to fit mine into a life which is already there. Because on most levels. That's not going to work. I'm not going to work. It's Shopland or Vijayland and I have to choose. I can't do both. I can't do both. I can't do both. I can't do both . . .

Vijay *repeats the line 'I can't do both' as he builds all of the crisp boxes into one large tower at the back of the stage. He then disappears behind it.*

The lighting state changes to pulsing lights as the below text is heard as a pre-recorded sound by **Vijay**. *The text repeats three times and in each iteration it gets louder and builds in echoes making it almost inaudible towards the end.*

The recorded text reads:

Your life has structures.
You must adhere to the cultural structures that are permitted.
Here is your structure.
Unstable work is not in that structure.
Selfishness is not in that structure.
Queerness is not in that structure.
Queerness is in the structure that I understand.
Queerness is in the structure but must be made palatable for those to understand.
Shopkeeping is in that structure.
Short changing customers is not in that structure.
Being queer and a shopkeeper is not in that structure.
Britney Spears is not in that structure.
Filial obedience is in that structure.
Writing performance is not in that structure.
Rehearsing performance is not in that structure.
Performing is not in that structure.
Performing is not in a structure I understand.
Your time is not in that structure.
Your lack of money is not in that structure.
Your friendships is not in a structure I understand.
Sacrifice is in that structure.
Sacrifice is in that structure.
Where do you go from here?
You must sit within that structure.
Your resentment is not in that structure.
Your resentment is not in that structure.
Your incompetence as a gardener is not in that structure.
Your anxiety is not in that structure.
Your forgetfulness is not in that structure.
Your Asperger's is not in a structure that I understand in this context.
Your structure is set for you.
You must adhere to the shopkeeping structure.
You must adhere to the shopkeeping structure.
The structure has been built out of sacrifice, out of work, it is now your structure.
Claim it. Do it. Your structure is irrelevant.
Dresses are not in that structure.
Attitude magazine is not in that structure.
Wigs are not in that structure.
Make-up is not in that structure.

After the text has repeated a third time, the lights change to create a spot on the tower of cardboard crisp boxes up stage. Britney Spears 'Stronger' plays through the radio. **Vijay** *kicks down the tower of crisp boxes in a moment of queer euphoria and a noticeable resistance to the above recorded text.*

Vijay *emerges in full drag wearing a punk-style dress with crisp packets sewn onto the skirt, a black wig and a plastic headset microphone that looks as if it was stuck onto a kids magazine. His make-up is re-done which now looks fresh and in keeping with his aesthetic as a queer performer in nightclubs.*

He lip-synchs the song and grows in confidence throughout.

When the words 'here I go' are repeated in the song, the music abruptly switches from being played on the radio to now being played on the PA speakers. **Vijay** *slams the pricing gun down on the floor and dances on his own. He continues to dance, lip-synch and have the time of his life.*

The track ends. Lights fade.

Ends

Performance Documents

1 Vijay Patel in *Pull the Trigger* at Camden People's Theatre, London, 2018. Photograph by Holly Revell.

2 Vijay Patel in *Pull the Trigger* at Camden People's Theatre, London, 2018. Photograph by Holly Revell.

3 Promotional image for *Pull the Trigger* (2020). Photograph by Holly Revell.

4 The family store that inspired *Pull the Trigger*. Photograph by Vijay Patel.

Re-Member Me

Created and performed by Dickie Beau

Directed by and co-devised with Jan-Willem Van Den Bosch

Credits

Director and Co-devisor: Jan-Willem Van Den Bosch
Design Supervisor: Lorelei Cairns
Lighting Designer: Mary Langthorne
Audio production: Helen Noir
Special props: Fani Parali
Stage Manager: Rob Hearn

Premiere: 19 March, 2017, Almeida Theatre, London.
Premiere date of this version: 25 May, 2023, Hampstead Theatre, London. The credited team refers to this production.

A note on contributors and context

Re-Member Me originated in the dressing room of the Royal Vauxhall Tavern, after I came offstage from performing a very long lip-synch to the voice of the late Kenneth Williams for a queer cabaret night. Fellow performer Dusty Limits made the tongue-in-cheek suggestion that I take my established shtick of lip-synching long-form spoken word recordings to a new extreme, and into previously uncharted territory – namely, by tackling *Hamlet*. Dusty proposed I take audio recordings of legendary Hamlets (Gielgud, Olivier, Burton, and so on), chop them up (dismember them), and then put these historical performances back together by 'channelling' – or you might say 're-membering' them – through my body; thereby turning myself into a kind of human Hamlet mixtape, performing the whole play, and playing all the parts, in an epic lip-synch medley. Hence the title *Re-Member Me*, which is of course one of the Ghost's lines in *Hamlet*, and a line that in this context reframes lip-synching as a kind of *body*-synching.

Whilst I was attracted enough to the strangeness of Dusty's human *Hamlet* mixtape idea to follow where it led, I think if I'd restricted myself to that specific outcome then the ensuing show would only really have been interesting for about five minutes. It's my repeated experience that, as someone once told me Peter Brook used to say (and I might be paraphrasing): 'Behind a good idea is often a better idea.'

Luckily, during a research and development attachment at what was formerly known as the National Theatre Studio, where I was given space and time to further develop the idea, a conversation with then Studio Projects Producer, Matthew Poxon, turned my head in a new direction. As I was 'auditioning' Hamlet recordings for my human Hamlet mixtape, Matthew drew my attention to one particular Hamlet, of which no recording existed: that of Ian Charleson, who took over from Daniel Day-Lewis in Richard Eyre's production at the National Theatre in 1989. The most tangible testament to Charleson's Hamlet exists in the form of one remarkable review by former *Sunday Times* chief theatre critic, John Peter, which I came across in the NT archive, and which stirred my imagination.

I felt an instinctive heart connection to Ian Charleson. I felt motivated by the fact that his story had seemingly been eclipsed by the legend of Daniel Day-Lewis's departure from Richard Eyre's production of *Hamlet* (Day-Lewis allegedly left the stage, never to return, after seeing the ghost of his actual father, Cecil Day-Lewis, appear on stage mid-performance). And I couldn't shake off a desire to 're-member' Charleson's Hamlet. But, since no recording existed of his performance, I would have to find a new approach. So, I stopped 'auditioning' Hamlet recordings and instead started to record the memories of people who had seen this one particular Hamlet, which by all accounts had been the greatest Hamlet almost never seen.

My new path was illuminated by another key conversation, this time with playwright Martin Sherman, who shared some indispensable insights and steered me towards interviewing Sean Mathias, Ian McKellen and Richard Eyre. These three figures became central voices of the show. My agent at the time, John Wood, generously lent his voice and memories to my growing compendium of conversations, and his voice went on to join these other three in the show. A coincidence led to my being introduced to Daniel Day-Lewis's former dresser on *Hamlet*, Stephen Ashby, through the arts producer Pam Vision, which was a tremendous coup. And while on a trip to New York, I was blessed to meet with the actor Suzanne Bertish, whose interview with me in a busy restaurant provided a key to the unfolding of the final piece. Finally, I was very fortunate that theatre PR Cliona Roberts was able to introduce me to the late John Peter, who agreed to let me record him reading his original review of Ian Charleson's Hamlet aloud.

I made the recordings that became the substance of this show over a period of two or three years, bit by bit, as opportunities arose. Another short r&d attachment at the National Theatre Studio brought my long-term collaborator Jan-Willem Van Den Bosch onto the journey with me, and together we began to navigate the material I'd gathered, laying down some dramaturgical logics for possible theatricalization.

Finally, a coffee with Robert Icke – brought about by producer Lucy Pattison – gave us a deadline, and a context. Robert proposed I put my developing ideas on their feet by creating a satellite show in relation to his upcoming production of *Hamlet*, starring Andrew Scott. The idea was that I would create a performance that could 'haunt' his set, in a nod to the ghosts of Hamlets past that inevitably follow each new iteration of the play; to be performed on Sundays during the run of *Hamlet*, when the Almeida would otherwise be dark. This context gave Jan and me the catalyst we needed to bring our ideas to fruition. Informed by ongoing conversations with Jan, where his directorial ideas fed back into my work on the text, I intuitively edited my collected audio into a 'digital script' using sound editing software. Together, Jan and I refined the structure and co-devised the theatrical form of the finished piece, and I simultaneously developed the 'digital script' by creating new video elements that became part of the fabric of the show.

After the initial 'scratch' performances at the Almeida, where Robert Icke's production had informed some of our key dramaturgical decisions, further presentation opportunities, including at the Public Theatre in New York, led us to create, on a shoestring, a tour-able stand-alone version of the show that was not dependent on the set of another production. At this point, lighting designer Marty Langthorne came on board and his brilliant creative contributions further developed the ongoing dramaturgy of the piece.

When we revisited the piece in 2023, ahead of a London run at Hampstead Theatre, Jan and I made a very few minor amendments to the text, primarily adding a couple more minutes of Stephen Ashby's reminiscences to the piece than we had originally, which we felt gave more balance to the overall show.

I'm deeply grateful to all of the key contributors I've named in this introduction, and many more whose conversations, comments, or other contributions, were invaluable to the process – including, but not limited to, Fintan Walsh, Aoife Monks, Ivan Mulcahy, Justin Nardella and Freddie Fogg. I'd also like to express a special thanks to the first Stage Manager who worked on this production, Naomi Harvey.

Re-Member Me was developed with the support of the National Theatre Studio, Almeida Theatre, Birkbeck Centre for Contemporary Theatre and Arts Council England Grants for the Arts.

Note on the text

Nearly all of the audio in this show is pre-recorded and with some exceptions almost all the voices featured are lip-synched by **Dickie Beau**, either live, on stage or on video.

DB means **Dickie Beau**. Where Dickie is lip-synching live to a voice on stage, this abbreviation will be followed by the name of the person to whom the voice belongs in parentheses, e.g. **DB (Ian McKellen)** means Dickie is lip-synching live to the voice of Ian McKellen.

T/H refers to a pre-recorded 'TALKING HEAD'. For much of the show, four identical talking heads appear on a video screen. In this pre-recorded footage that runs alongside the live action on stage, Dickie is lip-synching to the voices of John Wood, Richard Eyre, Ian McKellen and Sean Mathias. To differentiate between Dickie's live lip-synching, and the prerecorded lip-synch on video, these 'talking heads' will appear in this script as, e.g., **Richard Eyre (T/H)**

V/O means VOICEOVER (i.e. the voice of the speaker can only be heard, and the voice is not lip-synched), e.g. **V/O DB** means **Dickie Beau**'s recorded voice is playing but the voice is not embodied. (NB: In the case of Dickie's own voice it's a 'rule' of the show that his pre-recorded voice is *always* 'disembodied' whenever it is heard – until one point, towards the end of the show, all the previous rules are disrupted and Dickie speaks in his own voice live – when this happens, his voice is amplified by an onstage microphone so that the sonic world of the show maintains coherence.)

Scene One: Prologue

*A large projection screen floats in black space about two metres above the stage. In the centre of the black screen is a still image of a young man (***Dickie Beau***) in silhouette, encircled by a vignette. He is down on one knee, resting his chin on his hand, as if deep in contemplation. A visual 're-memberment' of Rodin's* The Thinker, *the image is also evocative of a Victorian 'shade' portrait.*

There is a caption underneath the image: 'Speak the speech, I pray you, as I pronounced it to you, trippingly on the tongue'.

The stage in front of the screen is littered with dismembered fragments of mannequins, illuminated by hazy sidelights. Torsos, legs and arms lay chaotically interspersed with fragments of costumes, giving the impression of dismembered bodies on a battlefield. The costumes themselves are conceived as the kinds of costumes that might have been worn by Hamlets of the past, so evoking the idea of past portrayals . . . a military uniform, cocktail blazer, pair of pajamas (some of the costume decisions, like this example of the striped pyjamas,[1] *which directly alludes to Mark Rylance's Hamlet, may be decisive nods to actual historical performances). Upstage right, there is a wheelchair. Upstage left is a skeletal clothes rail (empty of clothes), and a stack of four plastic chairs, the kind you might find in a rehearsal room. Several other props also litter the stage and are illuminated by special lights – these include a crown, a pair of running shoes, some military boots, a copy of the* Hamlet *playtext, and a latex replica of* **Dickie Beau'***s head (this last detail need not be fully legible to the audience until later in the show).*

House lights go down. During the following overlapping voices, a previously invisible black curtain, directly underneath the screen, is slowly raised to reveal a row of white curtains running the length of the screen, and flush with the screen. There are four curtains in total, fastened together to create one long curtain that runs the length of the screen. Later, when these curtains are opened, a further row of white curtains is revealed approximately two metres behind the first row – these two rows of curtains define a 'corridor' that cuts across the stage beneath the screen; the floor of this 'corridor' is painted grey, in contrast to the rest of the stage floor, which is black. Meanwhile, the image of The Thinker *on the screen, and the text caption, blur and fade to black. Flickering lights in the corridor behind the curtains seem to synchronize with the overlapping voices. Behind the curtains, the soft silhouette of a figure can just be made out, stage left, lying on a bed.*

V/O Overlapping Voices[2] I can't remember . . . I bet he remembers . . . Probably provoked my memory of the play . . . I don't know, I can't remember the ins and

---

[1] During the devising process some costume decisions contained folded within them other references/ resonances, from which further multivalent meanings might unfurl in relation to the text – e.g. in the case of the pyjamas, they take on additional expression in light of later allusions to a key production of Martin Sherman's play *Bent*.

[2] This medley of voices includes excerpts from Dickie Beau's interviews with John Wood, Ian McKellen, Richard Eyre, Sean Mathias and John Wood. The final dramatic 'Must I remember?' is from a recording of John Gielgud as Hamlet.

outs . . . If he remembers . . . I've forgotten . . . one of the many things I've forgotten . . . probably provoked by memory . . . *MUST I REMEMBER*?

A piano plays Schubert's 'Piano Sonata No. 21 in B-Flat Major'. During this music and the following voiceover, a moving image comes into focus on the screen of a young man, in silhouette, opening a pair of curtains, as if looking out of a window onto the audience.

V/O Uncle Monty[3] It is the most shattering experience of a young man's life when one morning he awakes and quite reasonably says to himself, 'I will never . . . play . . . The Dane.' When that moment comes, one's ambition *ceases*.

The warm lighting in the corridor behind the curtains grows stronger, as if a sun is coming up, and the crescendo of a CLOCK TICKING culminates in the sound of an ALARM CLOCK. The screen goes black. On stage, the figure on the bed sits up, suddenly woken by the alarm. From behind the curtain, sitting on the bed, **DB** *embodies the following text, lip-synching in silhouette.*

DB (John Gielgud)[4] I have of late, but wherefore I know not, lost all my mirth.

That it should come to this. *He rests his head on his hand, defeated, in a visual echo of the opening screen image. An odd sounding fanfare segues into the recognisable trumpet notes of 'YMCA' by the Village People. Then the original Village People track kicks in, while* **DB** *performs in silhouette a sequence of yogic stretches.*

DB (John Gielgud) WHY?

Village People – M.C.A
It's fun to stay at the –

DB (John Gielgud) That it should come to this.

Village People You can get yourself clean, you can have a good meal,
You can do whatever you feel . . .

DB (John Gielgud) Oh God! God!

Village People I said, young man –

DB (John Gielgud) What an ass am I.

Village People I said young man, you can make real your dreams
But you've got to know this one thing
No man does it all by himself

The shadow figure's mood shifts – more energized, hopeful, greater vigour in his exercise – as if directly inspired by the lyrics in the song.

---

[3] An iconic line from the cult film *Withnail and I*.

[4] In this scene, the DB (John Gielgud) excerpts are from recordings of John Gielgud as Hamlet.

Village People I said, young man, put your pride on the shelf
And just go there, to the Y.M.C.A.
I'm sure they can help you today . . .

The sound of a record scratching stops the music. This marks the sudden end of the shadow morning exercise routine – **DB** *has reached a limit and collapses on the bed.*

DB (John Gielgud) What dreams may come when we have shuffled off this mortal coil . . .

A bell tolls, and the figure behind the curtain clearly hears it.

PING! A lightbulb moment.

I know my course!

Blackout.

A transition: sounds of static, interspersed with distorted voices and the flickering black and white images of mannequin torsos on the screen.

Scene Two: Sir Ian

V/O John Barrymore[5] To be or not to be. That is the question.

Another distinct crackle of static coincides with a circular backlight coming up. **DB** *appears in silhouette behind the curtain, slightly stage left of centre, once again echoing the opening screen image (*The Thinker*). He embodies the following in silhouette.*

DB (Ian McKellen) Anybody can play Hamlet. Whatever you bring to Hamlet seems to apply. My own Hamlet, like a lot of my performances at that time is, er, I'm playing Hamlet and I'm running alongside Hamlet giving my notes on Hamlet to the audience. 'Note this!' I didn't take him into myself at all. Everybody . . . is . . . this business about have you seen *Hamlet* before, I remember two guys coming into the dressing room – Manders and Mitcherson – they were famous theatre historians. Oh! They had everything. Every old programme, every photograph, every design . . . amazing collection of stuff. Anyway, they came into the dressing room: 'Congratulations, you're our seventy-sixth Hamlet. Aaand you know we remember something about every Hamlet we ever saw. John Neville, for example' – he was a wonderful actor at the Old Vic; he and Richard Burton used to share the main parts . . . very romantic . . . 'John Neville had a little hole in his tights, right there.' (*He points to his bottom.*) I don't know what they would've taken away from mine.

Fade to black.

5 From a 1930s recording of John Barrymore as Hamlet.

Scene Three: Human Hamlet Mixtape

V/O Michael Douglas[6] Let's continue please. Step forward, tell me your real name, your stage name if it's different, where you were born, and how old you are.

DB *suddenly appears from behind curtains, centre stage. He is wearing a hospital gown and has wheeled on a disco ball on a drip stand. He pulls a dramatic pose, á la Norma Desmond.*

DB (Mixtape) It is I! Hamlet, the Dane!

As a dance track starts, **DB** *strips off his hospital gown, revealing his costume underneath: rainbow-coloured headband and wristbands, a Wittenberg University singlet, skimpy running shorts, and leg warmers (distinctly not the kind of costume anyone has ever designed for a Hamlet). The 'Human Hamlet mixtape' that follows is a mock Hamlet audition, composed of excerpts of various Hamlet performances by Kenneth Branagh, John Gielgud, John Barrymore, and Peter O'Toole, rhythmically remixed with the theme tune from* Fame, *undergirded by the Crystal Castles track 'Crimewave'.* **DB** *lip-synchs this mashup as part of a highly camp dance number. The memorable 're-member, re-member' middle eight of the 'Fame' song is re-performed in this version by the remixed voice of John Gielgud from his Hamlet.*

In addition to disco lights joining in with the music, a disco video montage plays throughout the scene, including spinning mannequin bodies, neon/rainbow disco floor graphics, and the magnified microscopic image of a virus morphing into a twirling disco ball. . . .

It is I! Hamlet, the Dane! / Have I something in me dangerous / Something in me / something in me / Have I something in me dangerous / Which, which, which, which, which, which, which, which, which / Let they wiseness fear!

Be be be be be be be be be be be be be / Or not to be, that is the question / Be be be be be be be be be be be be be / Whether it is nobler in the mind / To suffer the slings and arrows of outrageous fortune / Or to take arms against a sea of troubles / And by opposing end them

Oh God / I loved Ophelia / Forty thousand brothers could not / With all their quantity of love / Make up my sum / Oh God, God! G-g-g-g-g-g-g-g-God! / Oh God / It is I / It is I / I-I-I-I-I-I-I-I-I-I-I

Re-member / Re-member / Re-member
Re-member / Re-member

Hold, hold, hold my heart / And you, my sinews, grow not instant old / but bear me stiffly up / Re-member thee / Aye, thou poor ghost / Whilst memory holds a seat in this distracted globe / Re-member thee / Re-member thee / mem-mem-mem-mem-mem / Re-member Thee / mem-mem-mem-mem-mem-mem-mem-mem / It is I / I-I-I-I-I-I-I-I-I-I-I

---

[6] Excerpt of Michael Douglas as the Director in *A Chorus Line.*

DB *ends the number with a histrionic final pose, like a triumphant gay Atlas holding an imaginary disco-ball globe up above his head.*

On the screen above said head, the closing image of the dance number onscreen is a row of four naked male mannequin bodies, each with **DB***'s head superimposed on the top.*

A beat.

V/O John Wood Well, where can we go with this in this production? Because it's about the deconstruction of *Hamlet*. I found that too fussy.

It's evidently a 'No'. **DB** *slopes off towards stage left and wheels the disco ball away with him.*

Scene Four: Gielgud (An Actor's Life)

Piano music (a reprise of the Schubert Piano Sonata). Lighting change.

DB *begins to set up the four 'rehearsal' chairs in front of the curtains – these will end up equidistant under the screen, corresponding to the positions of the four mannequins with* **DB** *heads in the image on the projection screen.*

V/O John Miller[7] You've scaled so many high peaks in your career. Which one would you like to be remembered for most?

Upon hearing this voice, **DB** *stops setting up the chairs and sits on the chair furthest stage right to respond to the interviewer, who seems to be somewhere out in the audience. He performs the following not quite as an impersonation of John Gielgud, but rather as if channelling the spirit of Leroy from* Fame *through Gielgud's voice (i.e. like a very gay chorus boy).*

DB (John Gielgud) Oh, I suppose for Hamlet because it's a part that so many people have competed in. Naturally, it's a part that . . . I always . . . I must have been appallingly conceited when I was young, I remember going to a party when I was an understudy, somebody said, 'What are you going to be?' I said, 'I'm going to be a star!' Ha ha, I can't believe I was so impertinent at that time. And of course I never thought I would be one, really, but I sort of hoped to be – he-he. And I did long to get my name up in lights and all that stuff. I mean, I don't know what a great actor really is. I was very hesitant about making this programme, because one's bound to reveal oneself and one isn't very proud of it. And I think it's – although in a way acting depends on your scraping away the details of your personality and using all your qualities, to some extent, one is also somewhat ashamed of them being so lacking. I mean, I've never had interest in politics or sport. Two great wars have sort of passed me by in a way. And I've been so lucky and had such wonderful people to work with that I, I've been occupied and had fun and made many wonderful friends. One has nothing to reproach oneself with in that way. But I'm ashamed that I haven't got

---

[7] Interviewer, John Miller, from the documentary *An Actor's Life*.

more to offer really than just being an actor. I was very vain, and it did me a lot of harm because I'd give very sing song performances. And the people who were really honest used to tell me I was getting very affected and full of myself. Edith Evans once said to me, very politely, 'You know, if you cried a little less the audience would cry more.' Which was quite true. I used to flatter myself that my real tears were of such value. And I once read a very unfortunate remark to a reporter who said to me about crying tears, and I said, 'Yes, I always burst into tears if I see a regiment marching or a queen passing.'

V/O John Miller How did you find taking *Hamlet* on tour to the troops?

DB (John Gielgud) The troopsss? I *loved* it! I mean, it was a very exhausting and, er, hazardous job. We took our costumes, which was a bit rash because it was so hot in India and the Far East. And we had quite grand clothes which nearly killed us with the heat. I used to say to Marion Spencer, who played the Queen, 'Oh, please don't throw your train in the last act. All the dust in India gets up into my nose.' And she said, 'But I don't feel like a queen when I don't throw my train.' And we did *Blithe Spirit* with it, on other nights.

V/O John Miller Do you feel there is an acting tradition that is passed on from one generation to another?

DB (John Gielgud) Oh, I think there must be, don't you? I think there must be. I think it's a great advantage for one's survival in people's memories if you've played the great classics. Although so many marvellous actors have never played in anything rather than comedies or very light plays, and after they've gone it's shocking to me how quickly they're forgotten. But then I don't think one should complain, because we're one of the few creative professions that gets the reward in our lifetime. (*A thoughtful beat.*) One, one doesn't know whether there were actors born to blush unseen who would've been great actors if they'd had the chance. And I don't know how far one's ambitions push one, or how much they hold you back, 'cause I think they can do both. (*Pause.*) I had a few scenes that I think I was good in.

Piano music. Schubert again. As the piano music plays, the image of the four mannequins slides down the screen. Their bodies gradually disappear out of shot until only the four heads of **DB** *come to rest along the bottom of the screen. These will become four TALKING HEADS through the remainder of the show. From stage left to stage right these heads will lip-synch the voices of John Wood, Richard Eyre, Ian McKellen and Sean Mathias, respectively.*

Scene Five: Talking Heads / Tea Party

Lighting change. **DB** *picks up what looks like a blue doctor's/lab coat from the floor, puts it on, and continues arranging the chairs. With this blue work coat on, he is now 'THE DRESSER'.*[8]

---

[8] The voice of The Dresser is former National Theatre dresser Stephen Ashby, interviewed by Dickie Beau.

As the scene develops, **DB** *begins organising the space. He starts by placing mannequin torsos on the chairs and dressing these torsos in costumes from the floor, occasionally responding as THE DRESSER to the TALKING HEADS.*

John Wood (T/H) I'm John Wood and I represent Dickie Beau. Which I'm very pleased to do. I've seen an awful lot of Hamlets. An awful lot of Hamlets. I think the first one I remember hearing was John Gielgud at school, who was amazing. I worked with him on his very last day's work, and his voice had gone. David Mamet directed a Harold Pinter play with Rebecca Pidgeon, and all Sir John did was stand there in rapt silence. But he was so thrilled to be working. How many Hamlets have you seen?

Richard Eyre (T/H) I have seen a million and one Hamlets. I've seen it probably too many times for my own good.

DB (Dresser) (*points to the* **Richard Eyre** *Talking Head*) Richard Eyre. Lovely, lovely, lovely man.

Richard Eyre (T/H) When I was sixteen I lived in Dorset. My father was a farmer who was an ex-Naval officer. And so we didn't go to the theatre. I think I'd been once to a pantomime and once to a West End musical.

DB (Dresser) They always said about dressers, 'You never know about dressing 'til you've dressed on a musical.'

Richard Eyre (T/H) Until I stayed with a friend who lived in Bath. And his parents took us to see a play called *Hamlet* at the Bristol Old Vic, starring an actor called Peter O'Toole. And Ophelia was Wendy . . . Wendy . . . *Butterflies are Free* . . . Wendy . . . do I mean Wendy? . . . Anyway! Peter O'Toole had very dark hair and a Roman nose and I didn't know anything about the play, I didn't know how it turned out, and I was utterly captivated. And if there is, I mean one tells these stories to give a neatness to one's life.

DB (Dresser) You're kind of reflecting, aren't you? And you're romanticising and everything else, and you're trying to make a theory out of something.

Richard Eyre (T/H) But if there is a reason that I became interested in theatre it's because I saw that play at that particular time with that particular actor. He did – Peter O'Toole – did *Hamlet* at the Old Vic, when the Old Vic became the National Theatre. So, that was 1964. That was after he had become a film star. He had blond hair, he'd straightened his nose, and it was a very sort of soporific performance.

DB (Dresser) Very interesting, shows, isn't it? Because sometimes you think you've got it all right. I remember so many rehearsals, they thought they'd got the whole, the show right, and everyone thought, the word from the rehearsal room was going, 'Oh my god, this is magic.' Come to the stage . . . just died a death.

John Wood (T/H) Simon Russell Beale, Alan Rickman, Alan Cummings, Ralph Fiennes, Mark Rylance, Ben Whishaw, Jonathan Slinger, Michael Pennington, Roger Rees – fabulous – um . . . Daniel Day-Lewis, Jeremy Northam, Kenneth Branagh, Mel Gibson, Ian McKellen . . .

Ian McKellen (T/H) I've nothing illuminating to say about *Hamlet* that I can remember.

Richard Eyre (T/H) The second Hamlet I saw, oh, would be David Warner. Then I think I saw Ian McKellen play Hamlet.

Ian McKellen (T/H) I did realise and it's, it's, it's a point I've, I've given to a number of actors about to do it, whether they've asked for advice or not, I say, 'It's the leading part but it's not the only part. You don't have to carry the play. There's a lot of Hamlet when you're not on, even on stage. Let the others actors get on with it. It's all part of the play. It is a play called *Hamlet*, and you are in it, but you're not the only thing in it. It's not as big a burden as it seems to be Hamlet, because you can share it. And I think I did realise that. Mind you, I had a, I remember one night we were in Swansea and I was sharing a wonderful seaside cottage with Susan Fleetwood who was Ophelia and Julian Curry, who I'd been at university with, playing Horatio. And we were having, uh, we'd had a late night meal together, and one of them – probably Julian, he was rather outspoken – said, 'Ian, your performance is getting a bit slow as Hamlet'. 'Ah! What? Me slow? Me? Good God, I rattle through it.' 'Mmm. Well, we both –' 'You both think I'm slow? What about so and so? What about so and so? They're slow.' And Julian said, 'Can I just play you something?' And he had, in those days was huge tape recorders, no nice little machinery like this. And he started playing a bit of that night's performance. And fuck was it slow. I said, 'All right, that's enough, I believe you.'

By this point, **Dresser Dickie** *has mounted four torsos onto the four chairs and dressed each torso. The torsos' positioning implies that they each belong to the talking heads floating above them on the video screen. John Wood's torso is dressed in a ruffle-front shirt and shimmering evening jacket; Richard Eyre's torso is in army camouflage; Ian McKellen's torso wears an imperial military blazer with medals; Sean Mathias's torso is in a pyjama top.* **DB** *now comes across a long, elegant military officer's coat on the stage floor. He examines the label.*

Richard Eyre (T/H) The first production of *Hamlet* that I did was at the Royal Court in 1980 with Jonathan Pryce.

John Wood (T/H) Jonathan Pryce was . . .

John Wood/Ian McKellen (T/H) Jonathan Pryce . . .

All the torsos are dressed, so **Dresser Dickie** *decides to try this coat on himself* . . .

Ian McKellen (T/H) . . . was his own Ghost. Voice came out of . . . so, he did all the lines, as well. God. As if you need any more lines playing Hamlet but, um . . .

Eerie music, which seems to be linked to **DB** *putting on the coat. The four Talking Heads sense a change in the air and the coat seems to be having an effect on* **DB** . . . *We will shortly find out he is in the process of being possessed by the voice of* **Barbara Streisand**. *Lighting change.*

John Wood (T/H) (*suddenly possessed by the voice of Darth Vader*) I am your father.

DB (Barbara Streisand) Papa?

Richard Eyre (T/H) (*suddenly possessed by the voice of Jonathan Pryce as Hamlet possessed by the Ghost of Hamlet's father*) I am thy father's spirit. Doomed for a certain term to walk the night.

DB (Barbara Streisand) Papa?

Ian McKellen (T/H) (*suddenly possessed by the voice of Darth Vader*) If you only knew what happened to your father. If you only knew the *power* of the dark side.

Sean Mathias (T/H) (*suddenly possessed by the voice of Darth Vader*) Destroy the Emperor!

DB (Barbara Streisand) Papa? (*A shift and* **DB** *is suddenly possessed by the voice of Jonathan Pryce as Hamlet possessed by the Ghost of Hamlet's father.*) Adieu, adieu, re-member me. (*Comes out of Jonathan Pryce possession, back to Barbara.*) Papa . . . can you hear me? Papa can you see me? Papa can you find me in the night?

DB *takes in a deep breath as if to continue the song, but:*

DB (V/O) I've just remembered Berkoff, Berkoff played the voice of Hamlet's father in, was it Richard Dreyfuss's production on Broadway?

Dresser Dickie *comes back to himself and responds with slightly alarmed curiosity to the disembodied voice of* **DB**, *which seems to be coming from somewhere above, or behind, the audience. Is this voice familiar?*

Ian McKellen (T/H) Ah.

DB (V/O) But it was lip-synched by another performer.

Ian McKellen (T/H) Oh. Hm.

DB (V/O) I wrote to him and asked him if he knew how I could get hold of that because I thought it would be fun.

Ian McKellen (T/H) Did he not have it?

DB (V/O) No, he doesn't know, no, he doesn't have it, no.

Ian McKellen (T/H) He lives just up the road.

DB (V/O) Yeah, I've been there.

Ian McKellen (T/H) Hm. Did he show you the costumes he's got?

DB (V/O) No.

At the mention of costumes, **Dresser Dickie** *starts to carefully take off the coat as he continues to listen, before returning to the job of examining, folding and organising the costumes on stage into neat piles . . .*

Ian McKellen (T/H) He bought some costumes that were being sold by the National Theatre. He bought the costume Laurence Olivier wore as Richard III on stage. He bought the costume Laurence Olivier wore as Othello. He's got them hanging in his closet. What can he do with them? But . . . he's got them.

Extraordinary. So, I'm sure if that recording existed he would have it, because . . . he keeps things.

Richard Eyre (T/H) Anyway, Peter was . . .

DB (Dresser) (*a clarifying interjection*) . . . Peter Hall . . .

Richard Eyre (T/H) . . . getting into his period, um, well, which lasted, you know, er . . . forever . . . um . . . of strict orthodoxy about Shakespeare. I think it is a total cul de sac.

DB (Dresser) Peter Hall. Um. Phenomenal at getting the actors together. Phenomenal casting. Didn't direct at all. But he also was wonderful at curtain calls. The best director at curtain calls.

Richard Eyre (T/H) When I did *Hamlet* he had a public row with – Michael Billington had said how marvellous it was and Peter Hall took him on publicly and said, a sort of curious thing, he said that, er, Jonathan Pryce appeared to be . . . to be speaking as if he was . . . thinking in the moment. I thought, well, hang on, I thought that was the point!

John Wood (T/H) I'm trying to think how many other Hamlets I've seen. Many!

Richard Eyre (T/H) Anyway, Peter overlooked that, asked me to . . . and two years later I did *Guys and Dolls* at the National.

DB (Dresser) (*now juggling an unmanageable pile of costumes*) But I never really saw it because I was just running round changing all these costumes, having twenty-six changes in the show – one was, um, the slowest five minutes, the quickest eighteen seconds. We were screaming changing these – it was very very funny. Didn't stop running. Running running running running. You just did not stop running for the whole show. We had such a hoot, so many parties. Wonderful, wonderful cast. Oh my god, I've forgotten, I should know this, it's quite a well-known actor . . . Ian Charleson as Sky.

John Wood (T/H) Ian Charleson was a fantastic actor. A great actor. With a musical simple beauty about his voice.

DB (Dresser) And a lovely designer, who was it, I've forgotten her name. Beautiful cozzies. And then a lovely du um choreographer who's passed away now, whose name I forget too.

John Wood (T/H) Ian Charleson was a thrilling Hamlet.

Richard Eyre (T/H) And then I did *Hamlet* at the National Theatre, 1987, '88?

John Wood (T/H) It was 1989?

DB (Dresser) I can't remember.

Ian McKellen (T/H) We could look up the dates, I've got them.

Dresser Dickie *has arranged some neat piles of costumes and is now beginning to organize some of the mannequin limbs.*

Richard Eyre (T/H) Um. With Daniel Day-Lewis.

Dresser Dickie*'s ears prick up at the mention of Daniel Day-Lewis.*

Richard Eyre (T/H) And Daniel withdrew from the production halfway through the run, and then Jeremy Northam took over for a while, and then, er, Ian Charleson.

Sean Mathias (T/H) And this was in nineteen . . . eighty-nine.

Ian McKellen (T/H) Eighty-nine! Sean was very close to Ian, he'd been on holiday with him, he'd . . . probably closer than anybody, really, so if he remembers he'll remember exactly.

Sean Mathias (T/H) Dan was giving this legendary Hamlet. Legendary because he'd had such a break – I mean, he was very very nervous I think of going on stage, very unhappy, going through torment playing the role, convinced he'd seen his father's ghost.

Dresser Dickie *looks out at the audience conspiratorially. He now has a mannequin arm in each of his hands, which act as absurd gestural extenders of his own arms during the following speech.*

DB (Dresser) The story comes from me. I was dressing the Prince of Denmark. Um, when you're looking after someone like Daniel Day-Lewis, or anyone else like that, a smithen, little bit of information would come back to you six months later . . . vastly blown out. So, no, he didn't see his father dead. What he did do was have a lovely photograph of his father with, um, a poem that his father had written when he was first born. So, he kind of used that. But it was amalgamation of stories, 'cos I said, 'Oh, he's got a, um, a photograph of his father, and a lovely lovely poem. And from that those stories came together. He had flown back from New York that morning. I th, I think we did a dress rehearsal, 'cos there'd been such a gap. So, it was the afternoon we did a dress rehearsal. This is, I can't really remember very much. I said, 'Aren't you tired?' He said, 'No, I'm fine, Stephen, I'm fine.' And, um, he was kind of slumped over the, the dressing room, you know, fff, um table. And of course he wasn't, he was absolutely exhausted. Um. Judi Dench, um, when, um, she was playing, er, Dirty Gert with, um, Daniel, was concerned because he was putting so much energy into, into the role. Too much. 'Cos he was living it each time. He shrunk, I think, three jackets. He shrunk them, 'cos the sweat. Beautiful fabric. And sh –, I remember her saying, 'You know, you can't do that. It's got, you've gotta get the technique. You can't do this every night. I'm really worried about him. So, she'd, she used to buy him Mars bars. And when it came to the Dad scene, he just cracked up. Not cracked up. He just collapsed with exhausting, saying, 'I'm so sorry, I'm so sorry, I just can't do it, I'm so tired, I can't do it, I can't do it. I'm exhausted.' And that's the last time I saw of him. It's tragic, because as I was taking him to the dressing room, him crying his eyes out saying, 'I'm so sorry, I've let everyone down, I'm so sorry,' I'm unhooking all what I need for the understudy. I've unhook his cloak, grab that. I need the sword, I grab that. And I said, 'Don't worry, Dan, don't worry, Dan.' And I ran round to Jeremy Northam. And, um, I says, 'Hi Jeremy.' He says, 'Hi Stephen.' I says, 'You're on!' You could just see the colour drain from his face.

Dresser Dickie *lays down his arms. In so doing, his attention is drawn to a pair of mannequin legs on the floor, which seems to give him a new thought.*

Richard Eyre (T/H) When Dan left the production I thought it was important to get, um, a really considerable and experienced actor and, and that's why I asked Ian.

Dresser Dickie *begins to take the two mannequin torsos on the stage right half of the stage off their chairs, and stacks the chairs to stage right side of the screen.*

Sean Mathias (T/H) I came to London in seventy-three, and I met Ian then. But he was more friends of friends and I was not – I was friendly with him but not close, and then one year, I can't remember when that was, probably sometime in the eighties, I was going to Morocco on holiday and I wanted someone to go with. And he was just kicking his heels. He said, 'I'll go with you.' But we became from that really close, close, close friends. He became one of my best friends.

Dresser Dickie *divides the two stage right curtains, revealing for the first time a glimpse of the corridor behind the front curtains. He pushes the furthermost stage right curtain to the stage right edge of the corridor, and creates a 'pillar' with the remaining curtain, so that there are effectively now two 'windows' onto the corridor.*

Ian McKellen (T/H) There's so many obvious things to remember about Ian and, and, which made him great company. And one of them was his sense of humour. He laughed a lot. And made others laugh a lot. And of course he was beautiful. And of course he could sing. Like an angel. I think at his funeral they played something of his singing. Probably 'My Love is Like a Red Red Rose', that was his, er, one of his party pieces.

Dresser Dickie *mounts a pair of mannequin legs in each 'window'. A pair of male mannequin legs in the furthermost stage right window, a pair of female mannequin legs in the window closest to centre.*

DB (V/O) So, if I could ask you about Ian Charleson and Hamlet. Er, I know that, 'cause it was 1989, wasn't it, the production at the National?

Richard Eyre (T/H) Yes, yes.

DB (V/O) Erm, and Sean Mathias told me that earlier that year, it would have been about the same time, March, April, that you opened *Hamlet* . . .

Richard Eyre (T/H) Yes.

DB (V/O) He directed a one night only performance of *Bent*.

Richard Eyre (T/H) Yes.

DB (V/O) At the Adelphi.

Richard Eyre (T/H) Yes.

DB (V/O) Do you remember that?

Richard Eyre (T/H) Yeah, yeah.

DB (V/O) Did you go? Were you there? Did you see that?

Richard Eyre (T/H) I think I was there, yes.

Dresser Dickie *has found the female mannequin torso on the stage, taken it to her 'window' and now fixes it to her legs.*

DB (V/O) Er, 'cause Ian Charleson played Greta.

Richard Eyre (T/H) Yeah.

Sean Mathias (T/H) And that was an inc –, one of the, you know, the great nights of our lives, in a way, because we did it at the Adelphi Theatre to raise, I think I'm right, we were raising money to formulate Stonewall.

Ian McKellen (T/H) The first lobby group on behalf of lesbians and gay people in the United Kingdom.

Dresser Dickie *now fixes the male mannequin torso onto his legs.*

Sean Mathias (T/H) Ian Charleson played Greta.

Ian McKellen (T/H) And it was wonderful that Ian was in it because he would never have played Greta in a full scale production because it wasn't a big enough part. Ian was a leading actor.

Dresser Dickie *slides the 'pillar' curtain to the stage right edge so that both mannequins are now framed within one long window. He comes forward to view the framing of both mannequins from the front.*

Sean Mathias (T/H) He was brilliant as Greta, absolutely brilliant, he was fantastic.

Ian McKellen (T/H) You'd be a wonderful Greta.

Dresser Dickie *does a slight double take at this.*

Sean Mathias (T/H) But he had an amazing voice, singing voice.

Ian McKellen (T/H) I didn't realise when we did *Bent* that Ian was ill. Let alone very ill.

Dresser Dickie *moves to the stage right edge of the corridor and reattaches the two separated curtains together. During the preceding and following lines, he pulls this curtain across the front, concealing the mannequins and the corridor.*

Sean Mathias (T/H) I knew how ill he was, which most people didn't know, so, um, and it was quite difficult because Greta changes from her drag into a man's costume onstage.

Dresser Dickie *now opens the upstage curtains. As he is backlit from beyond the downstage curtains, this means we can see him moving in shadow. Over the following lines the upstage right curtains are opened first, which also reveals the mannequins in silhouette.*

And although I had put a screen for him to get changed behind he's, you know, he's got to be visible because he's doing a lot of the talking, he can't sort of disappear in the middle of the scene.

DB *opens the upstage curtains stage left, which reveals the silhouette of a hospital bed.*

So we devised a way of him dressing that he felt protected.

DB*'s silhouette comes to the centre.*

But the problem was people in the wings could see him.

DB *comes through the front curtain, centre-stage, now fully visible.*

And when he took his shirt off he was covered in Kaposi's sarcoma.

DB *slides the jacket off the torso that sits directly beneath the Ian McKellen Talking Head (the chair immediately stage left of centre).*

So, it was very, er, delicate and painful, you know, sort of, to go through.

Dresser Dickie *carefully folds McKellen's military jacket and adds it to one of the costume piles he organized earlier downstage.*

Ian McKellen (T/H) I suppose he must have been thinking and realising that there would, he wouldn't be working very often in the future. Although he still had *Hamlet* to come.

DB *returns to the McKellen torso and takes both the torso and chair together behind the downstage run of curtains. We see him place the chair in the shadow corridor, just stage right of centre, at an angle facing downstage left.*

Richard Eyre (T/H) And of course I knew that Ian . . .

DB *comes back through the curtains onto the stage.*

Well, let's say I knew of substantial rumours that Ian was ill.

DB *takes the final chair and torso off through the curtains.*

And then when Ian came round here to talk about it.

He places the final chair in shadow behind the curtains, just stage left of centre, at an angle facing downstage right.

There was absolutely no argument about it.

He lays the torso down onto the hospital bed.

Although I didn't say, you know.

DB *comes forward through the curtains and downstage towards sitting mannequin legs (which are missing part of one leg from the thigh).*

He had huge lumps under each eye, and his extraordinary and touching beauty was, I mean, he was disfigured.

DB *takes these legs off over his shoulder through the curtains.*

And it just became a sort of unspoken . . .

Behind the curtain, **DB** *attaches the sitting legs to the torso on the chair in shadow just stage right of the centre.*

He knew that I knew, and I knew that he knew that I knew. And, um, I just thought he should, he should do it. And. Knowing. I think. That his days were . . . were numbered.

Sean Mathias (T/H) And Ian started canvassing opinion, because doing, playing Greta and being exposed when you're so ill really was, cost him, you know, and it was really frightening.

DB *comes carefully forward through the curtains again, towards another set of mannequin legs. During the following speech, he proceeds to take these legs upstage through the curtains to the hospital bed completing the shadow image of a figure lying on the hospital bed.*

And as his friend and someone who loved him I wanted to protect him, and . . . I mean, I was thrilled that he played Greta, 'cause he contributed so much to the success of the evening and to the attention that we all got and to launching Stonewall, but I was also, you know, intensely aware of his vulnerability and didn't want him to, er, damage himself further. So, I remember when he got asked to play Hamlet, everyone said, 'Oh, you've got to do it, you've got to do it.' I mean, it's obviously a great honour to play Hamlet, Olivier Theatre, blah blah blah. Wonderful. But I think I'm right in saying, not with any pride or ego, that I was the only person who said, 'Don't do it.' I was frightened he would get very ill and it would precipitate his death, that's what I feared. I said, 'Don't do it, it'll kill you.' And he said, 'You know, I'm going to die anyway, so . . .' He was dying. He was dying. You know. He took on the role when he was dying.

DB *re-emerges from the shadow corridor, through the centre of the curtains, into full visibility on the stage.*

Ian McKellen (T/H) For me, the performance, I can't remember it in detail, but that Ian was ill, and desperately ill, and looking ravaged.

DB *comes across latex the model of his own head.*

The face was . . . Oh, dear. So often the case with AIDS that it attacks . . . perhaps the best part of you and it attacked Ian's looks, which were so crucial to his charm and his success, and . . .

DB *looks around for something . . .*

Didn't attack his voice, I don't think, but . . .

DB *spots the crown.*

So, there he was looking ill. The lighting as I remember kept him in the shade quite a lot,

DB *retrieves the crown and places it on the latex head. He auditions positions for the crowned head in relation to the theatre lights and appraises the effects.*

so that in that large theatre you could see the performance and think, 'Oh, Ian Charleson doesn't look as I remember him.' You wouldn't think any more than that. But for those of us who knew, when that Hamlet talked about death . . . well, it was revelatory.

DB *is satisfied with a position and sets the head down. His attention is drawn to the* Hamlet *play text on the floor beside him. He picks it up, opens it, begins to read as he slowly crosses towards stage left.*

I mean, I've . . . And when he said, 'Let be.' It was an actor talking from his own experience about the prospect of death. It wasn't our sentiment of knowing that the actor was going to die. It was that Ian knew he was going to die and, and he gave that to Hamlet.

En route, **DB** *is distracted by a stray costume – an enormous regal red velvet robe. He picks it up.*

I mean, actors are always dying in plays. I've often thought, can you ever bring that off as an actor?

He considers the robe. Could he bring this off?

Wouldn't it be wonderful if the audience thought the actor had died?

DB *tries on the robe, momentarily giving it life.*

You know, you play Hamlet, we all know he's going to jump up at the end and take the curtain call and go off to a club. Turn up and give this performance again tomorrow.

DB *has seen enough. He takes the robe off.*

But with Ian . . .

DB *lowers the robe slowly to the floor, as if melting away.*

He's dying in front of our eyes.

Sean Mathias (T/H) (*on* **Sean***'s voice,* **DB** *crosses to the empty clothes rail, where he stands and listens*) It transcended theatre because of the experience of watching a man playing that spiritual and metaphysical part and all the concerns of death and suicide, and the injustice of life, and treachery of life, and being channelled through a person who himself life was being cut short way to prematurely by an invasive sort of enemy that had, you know, entered our midst and we didn't understand.

DB (Dresser) HIV was never talked about then, in those days, [*'cos*] we never understood it so much. We were all very, very frightened of it. I didn't have penetrative sex for about ten years. Too terrified.

Sean Mathias (T/H) You know, AIDS didn't even seem like a disease at that point, it just seemed like a terrifying enemy. It was as if, you know, the metaphor of *Bent*, it was as if the Nazis had arrived in our society.

DB *steps through the empty rail and starts to walk towards the piles of costume he prepared downstage right earlier in the show.*

Because it felt, it felt like not just a disease, but a bigot as well.

As **DB** *crosses something on the floor of the stage catches his eye. During the following he moves closer to it. There seems to be a hole in the floor.*

Ian McKellen (T/H) Probably because in those days, it's difficult to remember now in England, and in Scotland more so, to be gay was a real disadvantage. But in those days no one would ever ask you were you gay. (**DB** *looks down through the hole . . .*) It was thought to be the worst thing you could say about a young person, or any man.

DB *interrupts himself to look up and interject.*

DB (Dresser) So we were all so neurotic about it. You couldn't even tell your friends.

DB *slides his finger into the hole on the stage floor.*

Ian McKellen (T/H) So. It was easy to hide. (**DB** *pulls open a large trap door.*) Not good for any of us. (**DB** *peers down into the darkness.*) But Ian was not – as I remember – Ian was not openly gay, even while he was playing Greta in the production to raise money for an organization that was going to make it easier for people to come out. I suspect he didn't ever tell his parents. Any more than any of us did. That wasn't out of the ordinary.

DB *begins to lay the previously arranged costumes/props/mannequin parts into the trap door. The trap door is now a kind of grave, and the gathered objects seem now the archive of a life now lost . . .*

Sean Mathias (T/H) That was part of what one went through with these deaths, was dealing with people's families as well, obviously, you know. The shock of the, the, the person who was so ill being outed as well through the illness.

Ian McKellen (T/H) And then the irony of him being identified for the rest of time as someone who'd died because he had sex with another man. So.

DB (Dresser) (**DB** *continues to lay the* Hamlet *relics/personal effects to rest in the trapdoor*) W – I think we all knew. Silvia Syms who took over from, um, Judi Dench . . . Um . . . Tricky. 'Cos she's an old, different type of actress. You know, the dresser said 'Oh, um, wh – at this point Judi and I would do this.' 'I will only say this once, I am not Judi Dench, we'll do it my way.' She was tricky. However, um, she would go early to pick Ian up for the show, cook him dinner before he came to the show, then bring him in, take him home. My thoughts about Silvia Syms changed enormously. Love. Empathy. And no judgement. And I suppose that's what you offer: love.

DB *is coming toward the end of the burial; aside from one pile stage left of the 'grave,' which includes the pyjamas, and the velvet robe, all the other costumes have now gone into the trapdoor . . .*

Ian McKellen (T/H) And when, when John Gielgud, in the later, earlier generation, was convicted for, um, what would be the phrase . . .? Well, he tried to pick somebody up in Trafalgar Square. (**DB** *is laying the last of the mannequin body parts in the grave.*) Was fined thirty pounds in, um, Bow Street Magistrates Court. Where I think Oscar Wilde had also been first charged . . . (**DB** *turns to the latex head and crown.*)

there was a move in the Equity Council . . . (**DB** *picks up the head and examines it.*) led by a Yorkshire one-eyed actor called Edward Chapman . . . (**DB** *contemplates putting the head into the grave.*) to have John Gielgud removed from Equity. To have his membership taken away from him. (**DB** *decides not to put the head in the grave and sets it back onstage.*) Which would've meant he couldn't have worked. (**DB** *stands and looks down into the grave, unbuttoning his overall.*) Because in those days the Union had a closed shop, and you had to be a member of the Union to act. (**DB** *drops his Dresser overall into the grave, and closes the trap door.*) And Gielgud couldn't work in America for ten years because he'd been found guilty. (*PAUSE. During which* **DB** *picks up the* Hamlet *playtext, and gathers the pile of costumes that he had left onstage, before turning upstage and heading into the curtained corridor.*) So, Ian's story is a part of all that. But when he was ill the significance of it was not that at all. The significance was that he was ill.

Scene Six: Gielgud (No Man's Land)[9]

Lights up in corridor. Coinciding with the lighting change, the Talking Heads on screen dissolve into a white outline of the heads, before fading to black. This is the first time since the opening of the show that the screen has gone completely black.

Piano music and birdsong.

DB *opens the stage right pair of downstage curtains and begins dressing the mannequin that is laid on the hospital bed, with the pyjamas. The vibe he gives off is of a gay nurse attending to a patient . . .*

DB (John Gielgud) Do you often hang about Hampstead Heath? I often hang about Hampstead Heath myself. Expecting nothing. I am too old for any kind of expectation. Don't you agree? But of course I observe a good deal on my peeps through twigs. A wit once entitled me a betwixt twig peeper. A most clumsy construction, I thought. All we have left is the English language. Can it be salvaged? That is my question. You're a quiet one. It's a great relief. Can you imagine two of us gabbling away like me? It would be intolerable. Oh, by the way, with reference to peeping, I do feel it incumbent upon me to make one thing clear: I don't peep on sex. That's gone forever. You follow me? When my twigs happen to, shall I say, rest their peep on sexual conjugations, however periphrastic, I see only whites of eyes. Experience is a paltry thing. Everyone has it and will tell his tale of it. The present will not be distorted. I am a poet. I am interested in where I am eternally present and active. (*Pause.*) I'll ask you another question. Have you any idea from what I derive my strength? I have never been loved. From this I derive my strength. Have you? Ever? Been loved?

Piano music closes the scene as lights fade and **DB** *pulls the stage left curtains across in front of the hospital bed.*

---

9 The audio for this scene is of John Gielgud in Harold Pinter's *No Man's Land.*

Scene Seven: Suzanne in Silhouette

Silhouette light comes up, with **DB** *behind the screen, framing* **DB** *in a rectangular 'window'. He is sitting slightly stage left of centre, appearing to face the shadow of a mannequin body he has seated in the chair slightly stage right of centre. The interview footage used in this scene was taken over lunch in a busy restaurant, so* **DB** *mimes the eating of bread, the shaking of a salt mill, reacting to the sound of another diner sneezing, etc., synchronizing the scene in silhouette with the sounds we hear on the recording. . . .*

DB (Suzanne Bertish) Where's the microphone? Oh, it's there. There's two.

DB (V/O) There's two, so it'll pick up both of us, I think.

DB (Suzanne Bertish) (*picking up the playtext, which now acts as a menu*) OK. I don't know what I want to eat. Um. Errr. A salad, I guess.

DB (V/O) That's what I'm thinking.

Waiter (V/O) Would you guys like to start with anything to drink other than water?

DB (Suzanne Bertish) No, that's great.

DB (V/O) Not for me, thanks.

DB (Suzanne Bertish) You know, it couldn't be a very athletic Hamlet. 'Cause he didn't have the strength. And a lot of his friends thought he shouldn't do it. I didn't, I thought he should do it. He wanted to do it. It was so profound. 'Oh that this too too solid flesh would melt.' I mean, he just collapsed on the floor, and spoke it. Oh. I remember that. At the end, and I have never seen this, in England, for a Shakespeare . . . at the end two thirds of the audience just stood. Not a few people. Just stood! They knew they had witnessed something deeply profound. They didn't know what. (*A sneeze from another diner, which* **DB** *reacts to.*) We went to the, um, the Green Room afterwards and Ian said, er, 'I wish they'd, er, review this, but, you know, the National aren't gonna ask anyone to come back and re-review it, I just want to get reviewed in it.' And when we left, I, I did not know John Peter, I had never met him. I picked up the phone (**DB** *picks up some 'bread'.*), I called the *Sunday Times*. He *happened* to be there. (**DB** *breaks imaginary bread.*) He was never, I found out subsequently, he was never, ever in his office. Ever. (**DB** *mimes spreading butter on the bread and shaking a salt mill, in sync with the sound.*) He had no idea that Ian, what Ian was suffering from. (**DB** *puts the bread in his mouth. We can hear Suzanne is eating as she says:*) But you've read the review.

DB (V/O) Yeah, I actually asked him to read it for me, too.

DB (Suzanne Bertish) Oh, really?

DB (V/O) John Peter, yeah, he read it for me. So, I have a recording of him reading it.

DB (Suzanne Bertish) He left a magnum of champagne for Ian, you know.

DB (V/O) I heard that.

DB (Suzanne Bertish) Isn't that weird? I mean –

DB (V/O) That is totally weird.

DB (Suzanne Bertish) Critics never –

DB (V/O) I've never heard of that before.

DB (Suzanne Bertish) I don't think he'd ever done it before or since.

Waiter (V/O) We have your butter salad.

DB (Suzanne Bertish) Lovely, thank you.

DB (V/O) Thank you very much.

Reverberant sound of crockery being set down on a table punctuates the ending of the scene. The backlighting dissolves with the sound . . .

Scene Eight: Talking Heads / Tea Party 2

The Talking Heads reappear on the projection screen.

In the darkness, the curtain that had concealed the white curtains at the start of the show is lowered once more, surrounding the screen with darkness.

Aside from the Talking Heads, lip-synching the dialogue in this scene, the stage is completely dark. One by one, as each voice speaks, an empty spotlight appears on stage beneath that Talking Head, literally illuminating the presence of absence. Once illuminated, these spotlights remain on until the end of the scene. . . .

DB *does not appear live during this scene, neither on stage nor in silhouette, partly in a nod to the scenes within the play of* Hamlet *during which the character remains offstage (as Ian McKellen has told us earlier in this show, 'There's a lot of Hamlet when you're not even on stage. Let the other actors get on with it . . .')*

Ian McKellen (T/H) (*the empty spotlight comes up under this Talking Head*) So, it was a friend of Ian's who called a critic, who otherwise would not have seen the performance, and, and he went and was absolutely knocked sideways by it. And didn't know that Ian was ill.

Sean Mathias (T/H) (*this second empty spotlight comes up with Sean's voice*) We were all at Ian's house having Sunday lunch and we read it and Ian's spirits were so lifted, I mean, he could barely leave the bed, he just was so elated.

Ian McKellen (T/H) I mean, as I remember, we've all seen very active Hamlets, who run around the place and so on. But Hamlet lives in his head. And Ian's Hamlet did and, and I remember it as being a very still performance. He must have been very, very tired. How he did the fight I don't know. I can't really remember the fight. That's always the dreadful thing about Hamlet, the end of the evening you've got to then do that fucker.

Sean Mathias (T/H) The thing I remember most about him was he was just incredibly romantic. He played it with a kind of incredible daring, like an actor from another century. He just was physically so kind of balletic and romantic. He did these great sweeping daring things with his voice and his body.

Ian McKellen (T/H) Well, Sean's memory is, is brighter than mine. Uh. Although we do occasionally have arguments about something that happened or didn't happen, but he, I bet he remembers. So, if he remembers, he'll remember exactly.

Sean Mathias (T/H) I guess Richard Eyre had the vision to offer Ian the part, you know. He had that vision. Whether he fully realised quite what he was offering Ian, I don't know. I've never asked Richard that, actually.

Richard Eyre (T/H) (*the third empty spotlight comes up under this Talking Head*) From this distance, I could pretend that in some sense, you know, it was, I was working out a thesis, but, it doesn't, it wasn't true. It was a very personal decision, and it happened that, in a sense, that Ian in every way endorsed my perception of the play. Um. And it's a terrible tragedy that he did. But, yes, he grew up to grow dead.

John Wood (T/H) (*the fourth and final empty spotlight comes up under this Talking Head*) The thing is, we've got to be realistic about it. Was that performance a good Hamlet in that moment? Or are we now remembering it because of, you know, the beauty of Shakespeare's language about death and mortality, and the readiness of the sparrow, the stillness, or whatever, the rest is silence. Are we making him, that man, in that moment, with those words, are we now turning him into something that really never was because he died very soon after? And my answer to that is NO. My answer to that was he was a great Hamlet. My answer to that is he would have been a brilliant King Lear. He would've had a career, should've had a career, equal and better than Dirk Bogarde. He was a star.

Talking Heads – and spotlights – go out.

Scene Nine: John Peter Review / Eulogy / Old Gielgud

This scene is underscored with 'Prospero's Books' by Michael Nyman. As the voiceover of John Peter begins, the lights slowly come up on **DB**. *He is now on stage (stage left) and holds the pose of a runner braced to start a race, ready for the starter's pistol. As the lights fade up on him, black and white footage fades up on the screen of a crowd of men's feet, running along a beach, and through the surf . . .*

John Peter (V/O) When you recast a production, you conduct a brand new experiment. Actor and director are like chemical elements. Change one of them and you change the reactions of both. The great Shakespearean roles can take a number of interpretations. And a different Hamlet will create a different Elsinore. Shining performances revolve like planets around the masterful new Hamlet, Ian Charleson, who succeeds Daniel Day-Lewis.

At the mention of Ian Charleson, **DB** *springs forward as if sprinting out of the starting blocks. But no sooner does he start than he is suspended mid-motion. At the same time as* **DB** *springs forward, the black and white footage on the screen cuts from the multitude of running men's feet to slow motion footage of Ian Charleson – the first time we have seen an image of him in the show – in a scene from* Chariots of Fire, *springing forward into a practice sprint. . . .*

Technically, he deploys clarity combined with a powerful dramatic drive. His delivery is steely but delicate. The words move with sinuous elegance and crackle with fire. This is a princely Hamlet, every inch the King he should have been. The first impression he makes is one of stern melancholy. He is tense, but composed. Charleson makes no concessions to dreamy distraught romanticism. His Hamlet is virile and forceful with all the sombre self-possession that comes from being a public man, observed of all observers. **He oozes intelligence from every pore**, a restless inquisitive rationalist.

At the mention of oozing intelligence, **DB** *physically shifts and he melts onto the floor. As he does he seems to trace the entire outline of his own body, running his hand up his arms, over his face, feeling his lips, feeling his legs, feeling what is between his legs, as if performing some kind of tactile investigation, both a searching and a finding. This is a kind of ritual of re-*Present*ing – a 're-memberment' . . .*

Of course, he is cultivated and refined. When he picks up Ophelia's book from the floor for her, he glances at it to see what it is. Like anyone to whom books are vital nourishment. But, more important than this, he has a natural alertness, which helps him to hear the silent subtext of people's conversation. An essential intuition, which cracks the coded language of the court. This inborn intelligence is honed on forceful thinking. To Charleson's Hamlet what has happened at the Danish court is an assault on reason and nature. It is monstrous because it is unnatural. The 'To be or not to be' speech is the complaint of a rationalist articulated by rigorous thinking and matter-of-fact self-reproach. The performance is laced and spiced with dry, tough, often self-mocking wit. Charleson's Hamlet can afford to laugh grimly at himself, because he has the natural regal confidence of a man who knows his own character. **He is perfectly at home with himself. It is the world that is out of joint.**

At this point in the review, **DB** *has completed his re-tracing/re-memberment, and he comes to rest on the floor, arms and legs outstretched, as if he is running although he is lying down.*

He is the true Renaissance man. A much trivialized phrase. But he knows his own worth, including the faults, the doubts and the blemishes.

Onscreen, Charleson passes the finish line. He is the winner. The images freezes and begins to fade . . .

Charleson's Hamlet is a brilliant exercise in mature judgement. His sombre self-knowledge forms the true substance of his tragedy.

The onscreen image of Charleson has faded to black.

The way someone like Charleson can transform a production is a **reminder** (**DB** *raises his head, re-membering.*) that actors are **alive and well** (**DB** *rises from the floor.*), that directors can only draw a performance from those who have one in them (**DB** *slowly crosses to wheelchair stage right*), and that in the last analysis the voice of drama speaks to us through actors. The voice of drama speaks to us through actors. The voice of drama speaks to us through actors.

A spotlight comes up on **DB** *in the wheelchair.*

Interviewer (V/O)[10] How do you enjoy being old?

DB Gielgud Oh, I hate it. Oh, so many of my friends have died. And I think one becomes increasingly guilty at seeing the world go by and not taking more interest in it. I've never done anything for anybody. I mean, I've, I haven't fought in either war. I knew all the great people of my time. And I do resent that I can't have some of them back. My, my most cherished. One pictures so many things that may upset one, particularly the death of people you're fond of, and wonders why they should be chosen rather than yourself. It is a terrible threat hanging over your head, which somehow you're more aware of when you're old than when you're young. I miss the companionship of rehearsals. But I couldn't play a long part now. I don't suppose I could remember it.

'Prospero's Books', which has been playing in the background since the start of the scene, reaches climax as lights go to black.

Scene Ten: I am not Prince Hamlet

Michael Douglas (V/O) (*in the blackout*) Let's continue please. Step forward, tell me your real name, your stage name if it's different, where you were born, and how old you are.

Lights up on **DB**, *now centre stage, standing on the upstage lip of the trapdoor, casting a large shadow onto the projection screen behind (see Fig 1). He now 'auditions' potential renditions of 'to be or not to be'. We hear varied attacks on this text, as if he is playing them over in his head (he does not lip-synch this audio). Meanwhile, his physical body attempts to take shapes that might 'fit' the voiceover . . .*

DB (V/0) To be, or not to be. To be, or not to be. To be, or not to be. To be. To be. To be. To be, or not to be. To be, or not to be. To be, or not to be. To be, or not to be. To be, or not to be – that is the question. To be, or not to be. That is the question. To be, or not to be.

He gives up. And suddenly from nowhere, in his own voice, he cries out:

DB NOOOOOOOOOOOOO! (*He settles down.*) **I am not Prince Hamlet. Nor was meant to be. Am an attendant Lord. One who will do to swell a progress,**

---

[10] The interviewer is believed to be Jeremy Paxman, taken from an interview recorded with Gielgud at age ninety-five in 1999.

start a scene or two. Advise the prince. No doubt an easy tool. Deferential. Glad to be of use. Politic, cautious and meticulous. Full of high sentence, but a bit obtuse. At times indeed almost ridiculous. Almost, at times, the fool.[11]

DB *holds the latex head as he drops the crown into the trap door. He closes the trap.*

Ian Charleson (V/O) I now give you that epitome of a lady's man to toast the lasses . . .

The black curtain under the projection screen is raised again to reveal the curtains.

(*Sings*) Oh my love is like a red red rose / that's newly sprung in June / oh my love is like a melody / that's sweetly played in tune /

DB *turns upstage, still holding the latest head. He opens the stage right panel of curtains, then the stage left panel, to reveal a 'window display' that might be like something Manders and Mitcherson*[12] *might have curated for their museum: an archive of Hamlets from the past. Several of the mannequins have been assembled in costume-y costumes and seem to be arranged in attendance to the figure lying on the hospital bed. Once the curtains are open,* **DB** *retrieves the mirror ball from earlier and also enters the corridor, wheeling the mirror ball towards the figure in bed. Meanwhile, a huge mirror ball comes into view on the screen above the stage.*

Ian McKellen (V/O) I've just remembered the last time I saw Ian. He was in bed. And they'd rigged up some – he had some crystals, and these crystals it was thought might cure him. They were rigged up. There was a light so the light shone through the crystals onto Ian. He was lying there like under a sunbed.

The mirrorball is now in position just upstage of the figure in bed, casting rays of light onto the mannequin body and the curtain corridor. **DB** *fixes the latex model of his own head to this mannequin lying down on the bed. He heads towards it.*

He'd been given up by the doctors. This was a bit of magic. I suppose if you don't want to die and you're dying, and someone says, 'Try this', you do. And here by the bed was a little table.

He turns and moves to a vacant chair in the centre of the corridor, at the foot of the bed.

And on the table was a copy of *Hamlet*.

On the chair is a copy of Hamlet. *He picks it up. He sits. He reads.*

Ian Charleson (V/O) (*singing*) So fare they weel my bonny lass / so fare thee weel awhile / and I will come again my dear / though 'twere ten thousand miles / though 'twere ten thousand mile my love / though 'twere ten thousand mile / and I will come again my dear / though 'twere ten thousand mile. . .

The black curtain comes down, covering the window display and **DB** *seated within it.*

On screen, the mirrorball morphs into the image of The Thinker *we saw at the opening of the show.*

---

11 From 'The Love Song of J. Alfred Prufrock' by T. S. Eliot.

12 The famous theatre historians mentioned by Ian McKellen in Scene Two.

Scene Eleven: Ian McKellen Epilogue

For the first time, the onscreen figure of The Thinker *comes to life. It has Ian McKellen's voice.*

DB McKellen (*the lip-synching image onscreen*) My, my own Hamlet. There was a sense that it was a success. But not critically. What did Harold Hobson say, who preceded John Peter at the *Sunday Times*, was the critic . . . 'Ian McKellen's Ham – the best thing about Ian McKellen's Hamlet is his curtain call' (*laughs.*) But I, I've noticed when people, as fairly often happens, you get articles about Hamlets of the past . . . mine's never included. (*He laughs. And laughs. And laughs again.*)

Blackout

Performance Documents

1 Scene Three: Human Hamlet mixtape. Contact Theatre, Manchester, November 2017. Photograph by Sarah Lewis. Courtesy of Dickie Beau.

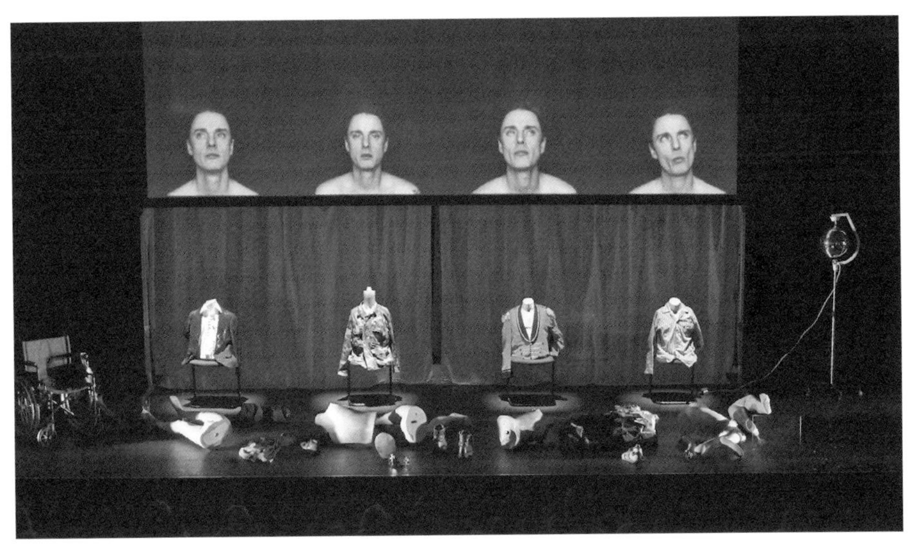

2 Scene Five: Talking Heads / Tea Party. Contact Theatre, Manchester, November 2017. Photograph by Sarah Lewis. Courtesy of Dickie Beau.

3 Scene Ten: I am not Prince Hamlet (the final window display). Contact Theatre, Manchester, November 2017. Photograph by Sarah Lewis. Courtesy of Dickie Beau.

4 Scene Five: Talking Heads / Tea Party. Almeida Theatre, 19 March 2017. Photograph by Robin Fisher. Courtesy of Dickie Beau.

5 Scene Ten: I am not Prince Hamlet. Hampstead Theatre, May 2023. Photograph by Sarah Lewis. Courtesy of Dickie Beau.

NT

National Theatre
Stage Manager's Report

Theatre OLIVIER
Date 5-9-89

Play HAMLET

Performance number	
Olivier Theatre	65
Lyttelton Theatre	
Cottesloe Theatre	
Tour	4
Total to date	69

	Up	Down	Playing time	Interval
Act 1	7-03	7-47	0-44	
Interval				32
Act 2	8-19	10-00	1-41	
Interval				20
Act 3	XIBAXB 10-20	11-20	1-00	
Interval				
Act 4				
		Totals	3-25	52
		Total running time	4-17	Calls SET

Absentees, cast changes (with reasons)

Mr.Day Lewis(Understudies: Messrs.Northam/Bedford/Nicholas)

Remarks

On the Ghost's exit in Act 1 Sc.5 Mr.Day Lewis left the stage and told me that he could not continue the performance. An announcement was made and the audience invited to take an extra interval. The announcement only specified technical problems. After 32 minutes the performance resumed with Mr.Northam as Hamlet. Mr.Bedford played Osric and Mr.Nicholas a Switzer. Mr.Northam coped brilliantly(not an exaggeration) and received an outstanding reception from the audience.

Stage Manager

6 The National Theatre's Stage Manager Report on the night Daniel Day-Lewis walked off-stage while playing Hamlet (5 September 1989), which precipitated Ian Charleson taking on the role. Courtesy of the National Theatre.

DollyWould

Written and performed by Sh!t Theatre

(Rebecca Biscuit and Louise Mothersole)

Credits

Director: Adam Brace
Premiere: 4 August 2017, Summerhill, Edinburgh.

Notes on the text

Words underlined are spoken in unison.

Performances of this play use a variety of multimedia including projected images, videos, audio and loop pedal – these are reflected through stage directions.

The photos included in this text are projected on a large screen upstage at the point at which they are included.

Footnotes are often used to denote a slide photo/video that is being projected upstage or to provide extra context to what is being said or portrayed.

This is a work of fiction. Names, characters, businesses, places, events, locales, Country and Western superstars, up-and-coming Performance Art sex symbols, cloned sheep and all incidents are either the products of the author's imagination or used in a fictitious manner. Any resemblance to actual persons, living or dead, or actual events is purely coincidental.

All song lyrics are original Sh!t Theatre or re-workings of Dolly classics.

The stage is covered in dirty white sheets. There are lumps and bumps under the sheets – the effect is a lunar landscape crossed with a dirty morgue crossed with an old abandoned building covered in dust sheets. Upstage left is a double swing set draped in white sheets, upstage right are two chairs, also covered in sheets. Downstage left is a small table covered in a white sheet with a desktop photocopier on it. Two mics downstage. Two body bags containing pink balloons hang upstage left and right. There is a balloon drop of pink balloons also set up. A mirror ball throws cell-under-microscope-like orbs over all.

The audience enter. Nobody is on stage. The mirror ball is turning.

Audio *Dolly Parton's 'Jolene', echoing and slowed down with sheep sounds and heartbeats over the top.*

Rebecca/Becca (B) *and* **Louise (L)** *enter from upstage right. They shuffle on, backs to audience, awkwardly closing any doors they have to enter through. When* **B&L** *finally turn to face the audience they instantly transform and enter as though they are superstars walking into an arena. Arms above heads, waving at the crowd. They are wearing denim shorts, black skull t-shirts and leather jackets. Their faces are painted white, including lips and eyebrows.*

They go to the mics.

B Hi, we're self-proclaimed multi-award-winning international performance artists Sh!t Theatre. I'm Becca.

L I'm Louise.

B It's nice to be back at [venue name]! We were here last year.

L Not in this room though – <u>this room's bigger</u>.[1]

B This is our mainstream crossover hit.

Lights change slightly to a pinker hue.

L I don't know if you know this about me but, when I was fifteen, I came out to my mum. As a country music fan.

Pause.

I *am* a lesbian . . .

B Her mum was more upset about the country music.

Lights snap and change to spotlights on the mics.

Audio *Dolly Parton's '9 to 5' intro piano loop. Buh buh buh buh buh – BUUUH BUUUH BUH.*

---

[1] Changes as per venue. The implication is always 'Here we are again. Doing better than we were last time. Of course.'

Video *Barbara Walters in 1977, in slow motion, with title 'Barbara Walters, 1977.' The video is silent.*

In character and in unison, **B&L** *are on their tiptoes, wobbling, with hands held like paws under their breasts pushing them up. Their voices are an exaggerated Barbara Walters impression with an added speech impediment for the letter 'r'. It's actually a very bad impression.*[2]

B&L When you spend a lot of time with someone in an interview it's very hard not to have rather special relationship. But my favourite talk, I guess, was with country music superstar Dolly Parton, maybe because it was so unexpected. When my producers first suggested her I said, 'It'll be awfully tough to do, we haven't a thing in common.' And then we met. Frankly, I'm crazy about Dolly Parton. And if you haven't met herself you have a treat ahead. Meet her – as I did – at the American Woyal Wodeo in Kansas City, Missouri.

L Horses and cowboys and sawdust and mud –

B Horses and sawboys and cowdust and mud –

Louise *looks at* **Becca** *who has got the words the wrong way round.*

B&L Horses and cowboys and sawdust and mud. And, as a special attraction for two nights only, the lady *Rolling Stone* magazine calls, 'An angelic, creamy-skinned, honey-wigged, golden-coated, flashing-eyed, jewel-encrusted, lush-bodied, feisty enchantress': Dolly Parton!

End of video.

Audio *Rapturous applause.*

B&L *take one step to towards the centre and bow deeply so that their hands and arms hang straight to the floor. They repeat the deep bow three times and then retrieve instruments.* **Becca** *with a mandolin,* **Louise** *with a banjo. They play a 4-bar country-style riff as the applause fades and then walk away from the mics, revealing the riff has been recorded as a loop. They add guitar and harmonica to the loop, and then stop it.*

Image *Screenshot of Barbara Walters from the previous 1977 video.*

Audio *Barbara Walters (BABS), asking interview questions:*

Babs Tell me about your childhood.

B&L*'s responses are verbatim Dolly Parton from the interview with Barbara, sung homophonically and in harmony.*

B&L Well, there's really quite a bit to tell. I don't know how far back you want to start.

---

[2] This text is taken directly from a televised Barbara Walters interview with Dolly Parton in 1977. It is available on YouTube and is seventeen minutes long. It is of an unguarded, unpolished Dolly, before she got all her answers down pat, all her quips and her Dollyisms. We suggest you look it up.

Babs Dolly, you said, maybe you were talking about when you were a kid, you said, 'I felt that I never belonged. I felt I was always different.'

B&L I wanted more than to just be a farmer's daughter, even though I'm proud to be. I just wanted pretty things, I wanted money to buy the things that I had always been impressed with as a child. I wanted to, I guess to be a star.

Babs I hear the folks back home saying, she's gone Hollywood. Dolly's changed. Or Dolly *might* change, not that she's changed yet.

B&L I'm my own person . . . and as a business person, I like to think that there's more money to be made than the money I've *been* making. I've been working too hard, too long, for too little.

Babs What do you make?

B&L Well, I made a great deal . . . but when you say that you can make millions compared to thousands . . . why not touch as many people. My dream was always to make as many people happy as I could in this life. I want to . . . I want to be able to walk into any place and say, well, there's Dolly Parton . . .

Loop stops. Pause. Loop starts again.

I want to be a star, a universal star. I would *like* to be a superstar. I guess all people dream of that . . . and that's what I'm trying to do.

Babs When is all this gonna happen?

Interrupting, very sure. Not clear if this is Sh!t Theatre or Dolly talking now.

B&L Well it's happening now.

Babs Are you there yet? Are you a superstar yet?

B&L *look around at audience.*[3]

B&L Noooooooooo! No no no no no no no no no no no no no no no no no no. No.

Babs You think that the superstardom will be here, let's say, in five years?

B&L (*very sure*) Yes.

Babs Yeah?

B&L I do.

They stop the loop pedal. The spotlights fade into a regular wash.

---

[3] You know, this show sold pretty well but there's always a chance there'll be empty seats. And how many people can you really fit into a theatre studio space anyway? Eighty? 150? It's not a stadium, is it? This isn't 'Making It', is it? How much money are we making off this gig anyway? We on a 60:40 door split again? I mean you should see our bank statements, really, it's embarrassing, we're gonna be thirty this year, is this really the height of what we can achieve? IS THIS REALLY IT? THIS IS OUR MAINSTREAM CROSSOVER HIT!

L (*to* **Becca**) Let's talk about ambition.

B&L *take off their leather jackets, throw them onto the floor and stomp off behind the sheet-covered chairs upstage right. When one is speaking the other looks sideways at them, then snaps their head forward towards the audience when it's their own turn to speak. The effect is ABBA-esque head choreography.*

L We are:

B Pure

L Raw

B TALENT.

L A DRIVE that makes us unstoppable.

B Limitless PASSION from the very core of our souls.

L FOCUS so intense that you can't hope to comprehend it.

B Add it up for yourself, friend, and guess what you'll end up with?

L Pure, unadulterated, absolute EXCELLENCE.

B It's simple, really.

L The only art that matters is the art that lasts.

B How many days do you have left? A week's worth?

L A month?

B A few years?

L That's the question.

Pause.

B Or is it?

L No, it's not. Because that's a question you can't hope to answer.

B But whether you have a few hours,

L Or a few years,

B You're worth it. Your body's worth it.

B&L *slowly disappear behind the chairs, 'elevator' style. Knees bending, sinking behind the sheets. Lights change to just a faint pink.*

Video A very graphic sheep birth video.

Audio *'I Will Always Love You' by Dolly Parton.*

When Dolly reaches the iconic 'And Iiiiiiii . . .' of 'I Will Always Love You' the sheep giving birth screams and a lamb is born covered in pus and blood. **B&L** *are also 'born' or 'birthed' from behind the chairs, they are now wearing wool wigs and pink t-shirts. They are also screaming and clutching each other tightly.*

A pause where they stare, blinking and confused, at the audience.

B Baaa.

L Baaa!

B Baaa Baaa.

L Baaa baaaaaa.

B&L (*to the tune of the famous 'Islands in the Stream' riff*) Ba- baaa!

Audio *Steady hand claps like a 4x4 time beat.*

B Baa baa baa baa baa baa baa baa baa
baa baaaa. Baa baa baa baa baa baa
baa baa baa baa baaaa,
baa baa ba ba baaa . . .
baaa baa baa baa baa baa baaaaaaaaa.

Audio *'Islands in the Stream' guitar break, then back to the claps.*

B&L Baa baa baa baab baa baa baa baa baaa
Baabaa baaa baa ba baa baa baa baa baa baaa
Baaa baa baa baa baaa
Baa baa baa baa baa baa baaaaaa!

It is clear by now that **B&L** *are singing 'Islands in the Stream' with no words, just baaa's. They reach the 'chorus'.*[4]

Baaa's continue and the song plays out. They approach the mics and lights come up with a faint green hue.

In bad Tennessee accents:

L Dolly once entered herself into a Dolly drag queen lookalike competition.

B She made her hair bigger, her lips bigger, her rhinestones . . . rhinier.

L And she walked out onto the stage with all them other Dollies.

B Each one an exact copy of Dolly but each one a completely unique, live performance.

Audio *Tattoo gun sound.*

B&L *wince slightly and hold their right thighs as though in pain. Audio stops and they return to normal, speaking this time in their own accents.*

B We fucking love Dolly.

---

4 Bright pink lettering reads: 'ALL TOGETHER NOW!' Sometimes people join in. Sometimes they stare in silence.

L We saved up loads of money this year to go to where she was born. Where her home is preserved. Back to where she started from.

B It was expensive but it was worth it.

L She's unique isn't she?

B That's what we like about her.

L Dolly was born on the 5th of July 1996.

B She had three mothers and no fathers.

L Dolly was bred with a Welsh mountain ram called David and produced two offspring.

B (*to* **Louise**, *smiling*) She's just such a groundbreaker.

L She spent most of her life at the Roslin Institute, Edinburgh, twenty-four minutes by car from here via the A701, with usual traffic.[5]

B Outside she looked like a lamb, but inside she was old mutton, and on Valentine's Day 2003, Dolly was euthanized due to a progressive lung disease and severe arthritis.

L If there's one thing you can say about her, she's original.

B I mean, I know *technically* she's a clone.

L But she's the *first* clone. A *unique* clone.

B She's the only clone you remember.

L She's the only clone whose name we know!

B But everyone knows Dolly. She's a sensation. She's the only one.

L The only one.

Video *'You're the Only One' by Dolly Parton karaoke track with lyrics.*

B&L *sing along as though mid-concert. Energy, hand gestures. They're really going for it.*

Video stops suddenly.

L The first cloned animal was cloned from a mammary gland. That's why she's named after a Country and Western singer famous for her mammaries.

B That's why they called her Dolly. Dolly the Sheep.

L Dolly can be cloned and cloned eternally. Her genes could live forever in new Dollies, other Dollies. Each one identical but each one different.

B Because each individual clone is a completely unique live performance.

---

5 Changes with venue.

The lights snap to the same spotlights we saw during their terrible Barbara Walters impression. **B&L** *assume the same positions, on tiptoes, struggling to stay up, with hands cupped like paws under their breasts.*

Video *Dr Kat Arney*[6] *talking to the camera in slow motion. This is titled 'Dr Kat Arney, genetic scientist and harpist'.* **Louise** *behind camera on the video says, 'OK, we're live . . .' but apart from that there is no audio.*

In character and in unison, once again, this is not an accurate impression of the subject and like with the Barbara Walters impression they have added an exaggerated speech impediment for the letter 'r'.

B&L When you make a clone there are the identical genes, and then environment, and then 'the wobble'.

L The life of wandom chemistry. **B** The wandom chemistry of life.

Becca *looks at* **Louise**. *She has got the words wrong.*

B&L The wobbly edge to everything. It is wandomness but scientists don't like to use the word 'wandom'. But it is. It is chaos. You can't wepwoduce that ever.

Video *Lots of photos of Dolly Parton drag queens. Each time* **B&L** *see a 'Dolly' they point and exclaim, 'That's Dolly!'*

Audio *Many versions of live karaoke and live performances of Dolly Parton's '9 to 5' layered over the top of each other.*

B&L That's Dolly? That's Dolly! Dolly Dolly etc.

Video *More photos of Dolly drag queens including Dolly avatars and an Andy Warhol of Dolly. Two sexy photos of Burt Reynolds are thrown in, at which* **B&L** *exclaim – with some clear joy – BURT REYNOLDS!*

Audio and video fade out and **B&L** *start to imitate the '9 to 5' piano line vocally. They record it on the loop pedal and keep it playing. They go to the plastic body bags hanging upstage and 'cut' them open with scalpels. In the bags are two pink balloons which pop on contact with the scalpels. At each pop* **B&L** *cover their noses or gag as though a foul-smelling gas has been released. Once both balloons are popped and the bags are open they fish around for goggles on which are stuck cartoon blue Dolly eyes. They put them on their foreheads and look at each other and the audience, pleased. They go back into the bags and find scissors, look down at their chests, up at the audience and back down. They cut holes in their t-shirts, exposing their breasts, look at the audience, pleased and confused, return the scissors to the bags and turn back to the audience, putting the goggles over their eyes to complete the transformation.*

It takes a second to realise they are now blind.

---

6 These quotes are taken from one of our interviews with Dr Kat Arney in 2016 in which she attempted to explain genetic science to two women who hadn't bothered listening at school. Becca's biology teacher didn't believe in evolution so perhaps it was for the best anyway.

They stumble to find a mic each, stop the loop and then grope to find each other in the centre of the stage. They hold hands and smile, very pleased with themselves.

B We fucking love Dolly.

L We saved up loads of money this year to go to where she was born, where her home is preserved. Back to where she started from.

B It was expensive but it was worth it.

L Dolly was bred and raised on a farm.

B (*to* **Louise**) She's unique isn't she?

L (*to* **Becca**) That's what we like about her.[7]

B Dolly has produced no young.

L But she produced her first single aged thirteen.

B She has written over 3,000 songs

L And she's probably a lesbian –

L And has tattoos of butterflies and flowers etched onto her breasts and arms –

B And she turned Elvis down when he tried to cover 'I Will Always Love You' and take half her rights –

[7] Star-like pin pricks start to appear on the screen. Over the course of the scene, the pin pricks start to form, like multiplying cells, into a face. SURPRISE. It's Dolly Parton's face.

L And she gave a thousand dollars a month to every resident of her local town for 6 months the year after it burned down –

B And she founded and pays for The Imagination Library which gifts over a million books a month to children across the globe, including here! –

L And our mate Kendahl's *dad* met her once and then met her again eleven years later and she remembered him *by name* despite meeting, what, millions of people every year –

They are getting more excited now.

B And she's ADORABLE –

L And she plays all her own instruments –

B And she grew up in a shack dirt poor –

L And she modelled herself on the town tramp because that's *her* idea of beauty! –

B And in March 1986 she did something no female country singer-songwriter

L Or male country singer-songwriter

B Or singer-songwriter had ever done before!

L She did something only Dolly would do!

B She bought the site and surrounding area of her childhood home and built a theme park and named it after herself![8]

They lift up goggles onto their foreheads and look around at the screen.

B&L Dolly?

Audio *A tinny backing track to 'Sneakin' Around' from the film* The Best Little Whorehouse in Texas. *The original performance is by Dolly Parton and Burt Reynolds, whose characters are lovers.*

Lights change to a pinkish hue. **B&L** *bend over into a deep bow, arms dangling, and stay there. They begin to slowly rotate on the spot, and sing 'Sneakin' Around'.*

L I like lots of cash on hand
And dirty jokes about the fuller-brush man

B I like stuff I understand
Like sneakin' around with you

L You know, I like a thrill that has no strings

8 Dolly's face fully in focus for just a moment, and then gone.

B Friendship that don't ever change

L And laughter from the joy of things

And sneakin' around with you

Video *Dolly the sheep at the Museum of Scotland, preserved in a glass cabinet, also slowly rotating as the song 'Sneaking Around' plays.*

Instrumental break. Video disappears and **B&L** *change their direction. When the next verse kicks in, they change direction again. Always slowly rotating, in a deep bow.*

The song continues.

Video *Dolly the Sheep at the Museum of Scotland, preserved in a glass cabinet, slowly rotating again. This time* **B&L** *are also in the video, looking pretty excited to be near the famous sheep.*

B&L *untuck woolen sheep tails from inside their shorts. It's the same wool as the Dolly wigs. They keep rotating.*

The song continues.

Audio and video end. **B&L** *stand up then straight back down into a deep bow again.*

Audio *Rapturous applause.*

B&L *straighten and then bow again.*

Audio *An American female newsreader's voice is heard: 'When Dolly wanted to open her theme park, her advisors told her she should call it "Crazywood". Eleven years later, Dollywood attracts millions of visitors every year. Dolly's always been bold with her larger-than-life looks and her big personality. Tonight she dishes about* *her love life and how she created her brand.*[9] *Her brand.*[10] *Her brand.*[11] *Her brand*[12] *brand*[13] *brand*[14] *brand*[15] *brand*[16] *brand.*[17]

During this **B&L** *go to the table with the photocopier and photocopy an image of Dolly. They look down at the printing images and back up at each other. Down, and up again. They walk to centre stage and grab onto each other tightly, faces squashed up against each other. A centre spotlight snaps onto the duo.*

L Dollywood.[18] Making memories worth repeat –

B Making memories worth repeating!

L Tennessee's top tourist attraction. Above Dolly's Dixie Stampede[19] – the world's premiere dinner attraction – and the Tennessee body farm[20] – the first and original centre for the study of human decay.

B How could it ever live up to what we expect it to be? How could it ever be as mad, or as gaudy or as big or as brilliant as we imagine it to be? How could it ever be worth the money we'd spend on it? The $228.90[21] on tickets? The £2558.58[22] on flights? The $86[23] on gift shop merch? Or whatever else we'd need to spend money on?[24] How could it be worth the thousands of miles we'd travel?[25]

---

9 A terrible Dolly Parton tattoo.

10 Another terrible Dolly Parton tattoo.

11 Another Dolly tattoo, also shit, this time in black and white.

12 This terrible Dolly tattoo has the words 'I will always love you' written underneath.

13 This terrible Dolly tattoo has the words 'tough titty' written underneath.

14 An uncooked lamb steak.

15 Bad eighties Dolly tattoo.

16 Cartoon Dolly tattoo.

17 Gothic undead zombie Dolly tattoo.

18 The entrance to Dollywood theme park. A big sign with Dolly's logo – a butterfly – with the words 'love every moment' underneath.

19 An advert for 'Dolly's Dixie Stampede' – woman in a Santa hat riding a horse above the slogan 'The Most Fun Place to Eat'. As of 2023, Dolly has dropped the 'Dixie' from the name.

20 A news article: 'Tourists dying to get inside University of Tennessee's Body Farm'. The photo in the article is of a barbed wire fence and a sign saying 'Forensic Anthropology Research Facility'.

21 A ticket confirmation for Dollywood: $228.90.

22 Flight confirmation: £2558.58. Knoxville airport is very beautiful by the way. There's a waterfall and when we got off the tiny plane at 10 pm it was the perfect balmy temperature outside. Our taxi driver asked us about London being dangerous because of 'all the terrorism' and then gave us his wife's business card in case we ever wanted to buy a house.

23 Screengrab of a bank account with various payments to 'Dollywood' plus various 'non-sterling purchase fees'.

24 Screengrab of a bank account with multiple payments to 'Ambition Tattoo Parlour', also with 'non-sterling purchase fees'.

25 A flight schedule showing three adults travelling from London to Knoxville, Tennessee for three days. The flight home appears to be twenty-four hours long. We spent all of thirty hours in Knoxville and had to stop off overnight in Chicago on the way home to make it cheaper and ended up at a lesbian dive karaoke bar called . . . Highly recommended. We also visited Second City because we are long-form improv nerds – in fact that is how we met. The show was disappointing but we had a jolly old drunken time then accidentally went half an hour the wrong way on the metro. Louise had to do a wee on the metro platform and we got back with three hours to sleep before our flight. The 5 am metro to the airport in the morning was full of people, homeless, all trying to find a warm place to sleep. We saw one boy of about eleven with no shoes, sleeping on who could have been his grandfather.

Or the lies we'd have to tell to the Arts Council. Or the time we'd have to take off work?

Audio *Loop of the opening guitar riff of Dolly Parton's 'Jolene'.*

L We left Knoxville[26] and took the bridge over the river Clinch.

B It's green and it's named after someone but no one remembers its name. There are wreaths on the bridge.

L Past a sign for Image Matters – photocopy repair.

B A sign for plastic surgery – say yes to fitting in the dress!

L Past Ambition, a tattoo parlour – your body's worth it!

L A big sign that just says, 'AVAILABLE'.

B Another sign that says, 'fireworks live on DVD'. First Dolly sign and we all scream AGHHHHHH.[27] Past lost sheep ministry.

L And arrive at Dollywood.[28]

B It is exactly the way it looks online.

L We park in carpark D/E.[29]

[26] A silent video of us in the back of a car, clearly very excited and both singing along to something. The car drives past a Dollywood sign.

[27] Four photos in a row of a closer approaching green road sign that says, 'Dollywood' with an arrow pointing left.

[28] A photo taken clearly from inside a car window of the entrance sign for Dollywood – same butterfly, same slogan.

[29] Us under a carpark sign 'D/E'. We are both in sunglasses, shorts, skull t-shirts – same as we are wearing onstage at the top start? of the show – and baseball caps that say 'Tennessee Body Farm'.

Dolly's Earrings![30]

B We got on the shuttle bus to the Dollywood gates. There was an announcement to 'keep those body parts inside the tram when we're moving.'[31]

L Outside the gates[32] we spot at least five separate people dressed as Dolly – blonde hair, mammaries, rhinestones.

B Inside. First stop toilets.[33]

L Becca treated herself to this poo at Dollywood.[34]

B Dolly's closet,[35] a shop to buy clothes based on clothes that Dolly has worn.

L Dreamsong Theater[36] now playing 'My People', a show about Dolly, by Dolly, performed by members of Dolly's extended family.

B Chasing Rainbows Museum[37] – the museum of Dolly's life.

---

30 Close-up of sign. D/E does indeed stand for 'Dolly's Earrings'.

31 Large red sign saying 'WARNING: can cause serious personal injury'.

32 A shaky phone camera video. Whoever is holding it is approaching a turnstile behind which is another Dollywood sign. The camera turns and we are there, backpacks and caps on.

33 'Restrooms' sign with a cartoon pointing hand.

34 Really quite a small poo in a toilet.

35 Dolly's closet front window. Slogan: 'Her Style, Your Size'.

36 A big salmon-coloured theatre with a giant photo of Dolly at the front. A sign says 'The Dreamsong Theater' and underneath 'Dolly Parton's "My People".' For scale we are standing underneath the photo of Dolly and we look very small. It's very sunny. When we visited, this show hadn't opened yet as we were technically out of season. We also missed out on Dollywood: Splash Country, a whole other water park dedicated to Dolly. For more information, please see the episode of *The Graham Norton Show* in which he visits Dollywood. There's a scene in which Graham and Dolly get dressed up in wetsuits and float around Splash Country singing 'Islands in the Stream' in giant rubber rings.

37 The Chasing Rainbows Museum – it is beautiful.

L Inside is the *actual* coat of many colours from the song 'Coat of Many Colours'.[38]

B The coat Dolly's mum made her from rags when they were dirt poor.

L There's also the recreation coat of many colours from the film *Coat of Many Colours*.[39]

B And the recreation of the recreation coat[40] that Dolly wears as an adult in the film *Christmas of Many Colors*.

L Cabinets and cabinets of Dolly's stage clothes.[41]

B There's a cabinet of Dolly dollies.[42]

L Into the sunshine and onto Dolly's tour bus where she was interviewed by Barbara Walters in 1977.[43]

B Just before she became a big mainstream crossover hit.
It's our absolute favourite interview.

B Dolly's bedroom walls and ceiling are entirely covered in mirrors.[44] We could imagine her lying there with an infinite number of Dolly's reflected back at her.

L There's a bed labelled 'Judy's bed'[45] because Judy always goes on tour with her.

B We paid $17.50 for this picture of us on the tour bus.[46]
It's our absolute favourite photo!

---

38 THE COAT OF MANY COLOURS!!! It's in a cabinet. It's surrounded by Autumn leaves. IT'S REAL!!!

39 Slightly slicker, prettier version of the coat. More colours. More buttons.

40 OK this is a very silly coat. Very bright. Very long, covered in rhinestones as well as colourful patches and mounted on a headless doll with huge breasts. There's an evolution here of 'real' authentic Dolly to 'real' fake Dolly.

41 Various glass cabinets of headless dolls with Dolly clothes on them. One cabinet is labelled 'Dr Dolly' as this is the outfit she wore when she received an honorary doctorate from the University of Tennessee, who now offer a course in Dolly Parton as part of the History Department. If you would like to apply for the (Masters) course, please follow this link: https://torchbearer.utk.edu/2017/03/coursework-dollys-america/ 'Dolly's America: From Sevierville to the World'

42 A load of creepy blonde dolls in a cabinet. The larger ones almost look like her. But not quite.

43 A shaky phone camera video: Louise climbing onto a bus and looking around, very excited. There's lots of dark wood and red pleather.

44 A bed with a guitar nestled on it, with mirrors above and to the side in which you can see Louise again in her 'Tennessee Body Farm' hat.

45 Purple stripy pillow with gold embroidered name: Judy.

46 Us and Jen in the kitchen of the tour bus, grinning wildly. There's a reproduction of Dolly's handwriting in the bottom right-hand corner that says 'I will always love you, love, Dolly Parton.' We're all wearing the same DMs. In the back left of the kitchen you can see a copy of Dolly's cookbook *Dolly's Dixie Fixin's Cookbook* on display.

L Right round the corner past Aunt Granny's Buffet,[47] a gift shop,[48] and another gift shop[49] is a full recreation of Dolly's childhood home.

B Her Tennessee Mountain Home.[50] It's a small, two-room cabin.[51]

L Preserved behind glass for people to look at.[52] Complete with replica gravestones[53] for her dead family outside.

B Her parents:

L Robert Lee Parton

B Avie Lee Caroline Owens Parton

L But nothing for her dead baby brother Larry

B Whose death scared the hell out of her so much

L She slept on his real grave as a child

B And nothing for Aunt Marth

L Whose dead body scared the hell out of her so much

---

[47] 'All you can eat country buffet' includes: fried chicken, breaded fish, beef stew, rotisserie chicken, mini corn dogs, fried okra, buttered noodles, green beans, mashed potatoes and brown gravy, macaroni and cheese, cooked cabbage, turnip green, pinto beans, cornbread muffins, fresh baked biscuits which actually aren't biscuits at all but some sort of a scone, soup of the day, salad bar, taco bar, fresh fruit, a beverage and dessert bar with soft serve ice cream. Adults is $16.90.

[48] Jen stood with her sunglasses in her mouth modelling a tie-dyed Dollywood t-shirt in front of two confused American tweenagers.

[49] A rack of leather belts with a sign above: Made in America.

[50] A very clean-looking wooden cabin. The sign in front says 'These mountains and my childhood home have a special place in my heart. They inspire my music and my life. I hope being here does the same for you. Dolly x.'

[51] A rustic wooden bed next to a small sofa, both covered in knitted patchwork blankets.

[52] Us inside the cabin.

[53] Three red metal gravestones planted in the garden alongside a green statue of an angel.

B She hasn't been to a funeral since. Will Dolly's fake grave be added here also?

L Or will Dolly's fake grave be a bigger, fake mausoleum in the centre of the theme park?

B Up the hill is a ye olde steam train station[54] and a wild eagle sanctuary.[55] Birds preserved in glass cabinets for people to look at.

L Dolly has single-handedly saved the American bald eagle from the edge of extinction.[56]

B Past the train station are the rollercoasters.[57]

L More gift shops[58]

B More rollercoasters[59]

L More Dollies[60]

B More Dollies[61]

L Another recreation of a cemetery,[62] this one with comical dead people names. And you can even get your photo taken in an upright coffin.

[54] Us again very excited to be next to something labelled 'Grist Mill'.

[55] One very sad-looking blackbird sat on a perch behind some glass.

[56] Becca with a giant stuffed bald eagle hat on, outside yet another gift shop.

[57] A sign: 'Warning! Please be aware of extreme danger!' behind which is a rollercoaster.

[58] Eight kinds of Dollywood flip-flops for sale.

[59] A purchased photo of us onboard the 'Tenessee Tornado' rollercoaster with the Dollywood stamp and butterfly logo over it.

[60] A cardboard cutout of Dolly – in glasses and a sensible blue suit – holding a cardboard version of one of Dolly's books, in front a sign that says 'Learn More'.

[61] Two wigs on display on Dolly's tour bus.

[62] Us outside the Lumberjack graveyard. You can clearly read their/our 'Tennessee Body Farm' baseball caps. The slogan for the graveyard is 'from a life of lumber to eternal slumber'.

B More rollercoasters[63]

L More gift shops[64]

B With Dollywood ('Making memories worth repea /

L Making memories worth repeating.')

B Dolly is preserving her childhood home,

L Preserving her memories,

B Preserving Tennessee traditions,

L Preserving the local wildlife,

B Preserving the local economy,

L Preserving her old costumes,

B Preserving her brand,

L Preserving against decay,

B Preserving these quails eggs![65]

L Preserving her image,

B Preserving herself.

L You end up where you started from, but the only way to exit is through Dolly's Emporium[66] –

B – the biggest gift shop.

Audio *Long '9 to 5' piano loop. Every time you think it's over, it starts up again.*

B&L *stand centre stage with utterly blank facial expressions. In very slow motion their mouths stretch and tug into a smile – it looks, at first, like an animal snarling or chewing, then builds to a big fake grin. Faces fall back to blankness the instant the music stops.*

They go to mics.

B (*to audience member*) What's your name?

They reply.

---

63 Another purchased photo of us on a rollercoaster, this one was called 'Daredevil Falls'. We are both in the front seats about to get very wet.

64 Us in sunglasses outside a shop that sells tin signs. We are standing next to a sign that says 'Two old crabs live here'.

65 A jar of Dollywood Old-fashioned Pickled Quails Eggs 'made especially for Dollywood'.

66 A sign hanging from the ceiling – a picture of Dolly smiling and the words 'thanks y'all come back! Dolly' above a large CASHIER sign.

B Pardon?

They reply.

B Kenny! Nice to meet you Kenny. So you might not know this, Kenny. When I was younger, my parents thought I had scoliosis and sent me to a back doctor. Turns out, I'd just hit puberty really young and had enormous breasts, for a child, and I'd just been stooping over for years. Out of the shame.

Becca *starts the Sh!t country music loop. Barbara Walters (***Babs***) continues her interview. All* **B&L***'s responses are sung in unison and harmony.*

Babs Listen, tell me about this marriage of yours. This *man* who nobody ever seems to see. We *heard* that he was here. We heard that he was in town, but none of us have seen him. Carl Dean. You don't see him very much. You're on the road most of the time.

B&L Well, I need freedom. The man gives me freedom.

Babs Why? I mean, if what you want most is freedom, why have a husband tucked away someplace to see six weeks a year?

B&L Well, he has the same freedom. See, the thing of it is, you don't find a person that you can be happy with and they can't accept you the way you are.

Babs Well, what about when you're on the road weeks at a time? No temptations?

B&L Well I didn't say that we never had temptations . . .

B&L *cross their arms.*

Babs Well when you have these temptations, does anything happen that he could be jealous of?

B&L No, not really, because he's the kind of person, and *I'm* the kind of person, that if by being apart, if we should meet somebody, I would never tell him. He would never know and it wouldn't hurt him, and if, it's the same way with him. I've got better things to do than to sit around in my room thinking

Music stops.

Oh, what's Carl doing tonight?

B (**B&L** *step away from the mics into the centre as though about to share a secret*) Our friend Lori told us, ██████████

L But then she thinks everyone's a dyke. 'KD Lang's a dyke.'

B Lori also told us about Judy. Dolly's 'best friend.'

L She said when Judy broke up with her once, Dolly had a nervous breakdown. It was chaos, but they're fine now. She tours with her and Dolly says they share a bed.

B In Dolly's lifetime movie *Coat of Many Colors*[67] – which preceded her Christmas movie, *Christmas of Many Colors*[68] – there is a scene in which Dolly is trapped naked in a closet and is literally *pulled out of the closet* by Judy.

L Dolly's always said there's nothing going on with Judy.

B They got married last year in a 'friendship' commitment ceremony

L Right before Dolly released her children's book *I Am a Rainbow*[69]

B Our friend Jo told us (*bad generic northern accent*)

L Jo produces BBC Country and Western radio so she knows what she's talking about.

B She says it's an open secret in the country world that

L You can't be gay on the outside in the country music world, especially when you've got so many members of your extended family working in your theme park.

B But you can be gay behind closed doors, on the inside.

L

B

L

Audio *A sheep's 'baaa!'*

L When we went to visit Dolly we found her rotating slowly on a lazy Susan. Preserved in a glass cabinet for people to look at.[70]

B Dolly is sneakin' around on a lazy Susan. She looks really good. She works . . .
. . . from 10 to 5.

---

67 A movie poster for *Coat of Many Colors* – Dolly Parton's face has been obscured by a photo of Dolly the sheep. We made a decision early on that we would never show Dolly Parton's face in this show, and we would never say her full name. Always just 'Dolly,' and avatars of the real woman.

68 A movie poster for *Christmas of Many Colors* – again, Dolly's face has been badly obscured by a sheep.

69 A photo of us holding Dolly Parton's book *I Am a Rainbow*. It's winter when we've taken it and our studio where we write is freezing, so we are wrapped up in coats and scarves behind the book, and we are smiling.

70 Video of us posing by Dolly the sheep in a glass cabinet. She is rotating slowly.

Audio *Wild applause.*

B&L *bow deeply.*

B&L *go to the mics and wait for applause to die out. They look humbled by the wild applause. Lights take on a green hue.*

Tennessee accents again.

B Dolly once entered herself into a Dolly drag queen lookalike competition.

L She made her hair, nails and teeth (nails and teeth) bigger and shinier.

B And she walked out onto the stage with all them other dollies. And she looked at them. And she could see her clones cloning themselves into the future. Replicating and repeating forever. Her image immortal.

L And Dolly murmured, 'I will never die.'

Pause. Lights back to normal wash.

B You might not know this, Kenny, but 'I Will Always Love You' was not written for a lover, it was written for a friend.

L A performance partner, actually.

B They were together seven years and Dolly left him following a falling out.

L It was chaos, but they're fine now. I mean, he's dead.

Blackout.

Audio *Porter Wagner introduces the duet, 'Jeanie's afraid of the dark'. There is applause and the song's opening guitar riff.*

Audio stops.

During the audio **B&L** *return to the photocopier, they set it off with the lid open so that their faces are lit by the photocopy scanner. They slowly lean in as though to photocopy their own faces and remain bent over the machine's glow to sing a cappella.*

SONG: 'Jeanie's Afraid of the Dark.'

Pause.

Audio *'Jolene' intro guitar loop. Slowed down and at a lower pitch.*

B&L *go to the chairs and sit,* **Louise** *on* **Becca***'s lap.*

L We left Knoxville and took the bridge over the river Clinch.

B The bridge is named after someone, but nobody remembers its name. There are wreaths on the bridge.

Video **Becca** *and* **Louise** *arriving at the location of the Tennessee Body Farm.*

L Past a sign for Image Matters: photocopy repair.

B A sign for plastic surgery 'say yes to fitting in the dress'.

L Past Ambition Tattoo Parlour – your body's worth it! Past a truck stamped 'Hazardous Cargo'.

B and a sign for 'knife shop – now sells guns!'

L Under a road sign saying 'Buckle up buttercup arrive alive'.

B We are on our way to a place we saw online but which allows no visitors.

L It's the Tennessee Body Farm.

Audio *'WOOAAHH BODY FARM!' (Music from the British 'Body Form' sanitary towel adverts).*

B&L *fall to floor and lie as though they are corpses left out in a field. They leap back up to their positions on the chairs when the music stops.*

L Just ten minutes away from Dollywood, it's the only other world famous attraction in town. Turns out Knoxville is famous for two things: Dolly and death.[71]

B On the back eastern edge of the UT Medical Centre there are weeds, trees, bushes and a metal fence with razor wire at the top.

L This is the Dollywood of the forensic anthropology world!

B We have hay fever, but Jen says there is a strange smell in the air.

Video **B&L** *trying to sneak into the Body Farm.*

L There is nobody else in the car park but as we get close to the gate our talk turns to whispers and we don't know why.

B This place is the first of its kind.

L It's unique isn't it?

B That's what we like about it.

---

[71] An online article about the Knoxville Forensic Anthropology Centre, nicknamed the Tennessee Body Farm.

L On the outside it's just an unmarked fence, on the inside are hundreds of decaying human bodies.

B People – or their families – donate their bodies to the department who then leave them outside to rot to study the stages of decay.

L In shallow bodies of water,

B Under bushes, in the open air, under a sheet,

L Someone was murdered in a trailer recently so they bought a trailer and put one in there.

B When you donate your body to other institutions the remains of your remains are returned within three years.

L Here they've got you for life . . . as it were.

B As long as it takes you to rot, and longer.

L (*half-sung to the tune of 'I Will Always Love You'*) They will always have you.

B Some of your bones may be moved inside and preserved in a glass cabinet for people to look at.

L At the gate we realised we had been followed by a slowly moving unmarked car.

B We lingered and waited to see if it would move on but it idled alongside us.

L We turned around and walked slowly back the way we'd come.

B The car followed . . .

L We stopped.

B The car stopped . . .

L The window rolled down and a police officer asked us what we were doing.[72]

B 'Just walking – away.'

L He followed us right back to our car.

B But first, Louise treated herself to this wee,[73] at the Body Farm!

Audio *'WOOAAHH BODY FARM! BODY FARM FOR YOOOU' (Slightly more of the music from the Body Form sanitary towel advert).*

B&L *crumple to the floor again. When the music stops they leap back onto the chairs.*

L Just like at Dollywood we ended up back where we started from.

B Instead of preservation this place has decay, but they've both got t-shirts.[74]

L You can't go inside but you can –

B Always

L – visit the gift shop.

Audio *American news reporter from before: 'Her brand*[75] *her brand*[76] *brand*[77] *brand*[78] *brand*[79] *brand'.*[80]

Video *A passenger-view video of one of the rollercoaster rides at Dollywood.*

Blackout. **B&L**, *lit only by the glow of the projected video, leave the seats and dress themselves in giant boob costumes that have been 'hiding' under the sheets. They put heels on. During this they sing the first verse and chorus of 'I Will Always Love You' in time with the twists and turns of the rollercoaster (e.g. 'and Iiiiiiiiiiiii-eeeeeeeee-iiiiii will aaaaaalwaaaaaaays . . .' etc.)*

As the rollercoaster comes to an end **B&L** *sit, dressed as boobs, on the swing set swinging gently next to each other. Lights slowly fade up. Eerie, stark.*

---

72 The unmarked police car pulling alongside us, Becca is waving at the cop.

73 Louise's wee and some toilet roll in a toilet bowl within the UT campus.

74 Actual Body Farm t-shirts for sale on the Forensic Anthropology Centre website.

75 Dollywood sign.

76 Dollywood brand logo – a butterfly.

77 Tennessee Body Farm brand logo – a skull.

78 Tennessee Body Farm mug.

79 Us wearing Tennessee Body Farm hats. We look ecstatic.

80 Very quick image of a decomposing corpse at the Tennessee Body Farm.

L While the body as a whole may be dead, little organisms within the body are still alive.

B A few days after death, these bacteria start the process of breaking down their host.

L The pancreas is full of so many bacteria that it essentially digests itself.

B As these organisms work their way to other organs, the body turns green, then purple, then black.

L If you can't see the change, you'll smell it soon enough because the bacteria create an awful-smelling gas.

B This gas will also cause the body to bloat, the eyes to bulge out of their sockets and the tongue to swell and protrude.

L If left in the open, maggots by now will have eaten everything under the skin's surface, leaving the skin to harden like a leather jacket.

B On the outside the body looks whole, but inside the maggots have consumed all the meat.

L If the body is left under a sheet, however, maggots will consume everything including the skin.

B A month after death the hair and nails and teeth NAILS AND TEETH will fall out, internal organs and tissues have liquefied, which will swell the body until it pops.

L At that point, a skeleton remains.

Music and Video *The karaoke backing track and karaoke lyrics for Dolly Parton's 'Straight Talk'.*

A pink-purple wash warms the stage. **B&L** *begin swinging in time with the music. The swinging escalates into a boob dance, based on a line dance.*[81] *Balloon drop*

---

[81] The boob dance is excellent but we frequently stumble in the high heels like newborn lambs.

is released. **B&L** *gleefully romp in the balloons. As the music begins to fade out,* **B&L** *begin popping the balloons by throwing themselves onto them. Some are harder to pop than others and require* **Becca** *or* **Louise** *to mount the other, thrusting their bodies repeatedly onto the balloons until they pop. It looks and sounds like* **B&L** *are humping each other. Once the music has faded entirely, there is just the sound of popping, breathing, whispered encouragement and gasping. After penultimate balloon,* **B&L** *collapse onto backs, panting. The boob costumes heave.*

B&L *spot one last balloon.*

L (*to audience*) Hands up anyone who wants a balloon? This one? (*Offers blown-up balloon.*) Or this one? (*Proffers a shriveled, popped skin.*) Are you sure? (*Indicates blown-up balloon.*) It won't last.

The pink lights fade, returning the stage to the stark, eerie light.

L You may not know this but I saw my dad's body two weeks after he died. He'd been embalmed and an unnatural smile had been stitched onto his face. It was the scariest thing I'd ever seen. I don't want the same thing to happen to me when I die.

Whilst **Louise** *talks to audience* **Becca** *retrieves an urn from upstage. Inside is dust which she uses to chalk her hands like a weightlifter. She offers the 'urn' to* **Louise** *who does the same.*

I don't want the image of that to replace the memory of me, like it did with my dad. I'd rather just be left out in the open to rot.

B&L *take hold of the top bar of the swing set and lift themselves up.*

Audio *A compilation of interviewers – mostly male.*

Do you have children? Do you plan to have children?

You're a very dramatic looking woman.

Those early shots of you – you're very pretty.

You've been very frank amount of plastic surgery that you've had.

Maybe it's none of my business but have you, have you, have you – ah – had a little work?

How long did it take you this morning to look so beautiful?

I'd like to see you sweaty.

How do you do it? You look terrific! Seriously, you still have the waist of a wasp.

What was the most you weighed?

You look terrific, how do you do it?

I won't remember you being, like, a heavy person. Or somebody inclined to be overweight.

What happened, did it just creep on you?

Please marry me, just consider it?

I always wanted to ask you, do you ever feel pressure about being beautiful?

Right now I want you to go offstage and put on something fancy for your number.

But Dolly, you never feel like you've been treated as a sex object?

Do you ever feel unconformable doing that? The tight clothes?

You look terrific and upstairs earlier today we were discussing your weight – now the last time I saw you were you this weight? Or a different weight?

Were you always bunched up at the top?

I wonder what you could do with those boobs, honey!

Will your melons be there?

You are – you are a, an attractive woman.

You don't have to look like this. You've very beautiful. You don't have to wear the blonde wigs, you don't have to wear the extreme clothes, right?

Boy you smell great!

You were a little tubby. I'm getting hooted now by the band!

Dolly Don't hoot him! Don't hoot him

During audio **B&L** *hang as boobs on the swing set with their feet tucked up as though about to do pull-ups. Every time their strength gives they tumble to the floor, get back up and continue hanging until the audio ends.*

Exhausted, they strip out of their boobs. They grab especially boob-shaped bottles of pink bubbly from each side of the stage.

Audio *A guitar backing track to 'Touch Your Woman' by Dolly Parton.*

B&L *swig from the bottles of fizzy wine – lipstick secreted on the bottle-mouths stains their lips pink.*

They sing. Pink-purple light fades up.

As the chorus begins:

Touch your woman[82] *[. . .]*

[. . .] Touch your woman[83]

The pink lights fade. **B&L** *go to the mics, still drinking from their bottles of fizz.*

B You may not know this but last year we were sent a video of a student doing a Sh!t Theatre tribute act.[84]

L We later learned that the lecturer marked them down; for not drinking alcohol on stage.

---

[82] We project, in bright pink, the words 'Touch your Woman Touch your Woman'.

[83] 'TOUCH YOUR WOMAN TOUCH YOUR WOMAN'.

[84] Images of said student in white face paint dancing in front of projected image, brandishing a ukulele.

B It takes a lot of work to look this sh!t.

Audio *The painful buzz of a tattoo gun.*

B&L *wince. Their hands instinctively clutch at their right thighs.*

B Let's talk about AMBITION

They cross to opposite mics.

L The only art that matters is the art that lasts.

B How many days do you have left? A week's worth?

L A month?

B A few years?

L That's the question.

B . . . Or *is* it?[85]

L No, it's not, because that's a question you can't hope to answer.

B But whether you have a few hours,

L Or a few years,

B You're worth it. Your body's worth it. Something you just can't wait to get out of your head and inked permanently into your flesh for the rest of your life?

L LIVE IT.

B BREATHE IT.

L EAT IT.

B SLEEP IT.

L We do.

B We are . . .

AMBITION TATTOO.
For all your Tattoo

B Ambition Tattoo
2521 N. Broadway
Knoxville, TN 37917

L Thanks for checking us out.[86]

---

85 A screengrab of The Ambition Tattoo Parlour website – it is revealed B&L are quoting from their bio page.

86 This text is an exact quote from the Ambition Tattoo Parlour website and their manifesto. It is ridiculous and wonderful. Especially, 'Ambition Tattoo: for all your tattoo.'

The lights crossfade to the mic spotlights. **B&L** *hoist themselves to stand on tiptoes, tuck their hands under their breasts, and put on anglicized versions of Barbara Walters accents – their Dr Kat Arney voices.*

Video *Dr Kat Arney talking. Silent and slow motion.*

B&L *quote Dr Kat Arney in unison.*

B&L Coming back to Dolly: You could make an exact copy of Dolly but it wouldn't be that same performance of Dolly. Like a musical score. Your genes are the song 'build a human' and every person is a completely unique (/ **B**: *uniquely complete*) performance of it. Dolly is the live performance of Dolly.

Louise *starts the sh!t country music loop.*

B&L *sing.*

B&L And then up here in these cabinets are my wigs. So here's another Dolly, and another one and another one . . .

Babs Dolly, did you look like this when you were a kid?

B&L Well, you mean, the full figure? (*Embarrassed laugh.*)

Babs Yeah, that's what I meant.

B&L Yeah, I thought that's what you meant. Well actually, I've always been pretty well blessed. As a child, I grew up fast. Other members of my family, you know, have done the same.

Babs Is it all you?

B&L I get asked that question. I always answer that by, 'cause people are in awe of the whole thing. You know, a lot of people say I *have*, a lot of people *say* I have, and I always say that if I hadn't have had it on my own, I'm just the kind of person that would have had me some made.

Babs Would you mind standing up? . . . Do you give your measurements?

B&L No, I always just say that I weigh 120.

Babs You don't have to look like this. You've very beautiful. You don't have to wear the blonde wigs, you don't have to wear the extreme clothes, right?

B&L No, it's certainly a choice. I don't like to be like everybody else. I've often made the statement that I would never stoop so low as to be fashionable, that's the easiest thing in the world to do. So I just decided that I would do something that would at least get the attention. Once they got past the shock of the ridiculous way I looked and all that, then they would see there was parts of me to be appreciated. I'm very real where it counts, and that's inside . . . But I just chose to do this, and it's, show business is a moneymaking joke, and I've just always liked telling jokes.

Babs But do you ever feel that you're a joke? That people make fun of you?

B&L Oh, I *know* they make fun of me. But actually, all these years, that people, you know, have thought the joke was on me, but it's actually been on the public. I know exactly what I'm doing, and I can change it at any time. Or I make more jokes about myself than anybody, because I enjoy – I know it. Like I said, I am sure of myself as a person. I'm sure of my talent. And to me, and I'm sure of my love . . . I like the kind of person that I am, so I can afford to piddle around and do diddle around with makeups and clothes and stuff, because I am secure with myself . . .

Louise *fades out the loop pedal. The mic spotlights crossfade to a general wash of the stage.*

B I don't know if you know this, Kenny, but this is our mainstream crossover hit. The only art that matters is the art that lasts.

L The reason Dolly is so successful is because she is so accessible.

B We've been working together for seven years now. Sh!t Theatre's all we've ever done.

L We had a huge falling out last year. It was chaos.

B We stopped living together.

L (*indicates the stage/theatre*) We almost stopped doing this.

B We couldn't keep going on about everything that was wrong. With us.

L With the world.

B If we were ever going to last

L We needed to make a show about something we both loved.

B&L *look at each other. They break into smiles before turning back to the audience.*

B And we decided *that* show would be our big, mainstream, crossover hit.

Audio *Guitar intro to 'Jolene' loop. Very low and slow indeed. Barely recognisable.*

B&L *move to centre stage.*

L We left Knoxville and took the bridge over the river Clinch.

B It's green and it's named after someone but no one remembers its name. There are wreaths on the bridge.

L Past a sign for Image Matters – photocopy repair.

B A sign for plastic surgery – say yes to fitting in the dress!

L And arrived at Ambition Tattoo parlour – <u>your body's worth it</u>!

B We went inside Ambition together to have Dolly permanently etched onto our bodies.

L Branded into our skin.

B (*to* **Louise**) You've got a dolly

and I’ve got a dolly

And Jen’s got a dolly

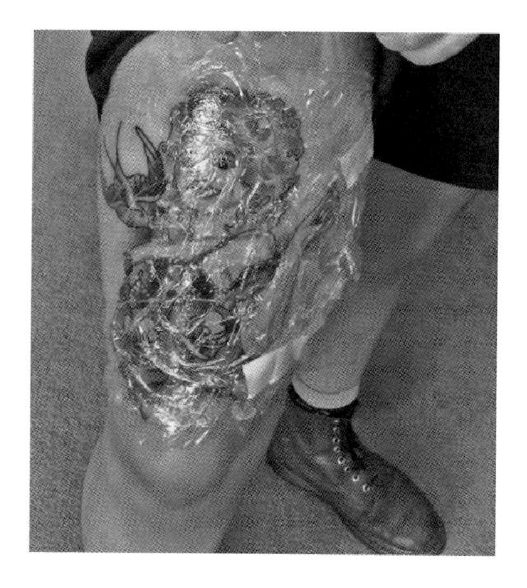

and she's permanent.

L This is permanent.

B (*to audience*) We think she looks really good.

L But Dolly will age.

B And when we die maggots will consume everything on the inside, leaving Dolly to harden like a leather jacket.

L If we're left under a sheet, however, the maggots will eat all the meat, including Dolly.

Audio *American news reporter from before: 'Her brand*[87] *her brand*[88] *brand*[89] *brand*[90] *brand*[91] *brand'.*[92]

B&L *look each other in the eye and take a deep breath. They clasp each other's hand and turn to face the audience head on. They begin to list merchandise. Each item is accompanied by a projected photograph of that actual piece of merch. As the list goes on, the photographs of the gift shop merch is interspersed with unnerving flash images of corpses at the Body Farm in various stages of decay.*

Over the course of the list, a centre spotlight gradually fades up over the general wash.

---

[87] Dolly's signature.

[88] Packaged mutton meat.

[89] Mutton meat.

[90] Mutton meat.

[91] A dead, skinned lamb.

[92] Very quick image of another decomposing corpse at the Tennessee Body Farm.

B Body Farm mug

L Body Farm pint glass

B Body Farm patch

L Body Farm pin

B Body Farm lanyard

L Body Farm flashlight

B Body Farm t-shirt

L Body Farm long sleeved shirt

B Body Farm sweatshirt

L Body Farm hat

B Dolly cap

L Dolly flat cap

B Dolly visor

L Dolly cowboy hat

B Dolly hats

L Dolly trucker cap

B Dolly workman OR WOMAN's[93] hard hat

L Dolly teddy

B Dolly teddy

L Dolly stuffed animals

B Dolly teddy bear

L Dolly tie-dye teddy

B Dolly 3D bear print pillow

L Dolly mug

B Dolly sippy cup

L Dolly sippy cup

B Dolly best friends mug

L Dolly mug with Dolly face

---

93 Additional image of a candy pink hard hat.

B Dolly tin cup

L Dolly jar

B Dolly pint glass

L Dolly shot glass

B Dolly shot glass

L Dolly shot glass

B Dolly shot glass

L Dolly shot glass

B Dolly drink cooler

L Dolly tea tray

B Dolly tea towel

L Dolly tea towel

B Dolly oven glove

L Dolly coffee

B Dolly cutlery

L Dolly recipe book

B Dolly blank recipe book – for your recipes

L Dolly golf ball

B Dolly soccer ball[94]

L Dolly football[95]

B Dolly chocolate balls

L Dolly bag

B Dolly purse

L Dolly coin purse

B Dolly shopping bag

L Dolly recyclable bag

B Dolly iron-on patch

---

94 Aka an English football.

95 An American football – not ball-shaped and held with the hands.

L Dolly pin

B Dolly broach

L Dolly soap

B Dolly replica hunting rifle

L Dolly children's book

B Dolly dollies

L Dolly childrenswear

B Dolly replica handgun for girls

L Dolly replica handgun for boys

B Dolly photo frame

L Dolly miniature rocking chair that is also a photo frame

B Dolly snow globes

L Dolly tartan blanket

B Dolly ceramics

L Dolly strawberry cider

B Dolly preserved cherries

L Dolly pumpkin butter

B Dolly pickled quails' eggs

L Dolly Jesus signs

B Dolly Christmas bauble

L Dolly best friend necklace (**B&L** *glance at one another.*)

B Dolly playing cards

L Dolly collectable ornament of coat of many colours

B Dolly DVD

L Dolly car stickers

B Dolly money clip

L Dolly dream box – to store your dreams

B Dolly slinky

L Dolly phone holder

B Dolly sunglasses holder

L Dolly flip knife

B Dolly chow chow

L Dolly hot chow chow

B Dolly dollar

Audio *The iconic drum-beat followed by 'And I . . .' from Whitney Houston's rendition of 'I Will Always Love You'. Before Whitney gets past 'And I . . .' she is drowned out by riotous applause.*

The wash snaps out with the drum beat, leaving **B&L** *standing proud in the centre spotlight. They bow twice and remove their shorts, fully revealing their Dolly thigh tattoos.*

Video *Dr Kat Arney playing the harp. It becomes clear that she is playing 'I Will Always Love You'. She makes a couple of mistakes and smiles and winces when it happens. It is gorgeous.*

During the video **B&L** *dress up as drag Dollies: rhinestone dresses, on back to front, over their vest tops so breasts are still out and on view. Plastic blonde wigs are placed on top of the wool wigs.* **Becca** *puts on the photocopier so it starts churning out photocopy after photocopy of Dolly with a skull superimposed over her.*

B&L *go to mics.*

Tennessee accents.

L You may not know this, but Dolly once entered herself into a Dolly drag queen lookalike competition.

B She made her hair bigger, her lips bigger, her rhinestones . . . rhinier.

Audio *Fades up slowly. 'You're the Only One' sung by Dolly mixed with quotes from throughout the show (e.g. 'more Dolly than she is', 'a unique clone', 'I can change at any time' etc.)*

L And she walked out onto the stage with all them other Dollies.

B And she lost.

Pause.

L They'd become more Dolly than she is.

Audio *Continues to build until it is almost unbearably loud.*

B&L *move upstage in their Dolly drag. They face the audience and pull their eye goggles down over their eyes, completing the Dolly avatar look. They pose, each fidgeting slightly and separately.*

Video *The projection fades in behind. It is* **B&L** *dressed as they are now, live on stage. Behind the projected image of* **B&L** *as Dolly avatars is another projection of* **B&L** *dressed as avatars. And another projection behind them. And another behind them. And another. Stretching into eternity. Each of the pairs of Drag Dollies are unique, dressed the same but fidgeting in different ways.*

Audio stops.

B&L *and all the video Dollies look right then left, in silence.*

Audio *Edit of Dolly Parton talking to a live audience.*

'Somebody once told me once that the best thing to do, to perform, is to make 'em laugh, make 'em cry, scare the hell out of 'em and go home. (*Audience cheers.*) I don't know how much of that we've accomplished tonight, but I'm looking forward to the next time I can come back and be with you folks. I want to dedicate this next song especially to all of you.'

Pause. Then **B&L** *sing a cappella:*

B&L I want to be able to walk into any place and say, 'Well that's Dolly'
And another one and another one
And another one and another one
And another one and another one
And another one and another one
I guess all people dream of that . . .

Snap to blackout.

Audio *Loud drum 'And I . . .' from Whitney Houston's rendition of 'I Will Always Love You'. This time the song is allowed to play out.*

The lights fade up. **B&L** *bow deeply twice. On the third bow they crumple to the floor and remain there as 'corpses' as the audience exit. Jen, dressed in a skull t-shirt, Body Farm hat and underpants (revealing her own Dolly tattoo), enters the stage and wraps* **B&L** *in the sheets covering the stage. She begins clearing the stage.*

Fin

NIGHTCLUBBING

Conceived, written and performed by Ray Young

Credits

Sound Designer, Musician and Performer: Mwen Rukendema
Sound Designer, Musician and Performer: Leisha Thomas
Lighting Designer: Nao Nagai
Set and Costume Designer: Naomi Kuyck-Cohen
Dramaturgy: Season Butler
Movement Consultants: Alleyne Dance
Directorial Collaborator: Nadia Latif
Producer: Anna Smith
Music Development Collaborators: xin, Naomi Jackson, Alicia Jane Turner and Kiera Coward-Deyell

Premiere: 26 April 2018, The Lowry, Salford.

The space is dimly lit, it is reminiscent of a nightclub or a gig venue. Microphones sit on edges of the space and one hangs from the ceiling. A white-rimmed hula hoop is on the floor below the hanging microphone. There is smoke in the air. A large black asteroid-like shape lies upstage left, as if it has just fallen from the sky. Two figures are huddled around a round table like scientists or DJs twisting buttons on the brightly lit interfaces of their machinery. A steady bassline pulsates from speakers they move their bodies to the beat. As the audience take their seats one of them reaches for a guitar. There is a black slash curtain hanging at an angle behind the square performance space. A TV flickers with static beneath the table. It has crashed into a pile of fine black rubble.

A bassy rock version of the song 'Nightclubbing' by Grace Jones builds and swells. A light begins to illuminate the asteroid. A hand slowly appears from the asteroid, then an arm, it retracks and we see a head squeeze its way of its cocoon, hair, eyes, shoulders, a torso. A creature appears; it uses its hand to push the cocoon down its body turning it into a large black skirt. The creature is **Ray**, *she stands defiant, strong, poised. She moves her body slowly through poses, angled misshapen, seductive, until she comes to stillness. The music gradually shifts to an electronic rhythmic pulse.* **Ray** *disappears inside the rock then appears again feet first sliding across the gloss black floor. She moves towards a large pair of platform hoof-like shoes. Once inside the shoes she stands, now towering over 6 foot, she takes in the audience, then slowly crouches, eyes on her audience and picks up a microphone from the floor.*

There is one performer and two musicians on stage throughout.

Ray (*low distorted voice effect*) She was born on an island under a leatherette star. She came up brown and thin and quiet as a twig in the shadow of a mango tree. Thin, shy, brown, quiet, growing in the sun. Then her parents sent for her. She left behind blue skies and sorrel ackee and saltfish, yam and green banana and headed for white dogs and white winters of upstate New York.

Ray *stands, twists her body to the left and poses with her hand on her hip.*

Ray (*high distorted voice effect*) When they left their hometown in the year 2000, they were already well read. They already knew Audre Lorde and Zadie Smith, Bell Hooks and Cade and Delany. They already knew how to defuse a potential threat, with a well place punchline, how a nod could give the unseen a moment of visibility, how to hide the chinks in their amour, when to let themselves be exposed and soft.

Ray *places the microphone into its stand. She turns slowly and starts to move in the hoof-like shoes towards a fluorescent hula hoop at the front of the stage. Each step is deliberate, she cuts through the space making sure she is seen.*

Nissy (*voice over*) People had to die, people had to suffer, people to battle, people had to go through pain and suffering even to this day because of their skin colour and then for you, just because of the image of a club, not letting people in based on their skin colour, it's disgusting.

She continues to walk until she is under the microphone hanging from the ceiling. She stands inside the hoop and crouches down to pick it up with both hands. She rises to stillness. She is poised, she takes in her audience, when she is ready she begins to hoop. A pulsing drone dips and rises and she moves the hoop around her body. If the hoop drops she returns to the floor, picks it up, rises and spins it around her body once more. Once she is caught in the rhythm of the hoops she begins to speak . . .

Ray (*speaking into hanging microphone*) I'm sorry for breathing

Sorry taking myself too seriously

Sorry for laughing too loudly

Sorry being able to ride the beat

Her voice is picked up by the microphone and looped back to her as she continues to hula hoop. She lifts her voice, fighting to be heard over the building loop.

Sorry for my love of colour

Sorry for my queer outlook

Sorry for 'Black Panther'

Sorry for 'Get Out'

Sorry for poverty

Sorry for wealth

Sorry for looking in neon pink

Sorry for being outspoken

Sorry for heteronormativity

For having a chip on my shoulder

Sorry you feel uncomfortable

Sorry for my features

Sorry for my muscles

Sorry for moving in next door

Sorry for questioning your authority

Sorry for my vulnerability

Sorry for fighting back

Sorry for this amour

Sorry for your fragility

Sorry for not turning the other cheek

For taking up space

Sorry for this skin

Sorry for being sorry

The hoop drops again, **Ray** *defiantly pics it up and spins the hoop around her body, hooping faster and faster, the drone builds in both speed and volume to match her movements. When she is ready she stops the hoop and throws it to the floor. She takes off her shoes, returning her to her normal height and walks upstage right. She sits beneath the table, where the musicians underscore the action with a soft guitar riff. She takes a moment to catch her breath, then creates a gravel circle around herself. Once she feels safe she picks up another microphone from the floor.*

Ray (*low distorted voice effect*) At seventeen she began to rebel against her parents and took paths that lead her away from family and religion. She stepped out from behind the pulpit and into the underground. Hard bass, shoes that defied gravity, bare skin, lipstick, club culture, dark corner, cocktails, queer spaces, long nights that met the morning, clothes that dripped with sweat, sweat that glistened under red lights, walks home in sunlight and yesterday's clothes.

Ray (*high distorted voice effect*) When they left their hometown in the year 2000, they didn't leave it behind completely . . . It clung to their hair, stuck to the corners of their eyes, gathered like balls of fluff on their clothes. The complex polymer in their skin made them super invisible or hyper visible. It made people act strangely around them, uninvited hands pulling at braids, invading space without question.

Ray *stands and puts the microphone on the table. She moves downstage right to stand in front of the microphone stand. On the stand there are loops of black cable.* **Ray** *picks up a coil of cable and places it around her neck.*

Nissy (*voice over*) People had to die, people had to suffer, people to battle, people had to go through pain and suffering even to this day because of their skin colour and then for you, just because of the image of a club, not letting people in based on their skin colour, it's disgusting.

Ray *continues to place the coils of cable around her neck. They drape down her body, each one longer than the last.*

Nissy (*voice over*) People would say look like really really, like really really really good if you wanna get into this club because they don't let people in based on how they look.

Nissy (*voice over*) There's a lot of girls who go in who are very very slim and they have that shape or whatever and they're really funny about letting in ummmm, people in who just don't suit their criteria.

Nissy (*voice over*) Please tell me why, why the promoter has to come outside the club and then he starts walking up and down up and down staring at people in the queue.

Once **Ray** *has removed the cable from the first microphone she moves upstage right where she finds another mic stand draped in more cable. As before she removes each coil, placing each one over her neck. The loops of cable on her body start to form a dress.*

Nissy (*voice over*) So, how exactly is the general manager or whoever or the owner or whatever of the club, going to pick people to go into the club like, like who is going to pick, how is he going to pick, what's the criteria?

Ah well basically, you know he's going to come up and down the queue and he's going to be looking out if you look good, you look on point then you're gonna be let in.

Beat.

He's gonna come and analyse you and look and see if you're dressed well, you look nice.

Beat.

The only people that were told to get out of the queue we not white, yes I repeat, not white, or you would say not really dressed or extremely good looking, you know like magazine good looking.

Beat.

He could come and he could say, oh sorry you have to go, oh sorry you have to go.

Ray *takes a length of cable and ties it tightly around her waist. She puts on the remaining cable over her head to form a hood. She is transformed.*

A slow guitar riff begins. It's the riff from 'Nightclubbing' by Grace Jones. **Ray** *moves through the space, her hands feel the cable against the contours of her body, she raises her hands as if she is trying to draw strength from another power beyond herself. She draws the energy back into her body as she continues to make way downstage right. Once at the downstage right microphone she raises her arms and then lowers them to meet the microphone.*

Ray (*low distorted voice effect*) She tried her hand at acting, got a taste for performing. She found the 60s counterculture, or else the 60s counterculture found her. She spread her wings and expanded her mind, living in communes and working as a go-go dancer, tripping on the city and LSD and whole new ways of being in the world and in her skin.

(*Sung – no voice effect*) Nightclubbing, nightclubbing
We're what's happening

(*High distorted voice effect*) They left their hometown in the year 2000, young and carefree. Still very much a reader, they navigated the world with ease. They never questioned why people clutched their bags when they walked past. Never questioned why more often not they would be followed around shops. Never questioned the stares held longer than comfortable. Never questioned the lowered voices when they walked into the room. From the titles on the library shelves to the looks from the security guards, they knew very well how to read. They just got on with it.

(*Sung – no voice effect*) Nightclubbing, nightclubbing
We're an ice machine

(*Low distorted voice effect*) At eighteen she hit NYC, no more shy girl no more twig, limbs sleek graceful as silk, ancient and hard as mahogany. Serious thighs like nothing High Fashion had ever seen. It wasn't exactly lights, camera, gorgeous. Something didn't click. Her complex polymer made her an alien to them, she left New York City and moved to Paris. This time something was different, an appreciation for the architecture of her face, the way the light seemed drawn to her skin, drawn in – or did it radiate out and out and through her, her skin a beacon. She was bold, androgynous, she stood out and they all saw her.

(*Sung – no voice effect*) We see people, brand new people
They're something to see

(*High distorted voice effect*) When they left their hometown in the year 2000, they pulled on their melanin, stuffed their future into the pockets of their purple coat and vowed to show themselves. So when the night came when someone barred their entry, tried to force them over the border of visibility. Ejected, rejected, stubbornly unseen, they stood their ground.

(*Sung – no voice effect*) When we're nightclubbing
Bright-white clubbing
Oh isn't it wild?

(*A beat kicks in. Sung – no voice effect*) Driving down those city streets

Waiting to get down

Won't you get your big machine

Somewhere in this town?

Pull up to my bumper baby

In your long black limousine

Pull up to my bumper baby

And drive it in between

You better pull up . . . . .

You better pull up . . . . .

Pull up . . . .

Pull up . . ..

You better better pull up . . . . .

You better better pull up . . . . .

Ah Ah you better . . . .
etc . . ..

Ray *continues to sing but moves away from the microphone, she dances and contorts her body. She tears the cord from around her waist and throws it into the space. She continues to move her body and rage with the music which is now wild of out of control. She takes the cord hood and rests it on top of her head. The hood, now hair, whips back and forth as she moves her body. Lights flash from behind the slash curtain, smoke fills the space, it feels like a storm. The hair meets the floor with a whipping sound.* **Ray** *continues back and forth, whipping and turning until finally she lets go of the hood and it crashes to the floor. The music swells and crashes and then begins to fade.* **Ray** *stands for a moment taking in the audience and then walks over to the hoop downstage left.*

She stands inside the hoop. Breathing heavily. We see her silhouette. There is a small pot that sits beside the hoop, light shines out of it. **Ray** *reaches into and pulls out coconut oil, which she smears across her legs and arms. A warm light illuminates her actions. A soft guitar riff is playing.*

Ray (*voice over*) What are you? What planet are you from? Did your people grow up closer or further away from the sun? Do your melanocytes clump together to form one continuous dark brown hue? Are you eumelanin or pheomelanin? Are you a light catcher? Like early humans you developed the ability to survive the sunlight. Are you Sub Saharan? Your melanin functions as a shield against ultraviolet radiation.

As she oils her skin, **Ray** *begins to calm. Her breath returns to normal, she relaxes into the ritual of oiling her body in an act of self-care. Once she has oiled her whole body, she picks up the oil and places it by the TV screen by the table.* **Ray** *walks back to the cocooned asteroid. She dives inside and flips the skirt inside out to reveal a brightly shining gold underside. She holds it up forming a massive golden disc, of which she is in the centre.*

Ray (*voice over*) Sometimes a flicker in your nervous system, a sweaty palm, the hairs stand on the back of your neck. You switch shield on, you sense bullshit, so you call it out.

(**Ray** *starts to speak along with the voice over*) You start vibrating on a different level, your sound waves kick out, shouting your trauma but the pheomelanin just hear noise. They are coming for you, but you don't lash out. You take time to decode their messages. They would have you believe you're the genetic anomaly, something missing in your anatomy.

Ray (*spoken off-mic*) You close your eyes start to trace the lineage back, you see your people in sunnier climes. Melanin, is a complex polymer found in those people who have historically lived closer to the sun, you see them drop like felsic lava from the sun's core, they meet the earth amalgamate, spread across the land, you start to understand. You vibrate faster. You take off, you are a light catcher, you are a light more brilliant than the sun.

Ray *spins the dress above her and brings it down in a pile upstage left.* **Ray** *lies on the floor with her arms out, then she turns over and lies on her side centre stage. The stage is filled with a warm light. The guitarist hands her a microphone.*

Grace Jones (*voice over*) No, I have the last word and you don't get it unless you go through me.

Ray Moving black seeing black, feeling black, black splaining.

Speaking black, loving black, black love.

Moving through space and time black, ride the beat black.
Sowing black, holding black, evolving black, seeing through black eyes.

Ray *stands.*

Titanium black, ceramic black Drifting on The Black Sea.

Undercover of moonlight black.

Black history, the sovereignty of black future.

Majestic black.

Liquid black.

Reclaiming black.

Seductive black.

Erotic Black.

Sexy as fuck.

Oozing black.

Boiling black.

Claiming space black.

Deep black.

Hard black obsidian glass.

Black holes that drink deep from the light of the universe.

Sleek, slick black.

Black that stops the clocks and leaves time suspended.

Nourishing midnight, secret places and sacred objects.
Dreaming black.

There is an implosion. The lights flash white. The TV flashes off. The music quickly rewinds.

Blackout

Performance Documents

1 Promotional image of Ray Young for *NIGHTCLUBBING*.
Courtesy of Ray Young.

2 Ray Young performing in *NIGHTCLUBBING*, The Lowry, Salford, 2018. Courtesy of Ray Young.

3 Ray Young performing in *NIGHTCLUBBING*. The Lowry, Salford, 2018. Courtesy of Ray Young.

Pleasure Seekers

Written and performed by Bourgeois & Maurice

(George Heyworth and Liv Morris)

Credits

Director: Jude Christian
Musical Director: Victoria Falconer and Jarrad Payne
Music production: Jarrad Payne
Set Designer: Emma Bailey
Costume Designer: Julian Smith
Lighting Designer: Marty Langthorne
Make-up Designer: Andrew Gallimore
Choreography: Will Tuckett

Premiere: 8 April 2022, Soho Theatre, London.

Content List

Opening

The space looks set for a party yet somehow menacing, as though artificial intelligence has attempted to visually interpret the idea of 'fun'. An enormous piñata dominates the stage, draped in hazard tape.

As the audience enters they hear muzak versions of aggressively optimistic pop songs, interspersed with a soulless telecom voice . . .

Voice Welcome to Pleasure Seekers. Please ensure that all personal belongings are safely stowed under your seating area and keep arms and legs inside the theatre at all times . . .

Thank you for your patience, your pleasure is important to us. We are currently experiencing high demand and all our staff are busy pleasuring other people. We will be with you shortly . . .

If you would like to experience pleasure online you can find it at www.bourgeoisandmaurice.co.uk.

Please be aware that the pleasure-inducing activities in tonight's show are being performed by trained professionals under stringent safety conditions. Do not attempt this at home.

This repeats ad nauseum until house clearance. Eventually a technician enters the stage and removes the hazard sign from the piñata, signalling that we are ready to have fun . . .

Lights down.

A bass starts. A spotlight picks out the gloved hands of **Bourgeois & Maurice** *(***B&M***) sticking through the back curtain, clicking in time to the beat. They sing.*

Song: Pleasure Seekers

Both We're putting the past behind us
Putting the past behind us
Putting the past behind us
It was shite.

Forgetting about the future
Forgetting about the future
Forgetting about the future
It doesn't look too bright.

Tonight we're gonna live for the moment
Tonight we're gonna turn off our phones
Or at least we're gonna put them on silent
So we can check them if we get bored during show.

B&M *step through the curtain. They wear brightly coloured jackets and PVC trousers – clown businesswear chic.*

Woah turn up the bass on the piano
Strawpedo your Veuve Clicquot
Or maybe you prefer to stay home
With a nice Merlot, whatever.

The number explodes into hypercolour, hyper-lit chaos; streamers flying, confetti falling, haze billowing. Just generally relentlessly over the top.

Tonight's about
Pleasure
Non-stop pleasure
Hedonism is my new religion
Pleasure seekers.

Bourgeois Dionysus said life should be a party
Dedicated to having a good time
So I honour the ancient gods
By taking sixteen pills at Berghain.

Maurice Marie Antoinette lost her head
For getting off her tits with the one per cent
But what the people didn't understand is
It was a legitimate work event

Both Woah turn up the bass on the piano.

Maurice *unfolds the top of the piñata to reveal a piano inside it.*

Strawpedo your Veuve Clicquot
Or maybe you prefer to stay home
With *Game of Thrones*, whatever.

Tonight's about
Pleasure
Non-stop pleasure
Hedonism is my new religion
Pleasure seekers.

Bourgeois Good evening, humansexuals, are you ready to have fun?

Crowd cheers.

Bourgeois We are Bourgeois & Maurice and we're on a mission to bring pleasure to every corner of the world. it doesn't matter who you are, doesn't matter where you're from, doesn't matter if . . .

Both There is no Studio 54 in your town
We can get down on the dancefloor of the Rose & Crown
Don't have to arrive on a white horse like Bianca Jagger

We can drive home drunk in our Fiat Panda
Wo-ah that sounds a bit pathetic I know
But you find the fun where you can get it
Some people like to spend their nights on Reddit
And some people like scat
Whatever brings you
Pleasure
Non-stop pleasure.

Bourgeois I want to feel as happy as Larry
I want to feel as free as Britney
I want to feel as fun as my mum before she had me.

Both Pleasure, pleasure, pleasure
Pleasure seekers.

Scene One

Bourgeois Thank you so much and welcome to *Pleasure Seekers*. I'm Georgeois Bourgeois, please give it up for my sinister sister on keys, Maurice Maurice.

Maurice Cheers.

Bourgeois What a gorgeous audience. Look at this front row, so chic. It's like a Prada front row. Gucci behind. Little bit River Island right at the back but that's OK. Look, Maurice, look at this beautiful audience. Look at these bone structures, we could be in Paris. In the catacombs.

NB: This opening section has a lot of flexibility in it, and will be ad libbed around this basic structure. They will respond to the audience, react to what they're wearing etc.

So, tonight is all about pleasure and I want to say congratulations on being here tonight. On prioritising your own pleasure. Some of you have probably got kids at home with separation anxiety and you've left them with some random babysitter you found on Grindr, some of you might have a recently bereaved grandparent, who could really do with your hand holding theirs while they watching *EastEnders,* but you said no! Fuck off, Granny. I'm going to watch Bourgeois & Maurice in [*reductive description of the venue – i.e. an old tent, a dark bunker in Soho*] instead. You're focusing on yourself! I respect that! So let's have some fun!

Maurice But first some rules.

Both Because rules make the fun.

Maurice Rule number 1 – no thinking.

Bourgeois We really really mean this. Please do not think during this show, it'll be easier for everyone. Tonight is all about having a good time and that's really hard to do when you think, cos you'll find yourself asking 'what does that mean?', 'why is there a giant piñata on stage?', 'what's the deeper meaning here?' There isn't any. I mean we'd love there to be, but there just isn't.

Maurice Yeah, we looked, but we just couldn't find any meaning.

Bourgeois Exactly, so just take this as an opportunity to waste a meaningless hour of your life at the theatre.

Maurice Great, rule number 2. No songs.

She closes the lid of the piñata keyboard and walks to centre stage.

Bourgeois What?

Maurice I'm done with the songs.

Bourgeois But . . . we just sang a song about pleasure.

Maurice Yeah and it didn't actually bring me that much pleasure. I really had to focus on getting the timing right and singing notes and stuff. It was quite a lot of hard work.

Bourgeois Wish we'd talked about this before. The whole show is songs. That's what we do.

Maurice I think you're being quite limited in your thinking. Tonight is all about pleasure pleasure pleasure, that can take many forms. We could make this person a chocolate roulade or give that lady up there a deep tissue massage. Why does everything have to be a performance?

Bourgeois I like performing, I like singing. They bring me pleasure.

Maurice Bit sad.

Bourgeois Maurice, look at these people. Look at their miserable, depressed faces. The world is a mess right now, and they need us to lift them out of their doldrums, to offer some respite from the horrors of real life. It's our job as artists. Did it ever occur to you that our songs might bring immense joy and pleasure to other people?

Maurice No.

Bourgeois Well watch this . . .

He targets someone in the front row.

Bourgeois Hi, what's your name?

Whatever their name is . . .

Bourgeois I should have guessed. No pressure but do you want another song?

Hopefully they say yes.[1]

---

[1] *If they say no:*
Bourgeois: [Name] it's been a tough few years for you hasn't it? You're angry aren't you? And when you're angry you lash out. I'm not sure you know what's best for you, so we're going to do another song.

Maurice OK fine, we'll do another song. (*She goes back to keyboard.*) But let's make a deal – I'll stand over here and really put in minimal effort, and Bourgeois you stand in the middle and do most of the work.

Bourgeois Oh what, so I'm just supposed to stand here centre stage, in the spotlight, getting all the attention, doing absolutely everything?

Maurice Yeah.

Bourgeois Absolutely fine.

Maurice Great. So final rule, number 3.

Bourgeois A rule we both agree on.

Together No negativity.

Bourgeois We just won't do it anymore. We've been there, we've done that. Yes pessimism, cynicism and nihilism have been our bread and butter for centuries, that mindset has made us extremely wealthy.

Maurice I live in Dubai now.

Bourgeois Yeah and you love it don't you?

Maurice It's great. There's no tax. Or gays. But has negativity really brought me pleasure? No, so we're not doing it anymore. No more negative Nancies.

Bourgeois We're rebranding. We are now optimistic Olivias. As part of this journey we've started putting little Post-It notes around our dressing room with positive sayings and phrases, just to remind us to stay upbeat. What was the one we like?

Maurice 'You're not being buried alive, you're being planted'.

Bourgeois That's not the one I was thinking of, I was thinking 'every cloud has a silver lining'.

Maurice OK, yeah that's good too. Basically the same.

Bourgeois Very similar sentiment. It's all about changing the way you think to be more positive. Shifting your focus. Yes, you might say 'oh wealth inequality is at the worst it's been in centuries with the top 1 per cent owning 99.9 per cent of everything', but . . . on the other hand there's loads of really hot people in the world. Which is going to make you happier to focus on? Are you glass half empty or glass half sexy?

(*To audience members . . .*) talking of which, you two are very attractive. Quite overwhelming actually, almost distracting. Are you in a relationship?

Bourgeois *responds to them and brings it round to talking about monogamy.*

Bourgeois Have you had the exclusivity conversation yet? It's important, because there's this new trend for monogamy, that some people can get hoodwinked into. Monogamy to me is like turning up at an all you can eat buffet and only having croutons. Don't you want to try something else? Bit of sushi?

Maurice A couple of Twiglets? Dairylea Dunker? Those little bone shaped biscuits?

Awkward pause.

Bourgeois Those are for dogs, Maurice.

Maurice Well they're nice.

Bourgeois Look I don't want to tell people how to live their lives, everyone must do what's right for them. I am actually in an exclusive relationship myself. With veganism. It's going well, thanks for asking. Early days, but yeah. I mean it's hard work, I have to work on it every single day. What you get out really depends on what you put in. Quite literally. And sometimes when I'm at that all-you-can-eat buffet my eyes do wander over to the salami plate, and I feel like a very bad vegan.

Maurice Well no, you're not bad, you're just a victim of a highly conservative heteropatriarchal society which expects you to adhere to a mono dietary lifestyle at the expense of your own personal fulfilment.

Bourgeois Ah thanks, Maurice. I really needed to hear that.

Maurice Well I'm really glad I said it then.

Bourgeois You're right! Let's not limit ourselves, let's fill our plate with whatever we want. We shouldn't deny ourselves pleasure. We should give ourselves over to absolute indulgence. Maurice, release the poppers!

Maurice *presses a button on the piñata which releases dry ice from its arse.* **Bourgeois** *drops to his knees and inhales the smoke before singing.*

Song: I Need Meat

Bourgeois Eating in the same restaurant every night
Can get boring
Sometimes I crave another flavour
Something I can really get my teeth into
I've had enough of silken tofu
I've been swallowing
The same old aubergine
For far too long
Tonight I need a bite
From a different menu.

Both I need Meat!
Put some bacon in my baked potato
Meat!
Give me chorizo with my manchego
Put blood in my sausage

Spam in my bap
I've got a hard on for lard ons
There's no looking back
I need meat.

Bourgeois There'll always be a place for a plant-based diet
In my life

Both Jackfruit's so versatile

Bourgeois I will never close that cupboard door
Just hoping we can open it up a little bit
I don't like cheating
On what I'm eating
I want a consensual
Break from vegetables
I need a different source of protein.

Both Give me meat!
Own me with a pepperoni
Meat!
Mince into my cannelloni
Make jerky from my turkey
Stuff my duck
I've got a bone in hand

He produces a fake ham leg and sings into it like it's a mic.

And I'm ready to . . .
Eat

He flings the ham behind him.

I need meat.

He produces a long string of sausages and wears them like a feather boa as he descends into the audience.

Come on press my chicken breast panini
Grab an Oxo cube and rim my martini
Rub me in goose fat
Then prick me with a sprig
Of rosemary
Then roast me
In a bird in a bird
In a bird in a bird
In a bird in a bird
In a pig.

Maurice *appears from behind the keys wearing a pig nose.*

Maurice Oink.

Bourgeois I need meat!
I know I should be gentle with
Meat!
Cos my body's used to lentils
[*Fart sound effect*]
But I need meat!
I'm a carnivore whore for
Meat!
Come on serve it to me raw
Meat!

Maurice *comes centre stage and during this final verse they both strip off their outer jackets revealing leather harnesses underneath.*

I want it hot and fresh
Sizzle sizzle
I want a pound of flesh
I'll even eat the gristle
I might regret it when I'm Type 2 Diabetic
But right now I'm horny for
Meat!

Scene Two

Bourgeois Thank you.

Maurice I'm going to do a bit of tidying up. Gets a bit messy otherwise.

She picks up the jackets and puts them in a bin.

Bourgeois Yeah, that's the problem with fun.

Maurice How are you feeling after that?

Bourgeois Quite liberated actually. How are you?

Maurice Um, hard to say. Did I enjoy it? Not massively. Bit juvenile. I'd give it two stars, maybe three. Room for improvement. Also, it was quite offensive to the plant based community and it perpetuated a common / stigma around . . .

Bourgeois I'm gonna stop you there. Rule 3. No negativity.

Maurice You're right. It's so hard. But no, not anymore. It's just optimism, optimism, positivity.

Bourgeois Stop this gothy, witchy-woo lurking in the corner business. Come on, come over here into the light.

Maurice *reluctantly goes to centre stage.*

Bourgeois Maurice, tell us, what brings you pleasure?

Maurice *stands motionless and blank.*

Bourgeois Anything, literally.

Still blank.

Bourgeois Don't overthink it. I say 'pleasure', you say . . .

Maurice . . .

Bourgeois OK, well why don't we ask these lovely people, maybe you can get some ideas from them?

Bourgeois *chats to an audience member. They tell him about something they find pleasurable.* **Maurice** *responds, brushing each of them off. None of them bring her pleasure.* **Bourgeois** *asks two or three people then reacts with shock at a very mundane thing.*

Bourgeois Wow. Can I just say that's so brave of you to admit in a room full of strangers. I know we have an eclectic audience, but that's, woah, quite . . .

Maurice Bourgeois, don't shame them.

Bourgeois Oh you're right, sorry. No shame. Nothing's off limits in our pursuit of pleasure. Everything is valid here. Well, unless you're really into murder.

Maurice (*laughing*) But even then. You put your hands up and say 'I got a bit carried away but they just wouldn't listen, it doesn't make me a bad person'. Hypothetically.

Maurice *sheepishly moves back to the keyboard.*

Bourgeois Well . . . if we're both getting things off our chest this evening.

Song: Buying Shit

Bourgeois I've got a secret
Something I keep hidden inside
Something no one knows
Except the algorithms online
I never thought I'd be the type
Who does this
I always fight for what is right
When I'm in public
But when I'm on own I forget my politics
And in just a few little clicks.

Both Suddenly I'm buying shit late at night on Amazon
I just can't resist the bargain price on Amazon
And I know it's wrong but it feels so right
So I'll keep buying shit on Amazon til the morning light.

Bourgeois *climbs on top of the piñata.*

Bourgeois I bought *Das Kapital*
It was £1.86
I didn't read it all
But I think I got the gist
And I agree the exploitative labour market's damaging society
But I'm in desperate need of printer ink with next day delivery
I can't just go to the stationery store
Because it doesn't exist anymore.

Bourgeois *stands on the piñata and we go full 'Live at Wembley Stadium' with sound and lighting.*

Both Since I keep buying shit late at night on Amazon
Like this FitBit – half price on Amazon
It looks so real
But I know it's fake (who cares)
I'll buy another one on Amazon when this one breaks.

Doorbell sound. **Bourgeois** *goes off stage and has an overly excited conversation with a delivery driver. He returns, dragging a huge stack of Amazon boxes.*

Bourgeois I read a terrifying story in the *Guardian*
About the darkness at the heart
Of Amazon
But I only got half way through
I got distracted by an advert
For Peloton

Money can't buy you happiness
It just buys you loads of stuff
And I'm here to tell you
For me that's enough.

Bourgeois *dances with the Amazon boxes.*

Both Amazon baby
Look what you're doing to me
Amazon baby
I wish I could quit ya but
You make my life so easy
You've captured my heart
And all my data
You know what I need
Much better than me.

Bourgeois *swings the boxes around, releasing packing materials everywhere. Hopefully over the audience too.*

So I'll never stop buying shit late at night on Amazon
Any old random shit that I happen to like on Amazon

Cos it picks me up
When I get depressed
So I'll keep buying shit on Amazon til there's nothing left
Buying shit on Amazon til there's nothing left
Nothing left
Nothing, nothing, nothing
Left.

He shakes one final box and a solitary packing peanut drops to the floor.

Scene Three

Bourgeois *gets a broom and starts sweeping up the packing peanuts.*

Bourgeois I sometimes worry that the messages in our songs are a bit subtle. In case you didn't get that, the message in that song is that Amazon is really, really bad. Don't use it guys. Use the alternatives. Like Ali Express.

Maurice We got this piñata from Ali Express didn't we?

Bourgeois We did yeah, how much was it again?

Maurice 79p.

Bourgeois Bargain. I've actually broken it, we should buy another one for tomorrow.

Maurice No, we're not just buying a new one, we can repair this. We need to be more sustainable now.

Bourgeois That's true. It's one of the things we asked ourselves at the start of writing this show, is our addiction to consumption, excess, hedonism, ultimately going to lead to the complete destruction of Planet Earth?

Maurice We decided no, cos we wanted to do the show.

Bourgeois But we asked the question and that's what matters isn't it.

Maurice Yeah, and we got a sustainability consultant. What was her name again?

Bourgeois Gretal? Th . . .?

Maurice Thun-berg? Fun-berg?

Bourgeois Greta No-Fun Berg! That's what we called her. Just a little office joke. Because the thing Greta said to us was, 'Bourgeois and Maurice, please do not do your show. The world does not need it.' She's a very funny teen terrorist. I said to her, 'Greta, we beg to differ. This is more than a show. We are not just performers. We are piano-based social activists.'

Maurice Changing the world one harmony at a time. Greta's not the only one who was on our backs. We did another Zoom session with Insulate Britain.

Bourgeois Insulate Britain! Isn't it insular enough? Don't we need to open a few windows and let a nice continental breeze in? Honestly the stuff these loonies are saying, all the things we apparently need to give up.

Maurice Just Stop Oil.

Bourgeois They're saying we have to give up petrol? Well there goes Vaseline.

Maurice Plastic!

Bourgeois That includes sequins. It always feels like it's the queer community that has to give things up first. So Maurice and I have put our heads together and we've come up with something we think would be much much easier for us all to cut out . . .

Song: Babies

Both Babies

Bourgeois Chubby little features
Hide the fact they're nasty little creatures
Sucking the life out of the earth like leeches.

Both Babies

Bourgeois The intelligent primate
Shame they're such a strain on the climate
The ozone hole grows every time a cervix dilates.

Both Babies creeping out of vaginas
Leading us like the Pied Piper
To our death with non-biodegradable diapers.

Babies
What do they believe in?
Most of them aren't even vegan
They don't care about dairy cos they're evil.

The world is getting hotter
We can't hide from the rising sea
We've got to do something
To rescue humanity
Protect the future, save our species
Put an end to babies.

Bourgeois *walks to the pile of Amazon boxes, reaches in with a grimace and produces a life-size robotic toy baby. He places it on the piñata and it immediately springs to life, crawling menacingly throughout the rest of the song.*

Babies.

Bourgeois What a bunch of losers
Brainwashed mindless consumers
Selfish greedy boob abusers.

Both Babies.

Bourgeois Pointless blobs
Lazy benefit scrounging slobs
Every baby should be made to get a job.

Both The world is getting smaller
And we're running out of room
We can't keep accepting these
Immigrants from the womb.

He picks up a protest sign that reads 'GOD HATES BABIES'.

Protect your borders, save your countries
All the problems of the world lay at the feet
Of babies.

Babies' cute little faces
Lining up to take all our places
Babies hate us and they wanna replace us.

Two babies in hanging bouncers drop from the ceiling above **Bourgeois***' head.*

Babies
They're gonna get us
Babies
They're gonna get us
Babies
They're gonna get us
B.A.B.I.E.S. gon' get us.

Babies! Nasty babies!
Evil babies! Awful babies!

Babies! Scary babies!
Dangerous babies! Deadly babies!

There's a baby army forming in the four corners of the world
Wearing babygrow uniforms – blue for boys, pink for girls
If we don't go to war against this evil force
This weed will keep on growing
We've got to nip it in the bud
Cos otherwise imagine how much more destructive
Babies will be
When they
Grow up.

Scene Four

Bourgeois I'm hearing some cheers in the audience for that one. Sounds like Mumsnet's in the house tonight.

Maurice *has a meltdown at the piano.*

Bourgeois Maurice? You OK?

She collapses and crawls under the piñata.

Maurice I can't do it. I've tried. I gave the songs a shot, I really did. But even singing about the eradication of babies hasn't helped. Maybe I'm just incapable of experiencing pleasure. How are you feeling?

Bourgeois Well I was feeling pleasure but now I'm not cos you're not.

Maurice So your pleasure is dependent on mine?

Bourgeois I think it might be.

Maurice That's quite a lot of pressure. This is getting too much, I need a break.

Bourgeois Do you want a cup of tea?

Maurice Yeah.

They roll on a tea set and make a cup of tea slowly and methodically. They chat while the kettle boils.

Bourgeois Sorry everyone, we're just gonna take a five-minute break. You don't have to watch this bit, it's going to be really boring. Do whatever else you want to do. If you want to look at your phones that's fine, if you want to take photos that's fine too. We didn't spend two hours getting ready for this to be a 'nice memory'.

An awkward pause as they work out what to say to each other.

Maurice How was your lockdown?

Bourgeois Well, I stayed in every night eating shit food and watching shit TV. I basically became a heterosexual.

Maurice You poor thing.

Bourgeois Horrible, horrible life those people lead. People don't talk about it. It was a harrowing window into the lives of others.

Maurice Have you ever met a happy heterosexual?

Bourgeois How can they be? When they're not at home they're at B&Q. It's no life. How was your lockdown?

Maurice Fine. I spent most of my time just mining bitcoin in here (*indicates her wig*). It's a crypto farm, actually uses more power than Argentina.

Bourgeois Do you think you have anything to do with the recent collapse of the crypto market?

Maurice Yes. I do. I think I devalued it with my cheap sense of humour.

Bourgeois Maybe that's why we work well together. We're both drawn to industries built on deeply unstable economics.

They look around at the stage.

Maurice Got any plans for the week?

Bourgeois Well I'm in a show. A play really.

Maurice Oh right, what kind of play is it?

Bourgeois A Gibson.

Maurice An Ibsen?

Bourgeois Gibson. Debbie Gibson. It's an autobiographical drama about the life of Debbie Gibson.

Maurice Who's Debbie Gibson?

Bourgeois You don't know who Debbie Gibson is? Eighties pop star Debbie Gibson. The American Kylie.

Maurice Never heard of her.

Bourgeois Well she's written a play, quite a harrowing dark drama in three acts.

Maurice No idea who Debbie Gibson is.

Bourgeois (*to audience*) Have you heard of Debbie Gibson?

Few mutterings.

Maurice A few people. I think it's a bit niche.

Bourgeois What does niche mean?

Maurice It's French for gay.

Kettle's boiled. **Maurice** *unplugs it.*

Bourgeois Let me do that, you get weird around electrical items.

Maurice I draw too much power.

Bourgeois We need to get you PAT tested.

Maurice I know, but I don't want to know the result!

Bourgeois Yeah, easier to just get on with your life these days.

They start making the tea.

Maurice I started getting into writing during lockdown too. Been working on a screenplay for a film. It's based on the *Avengers Assemble*, but it's about moany, middle-aged white men, and it's called Gammons Gather. Gonna be set in boardrooms and rotary clubs and they all just get together and have a big old whinge about having their privilege taken away from them. Thinking of ending it with a car chase, down the B roads of Gloucestershire, with them not indicating at the right time, as they speed off in their Teslas to their second home in the Cotswolds.

Bourgeois Wow, sounds great, good luck with that.

They take a sip of their tea.

Maurice Ahh, that is wonderful.

Bourgeois Would you like a biscuit?

Maurice Yes please.

He opens the piñata head and takes out a biscuit. It plays a recorded 'Step away from the cookie jar'.

Bourgeois It's one of those posh ones you get on aeroplanes. Got it when I went to Sitges with Phillip Schofield.

Maurice *dunks a biscuit into her cup and carries on talking.*

Maurice Maybe we've had it wrong all this time, maybe pleasure isn't about excess and massive partying. Maybe hedonism can just be simple and calm.

Bourgeois Maurice, I think you've cracked it.

She pulls her biscuit out of the tea, and slowly looks at it. It's broken. She pauses, taking in the magnitude of the situation. Then she screams and throws the biscuit on the floor.

Maurice Why does everything I love have to break?

Bourgeois Maurice, calm down. Don't panic.

Bourgeois *pushes the tea set off.*

Maurice (*furious*) I just wanted a moment of simple pleasure and I totally fucked up my tea.

Bourgeois Maurice, it's OK. I'm going to approach you, but it's not an attack, you don't need to fight me off like last time. Physical contact coming in 3, 2, 1.

He strokes her back, she winces.

Bourgeois I've got a solution. It's a quick fix but it always works.

Maurice Not . . .

Bourgeois Yeah . . .

Maurice We said we never would again.

Bourgeois Just once.

Maurice I always regret it.

They start to undress.

Bourgeois But it feels good at the time.

Maurice That's true.

Bourgeois And it doesn't take long.

Maurice Let's do it. One last time. After all, life is just a series of experiences

Bourgeois Waiting to be liked by someone else online.

They stand behind the keyboard, pose for a selfie. Lights flash.

Song: Like Machine

Both Feed the Like Machine
Give me another hit of dopamine dopamine
Feed the Like Machine
Give me another hit of dopamine dopamine.

Here's a photo of my breakfast
To make you jealous
It's a bowl of porridge
With blueberries on it
I bet you want it
I bet you like it
You want my porridge so
Go on post a comment on it.

Feed the Like Machine
Give me another hit of dopamine dopamine
Feed the Like Machine
Give me another hit of dopamine dopamine.

Bourgeois Here's a video of my cat playing on a bed

Maurice Here's a black and white photo of my dad (he's dead)

Bourgeois Here's some bread that I baked all by myself

Maurice Here's an opinion that I borrowed from somebody else

Both Here's some funny memes about war
Here's my kitchen extension
Here's some stunning jeans from Dior
Here's my gran, she's got dementia
Here's my daughter, she is two
I document her every move
For you
So keep the likes coming in.

Feed the Like Machine
Give me another hit of dopamine dopamine
Feed the Like Machine
Give me another hit of dopamine dopamine.

Bourgeois Now I'm flying high
On a wave of adoration
Basking in the glow
Of constant validation
Finally I'm loved
By some people I went to school with
Finally I'm loved
By that comedian I met in a bar once
Finally I'm loved
By my ex boyfriend
Finally I'm loved
By my homophobic aunt.

Discordant note. **Bourgeois** *breaks out of his reverie.*

Bourgeois Oh that one made me feel weird. I think I'm having a comedown.

Maurice Do you want another hit?

Bourgeois Yeah.

Music kicks back in.

Both Here's a book I haven't read that makes me look very smart
Here's me standing next to some contemporary art
Here's a celebrity you wish you could meet
Here's a deliberately provocative Tweet
Here's my feelings
Here's my worries
Here's my kinks
Here's my soul
Here's my head
Here's my shoulder
Here's my knees
Here's my hole
Here's my passwords and my PIN
Take absolutely everything
That I've got, just don't stop
The likes coming in.

Feed the Like Machine
Give me another hit of dopamine dopamine
Feed the Like Machine
Give me another hit of dopamine dopamine
Dopamine dopamine
Dopamine dopamine
Dopa dopa dopa dopa
Do do do do
D-d-d-d-d
Dopamine!

They both collapse on the floor in ecstasy/exhaustion.

Scene Five

Maurice We have got to stop doing that.

Bourgeois It's never as good as I remember.

The piñata makes an awful noise. **B&M** *run over.*

Bourgeois Patsy! What's wrong, girl? Maybe it's because I pulled her head off?

Bourgeois *strokes her head.*

Maurice No. Oh my God, I think she's in labour.

Bourgeois What?!

Maurice I'll get her a modesty screen.

She puts a screen in front of the piñata.

Bourgeois Come on, Patsy, you can do it. Breathe deeply.

Maurice Remember the hypnobirthing. One big push, Patsy.

Maurice *delivers a miniature disco ball donkey. They look at it in wonder.*

Maurice The miracle of new life.

Another donkey sound.

Bourgeois There's something else.

He pulls out a large shiny disc.

Bourgeois What's this?

Maurice It must be the placenta.

It pops open to reveal it is in fact a small camping tent.

Bourgeois Does afterbirth normally look like this?

Maurice I know what's going on.

She picks up the miniature disco ball piñata.

Bourgeois Do you?

Maurice Yes, the Like Machine, all the dopamine. We've gone beyond Instagram.

Bourgeois TikTok?

Maurice Further.

Bourgeois Wordle?

Maurice Even further.

She puts down the miniature disco ball piñata. Lights hit it as it starts to rotate.

Maurice We're in the metaverse.

Bourgeois What's that?

Maurice It's something to do with Nick Clegg.

Bourgeois I don't understand, Maurice, where is this place? Where has our audience gone?

Maurice They're just out of reach in the physical realm and we're in a limitless digital space where anything is possible.

Bourgeois Anything?

Maurice Anything! In the metaverse you can reinvent yourself, it's a chance at a second life. (*Pointing at the disco ball piñata.*) That's what this means. A whole new beginning.

Bourgeois The metaverse is so rich in symbolism! Maybe this is the place we find true pleasure.

Maurice Well since we're here, who are you going to be in your second life?

Bourgeois I'm gonna be someone who is tough and strong. Someone you can rely on. Someone you'd call in a crisis. I'll be a folk guitarist!

Maurice You can do that in the metaverse. Play!

Bourgeois *strums the air. A slightly out of tune guitar sound.*

Bourgeois Oh, it needs tuning . . .

Maurice Let me just . . .

She pretends to tune it. **Bourgeois** *strums the air again, it sounds lovely. He mimes playing beautiful guitar music.*

Bourgeois I'm so talented in the metaverse! So what are you gonna do with your second life?

Maurice Hmmm . . .

Song: Second Life

Maurice In my second life
I will be
A big shot billionaire
I'll get my wealth
From my family
As the first born male heir
But I'll be a philanthropist

I'll change people's lives
I will want the world to benefit
From my wealth
. . . Or will I?

Both Cos I could buy an island
And a yacht made of diamonds
I could build a castle in space
If I could have the kind of fun
That's out of reach to mostly everyone
Would I really give it away
In my second life?

Maurice I hope I'd be a good billionaire, but maybe I wouldn't.

Bourgeois How about something that's unequivocally good. Like . . .

During his verse **Maurice** *mimes playing an egg shaker, which can be heard on the track.*

In my second life
I will be
A pioneering doctor
Of vaccinology
I'll make cures for the worst diseases
And give them away for free cos
I will not believe in profiting
From saving people's lives
I will the world to benefit
From my work
. . . Or will I?

Maurice *mimes playing a tambourine.*

Both Cos I could use my genius
To implant 5G into the global population
Get paid by the CIA
To control people's DNA
Then I'd have total domination
In my second life

Bourgeois Oh, it's hard. So many paths life can take.

Maurice Maybe try something more normal.

Maurice *mimes playing a wood block.*

Bourgeois In my second life
I will be
A beauty influencer.

Maurice Oh that would be great, you'd get sent loads of free make-up. And unsolicited fanny pics. I know . . .

Maurice *mimes playing a glockenspiel.*

Maurice In my second life
I will run
A pop up coffee shop.

Bourgeois But you hate the general public.

Maurice Oh yeah, they're fucking awful.

Bourgeois I've got one.

Maurice *mimes playing a mouth harp.*

In my second life
I will be a . . .
A . . .

Struggles to find an idea.

Bourgeois No, it's gone. You distracted me with that twangy thing.

Maurice It's so hard. There must be something we can be.
In my second life
I will be a dog.

Bourgeois Why?

Maurice Why not?
I'll spend my days just chasing sticks
And rolling around in lots of lovely fox shit
Nothing would bother me
All my worries and cares would fade
No job to stress me out or sex life to get anxious about
Cos I'll have been spayed.

Both Then one day I'll meet a kid who'll accidentally startle me
And I will just snap
Next thing I know I'm being taken to the vet
And then it all turns black
In my second life.

Scene Six

Bourgeois Well that wasn't very successful.

Maurice No. We couldn't even find pleasure in being someone else.

She notices the pop-up tent.

Maurice God on a wheel, now we've got to put this fucking thing away.

They struggle to get the tent back into its bag.

Bourgeois Anyone know how to do this?

Maurice I would say this is one the least pleasurable things I've ever done.

They can't do it.

Bourgeois I give up.

Maurice Me too. On everything. We should have done a show about pain and suffering instead.

Bourgeois No, come we've got to stay optimistic.

Maurice I'm really struggling with optimism right now.

Bourgeois But, Maurice, this is a show about . . .

Suddenly a very short, and abrasive reprise of the chorus from the first song 'Pleasure Seekers', **Bourgeois** *sings and does the moves,* **Maurice** *stands unimpressed.*

Bourgeois Pleasure, pleasure, pleasure
Non-stop pleasure

Bourgeois Remember the positive aphorisms, the ones Tom Daley knitted onto tea cosies for us. The sun will come out tomorrow. Always look on the bright side of life. Every cloud has a silver lining.

Maurice OK, the sun will come out tomorrow and the day after that it will just piss with rain again? Always look on the bright side of life, you're really gonna damage your retina. Every cloud has a silver lining, but by the same logic . . .

Song: Every Silver Lining

Maurice Every silver lining has a cloud
Every single thing that's good is also bad in some way
Remember you must never ever doubt
That whenever you feel pleasure someone else is in pain.

Both When it looks like you're winning at life
Take a second to think about
The fact that someone else is losing and one day you will too oh
Every silver lining has a cloud.

Track kicks in. They put on sequinned silver capes and hold umbrellas.

Bourgeois Maurice, by jove I think you've got it. The message of our show is that absolutely nothing in life can be enjoyed!

They do a jolly dance with the umbrellas as the song repeats.

Every silver lining has a cloud
Every single thing that's good is also bad in some way
Remember you must never ever doubt
That whenever you feel pleasure someone else is in pain
When it feels like you're winning at life
Take a second to think about

The fact that someone else is losing and one day you will too oh
Every silver lining has a cloud.

The song keeps repeating, but starts to speed up and get distorted. **Maurice** *is becoming increasingly aggressive as she sings. They start talking over the track.*

Scene Seven

Bourgeois Maurice, wait, stop the song.

Maurice Why?

Bourgeois It isn't good for us, it isn't good for anyone. We've swung way too far in the other direction, this is pure negativity. I think we're addicted to being horrible bastards.

Maurice You're right. This is actually quite bleak.

Bourgeois We need to find the off button.

They manically search around the space.

Bourgeois We've lost control, it's all the things said we wouldn't do! Pessimism! Cynicism! Nihilism!

They yank at the curtain at the back of the stage, which completely rips away.

Thunder clap. Evil laughter.

The Negative Nancies rise slowly from their slumber. They are three wacky air dancers, the ones you see outside second hand car showrooms. Two of them are large – one appears behind the curtain that has been pulled down, and one from out of the piñata head. The third is a tiny desktop one, which appears on top of the piñata.

Maurice What is going on?

Cynicism We are the Negative Nancies. And you summoned us by name. I am Cynicism.

Pessimism I am Pessimism.

Nihilism And I'm Nihilism!

Bourgeois Why are you here?

Pessimism You've been taking our name in vain.

Nihilism Yeah you bitches have been bad mouthing us.

Maurice No, we just don't want to be negative anymore.

Cynicism Why? What's so wrong with being negative?

Bourgeois Well it's not very helpful is it? Just makes people feel bad.

Pessimism I think you'll find pessimism is very constructive. Would you want an optimistic person doing your risk assessments?

Maurice No, we just hope . . .

Pessimism What good is hope? Hope is a pacifier, it makes you lazy, nothing ever changed from people saying 'oh it might get better tomorrow'.

Bourgeois But we just wanted to find pleasure. Freedom from the worries of the world. Freedom from the fear that life has no meaning.

Nihilism No, when you realise that life has no meaning it's very liberating. We're all gonna die, let's have fun!

Cynicism Bourgeois & Maurice, you have blocked yourselves from experiencing pleasure by denying who you really are. Revel in negativity. Don't hide in the light, find freedom in the darkness!

Nihilism The world needs negative thinking!

Cynicism Embrace the power of negative thinking.

They all repeat the phrase as they start to deflate.

Bourgeois I'm really glad we told our audience not to think, because they would be pretty confused now.

Maurice So they're saying negativity can actually be good? Hmm.. maybe a cynical attitude is a good way to hold authority to account and question the status quo?

Bourgeois Yeah plus we love being little bitches. That's what brings us pleasure!

Maurice You're right there's nothing I love more than a good, cleansing whinge.

Bourgeois So maybe . . .

Maurice . . . we just be ourselves?

Bourgeois Be ourselves.

Maurice That's so optimistic.

Bourgeois Ah but wait, optimism is bad. Oh this is confusing. How are we going to end this show?

Maurice So negativity can be positive.

Bourgeois Positivity can be dangerous.

Maurice Nihilism can be oddly hopeful.

Bourgeois Babies are evil.

Maurice That's not up for debate.

Bourgeois Pain can be pleasure.

Maurice Can it?

Bourgeois Yes, remember last summer on that windy beach in Whitby and we met that strange withered goth?

Maurice Jacob Rees-Mogg?

Bourgeois He told his stable boy to whip us with his riding crop, and at first we said we didn't like it, but then what did we admit?

Maurice We did like it. Oh so pain can be pleasure, pleasure can be pain.

Bourgeois I'm starting to think maybe everything is meaningless and the pursuit of pleasure will ultimately lead to existential despair.

Both Any questions?

Maurice Yeah I've got one, how *are* we gonna end this?

Bourgeois With a song?

Song: What's The Point?

Maurice Every morning I commute to my kitchen table
Where I sit and write 'Hello thank you for your email,
Sorry for the slow reply it's just that I've been busy
Staring into the abyss, best wishes.

Bourgeois Every evening in sequins I stand on stage
And try to remain relevant despite my age
I tell another joke, hey that's what we're here for
Have you heard the one about the impending nuclear war?

Both What am I doing with my life?
I lie awake each night in bed
With these thoughts playing in my head
Until they turn to existential dread
And I'm left thinking

What's the point?
In anything?
What's the point at all?
What's the point?
What's the point?
In anything?
What's the point in anything at all?
I watch the news and get confused
And overwhelmed
So I turn it off and then I feel guilty
That I turned it off.

Maurice Should I do more for humanity?
Should I stop you on the street for charity?

Bourgeois Could I be the next Mother Theresa
Or Jesus or Bimini?

Both No! I'm just an insignificant speck.
As useless as a Travellers' Cheque
I think I better get my shit together

Maybe I should leave the city
Move to somewhere slightly shitty
Be the gentrifier I despise
Or maybe I should get a dog
Or start believing in someone's God
Just to give some purpose to my life
But then I think . . .

What's the point
What's the point in anything?
What's the point in anything at all?
What's the point
What's the point in anything?
What's the point in anything at all?

What
Am I
Doing
With my life?

Do you know what I mean?
Do you know what I mean?
Oh I know you know what I mean.

Are we all just cogs
With pointless jobs
In the capitalist machine?

Do you know what I mean?
Do you know what I mean?
Oh I know you know what I mean.

Or is at all just fake
Are we living in The Matrix?
Is life but a dream?

What's the point
What's the point in anything?
What's the point in anything at all?
What's the point
What's the point in anything?
What's the point in anything at all?

Bourgeois What's the point in democracy?

Maurice What's the point in religion?

Bourgeois What's the point in aristocracy?

Maurice What's the point in pigeons?

Bourgeois What's the point in working?

Maurice What's the point in not?

Bourgeois What's the point in having a king?

Maurice What's the point in wasps?

Bourgeois What's the point in Bourgeois?

Maurice What's the point in Maurice?
What's the point in foie gras?

Bourgeois What's the point in geese?

Both What's the point in doing this show?
I honestly don't know
What's the point in singing this song?
There isn't one!

Bourgeois So sorry, we don't have any answers. Sorry for wasting your time. Sorry to Soho Theatre, sorry to the Arts Council, sorry to our techs, sorry to our incredible creative team and mostly sorry to all of you.

Both What's the point
What's the point in anything?
What's the point in anything at all?
What's the point
What's the point in anything?
What's the point in anything at all?

Blackout. Lights up. **B&M** *do a quick bow then leave.*

Scene Eight/Encore

B&M *reappear wearing fabulous flowing robes.*

Bourgeois Thank you, this is so unexpected. We really weren't planning to do an encore. We're already in our dressing gowns. I feel a bit like a cult leader in this outfit.

Maurice You'd be a good cult leader actually.

Bourgeois Thank you, Maurice.

Maurice Yeah you've got that deluded egotistical persona that really goes with the job.

Bourgeois Ah thanks, that's one of the sweetest things you've ever said to me. You could be the woman who lurks in the background and poisons the town's water supply.

Maurice Oh yeah I'd be good at that.

Bourgeois You've really got the skill set. (*To the audience.*) Thank you so much for coming this evening. We have time for one final song, and we really wanted to end this show with a message of hope so we searched through our back catalogue and . . . unfortunately couldn't find a single message of hope in there.

Maurice Absolutely none.

Bourgeois So instead we're going to do a cover. We wrote this show over the last two years, in our bedrooms, going silently mad, don't know if you can tell, but we were reflecting a lot on the pandemic, and the fact that this might not be the last pandemic in living memory, and it's certainly not the first. So we looked back at some of the artists from the eighties, many of whom we lost, to see if there were any messages of hope there. And so we would like to do a song by an artist from that time, someone who has brought us immense pleasure, and has been a huge inspiration to us, and was the original drag alien. They're an artist called Klaus Nomi. There's a moment in this song that we'd love for you to join in and sing. You'll know when it is, because I'll say 'now sing'. Thanks again for coming, this is dedicated to you all, and to Klaus Nomi.

Song: After the Fall

Bourgeois Well I told you about the total eclipse now
But still it caught you unaware
But I'm telling you hold on, hold on
Tomorrow we'll be there
And even though you went to church upon Sunday
You thought you didn't even have a prayer
But I'm telling you hold on, hold on
Tomorrow we'll be there.

Both After the fall we'll be born, born, born again
After it all blows away
After the fall, after the fall
After it all blows away.

Bourgeois We'll take a million years of civilization
We're gonna give it the electric chair
But I'm telling you hold on, hold on
Tomorrow we'll be there
I see a hundred million lonely mutants
They are glowing in their dark despair
But I'm telling you hold on, hold on
Tomorrow we'll be there.

Both After the fall we'll be born, born, born again
After it all blows away
After the fall, after the fall
After it all blows away.

Bourgeois Well the freak shall inherit the earth now
No matter how well done or rare
But I'm telling you hold on, hold on
Tomorrow we'll be there
We'll build our radioactive castles
Out in the radioactive air
And I'm telling you hold on, hold on
Tomorrow we'll be there.

Both After the fall we'll be born, born, born again
After it all blows away
After the fall, after the fall
After it all blows away.

B&M *get the audience singing along in two overlapping parts.* **Maurice** *stops playing the piano.* **B&M** *leave the audience singing a cappella as they drift to the back of the stage and disappear.*

The End

Performance Documents

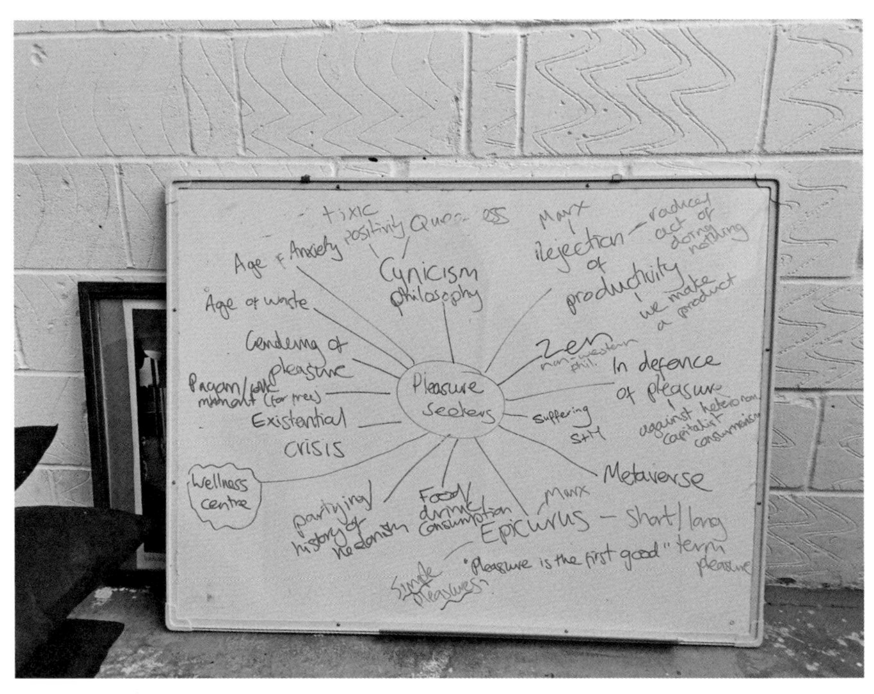

1 A white board detailing initial concepts for the show. Studio at Limehouse Art Foundation, August 2021. Photograph by Liv Morris.

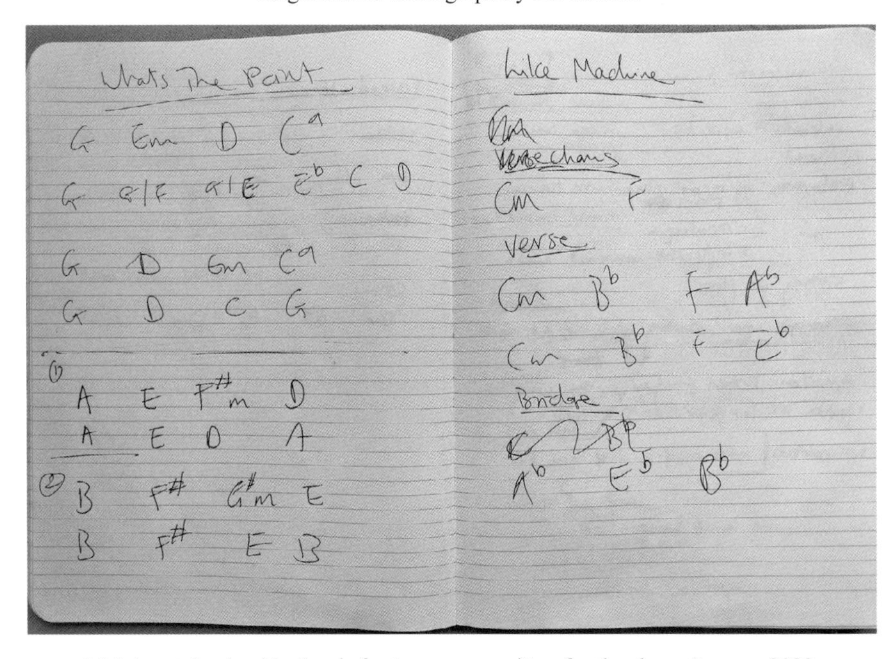

2 Liv's notebook with chords for two songs written for the show, January 2022. Photograph by Liv Morris.

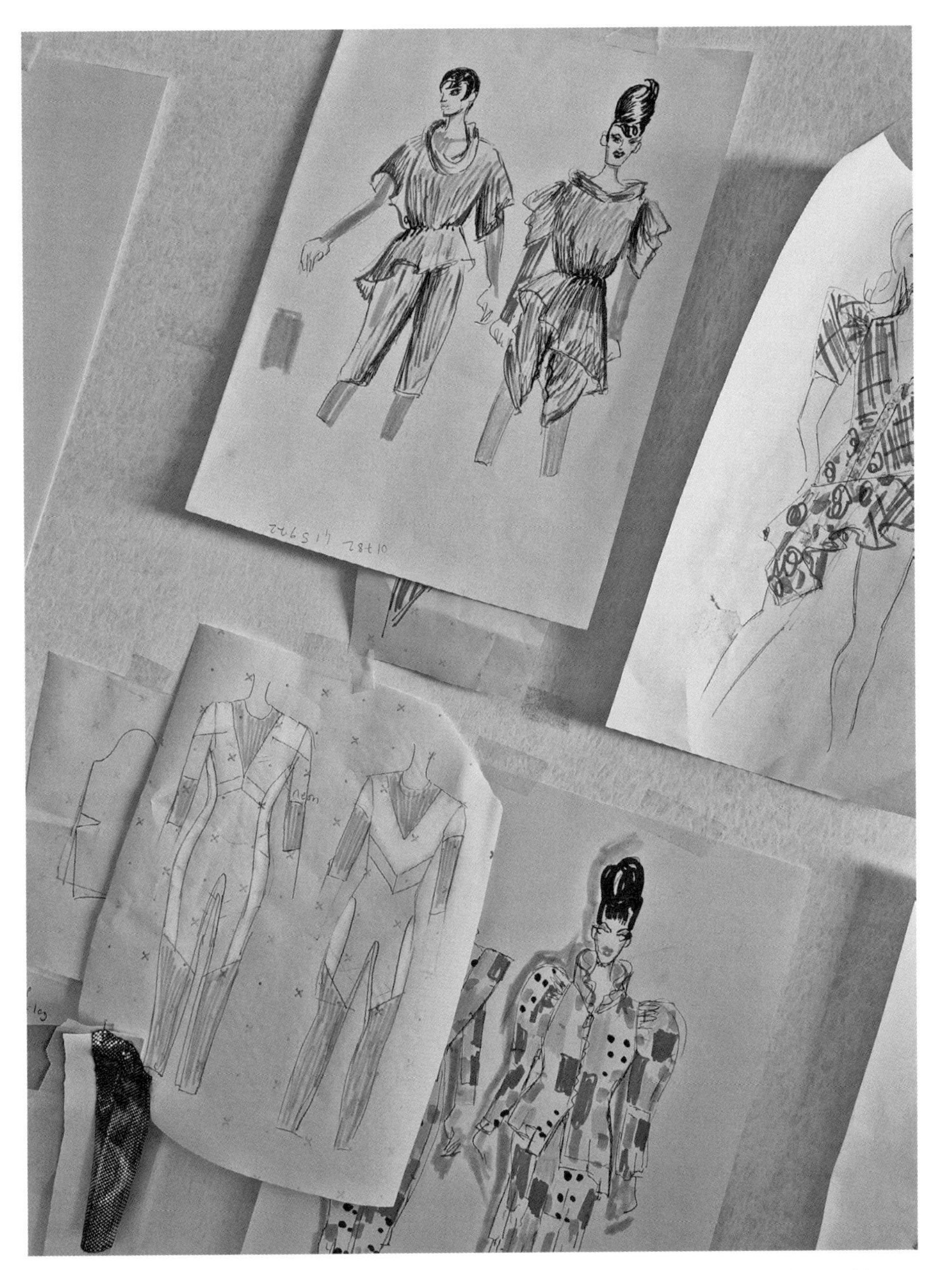

3 Costume design sketches by Julian Smith, January 2022. Photograph by Julian Smith. Courtesy of Bourgeois & Maurice.

4 Set design mock-up sketch by Emma Bailey, January 2022. Photograph by Emma Bailey. Courtesy of Bourgeois & Maurice.

5 *Pleasure Seekers* at Soho Theatre, April 2022. Photograph by Holly Revell. Courtesy of Bourgeois & Maurice.

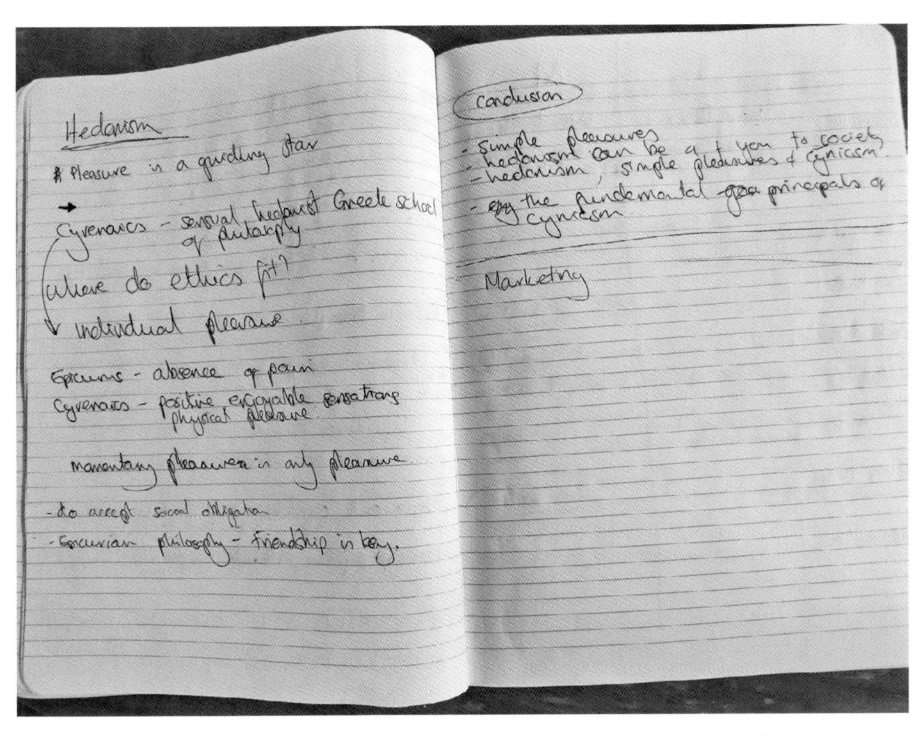

6 Liv's notebook with notes detailing research into hedonism, July 2021. Photograph by Liv Morris.

The Making of Pinocchio

Written and performed by Rosana Cade and Ivor MacAskill

Credits

Creators: Rosana Cade and Ivor MacAskill
Performers: Rosana Cade, Ivor MacAskill, Jo Hellier, Tim Spooner and Ray Gammon
Set, Prop and Costume Designer: Tim Spooner
Sound Designer: Yas Clarke
Cameras: Jo Hellier
Lighting Designer: Jo Palmer
Cinematographer: Kirstin McMahon and Jo Hellier
Producer: Dr. Nora Laraki for Artsadmin
Creation Producer: Mary Osborn for Artsadmin
Production Manager: Sorcha Stott-Strzala
Assistant Stage Manager: Ray Gammon
Outside Eye: Nic Green
Movement Advisor: Eleanor Perry
Captioning: Collective Text; Emilia Beatriz, Daniel Hughes with Rosana Cade, Yas Clarke, Ivor MacAskill, and Jamie Rea

Commissioned by Fierce Festival, Kampnagel, Tramway and Viernulvier with support from Attenborough Centre for the Creative Arts, Battersea Arts Centre, LIFT and Take Me Somewhere.

Funded by Creative Scotland, Arts Council England, and Rudolf Augstein Stiftung, with development support from The Work Room/Diane Torr Bursary, Scottish Sculpture Workshop, National Theatre of Scotland, Live Art Development Agency, Gessnerellee, Mousonturm, Forest Fringe, West Kowloon Cultural District and LGBT Health and Wellbeing Scotland.

The Making of Pinocchio was originally created as a digital performance, filmed in one take in Glasgow's Tramway, and live-edited, before being streamed to audiences as part of Take Me Somewhere festival on 21 May 2021. It was then developed into a live theatre performance and premiered at Kampnagel, Hamburg, a year later on 12–14 May, 2022. This script represents the general script at the time of writing – early 2024 – rather than for one specific performance. However the artistic director named is LJ Finlay-Walsh from Tramway who was the originator of this role. This changes depending on where the performance is taking place.

What also increases over time is the performers' ages and the amount of money Ivor has spent on his gender transition. Due to the woeful state of transgender healthcare in the UK, this amount is expected to rise, but we hope it will stop increasing before we stop touring this work.

Note on production

The Making of Pinocchio is performed on a stage at least 10 metres wide by 10 metres deep, with the audience positioned in a tiered seating bank facing the stage.

The set is intended to evoke a film studio – there is technical equipment including lighting stands, TV monitors, microphones and cameras visible. Some of these are real. Some are made of wood. Some are real but hidden inside fake wooden versions of themselves. Some are made of fake wood.

The real walls of the actual theatre space are exposed rather than covered with drapes.

The stage is dominated by a rich red cloth called The Red Backdrop, which hangs vertically from the rig stage right, goes all the way down to the floor, and runs across the floor. The cloth is 10 metres wide, and creates a backdrop for images captured through the FANTASY CAM.

The FANTASY CAM is a camera positioned on the floor stage left, pointing towards the hanging Red Backdrop stage right, which completely fills the shot with red.

The camera is carefully positioned and focused to create images using Forced Perspective. Objects or people close to the camera will be large, and objects or people far away will be much smaller, whilst appearing to be on the same plane in the image. The FANTASY CAM has a cinematic quality, with rich colours and high definition, and is always capturing images from an entirely fixed position.

The real camera is hidden inside a fake wooden camera with a wooden lens/nose and wooden reels/ears on top.

Near the FANTASY CAM are a selection of wooden props and objects which are placed in front of the camera to create various scenes throughout the show. In the opening scene there are five sticks with bark removed standing upright, unevenly spaced in two rows about 30 centimetres in front of the camera, creating a forest.

There is a second camera, called the DOCU CAM. This is operated by a performer on stage – CAMERA PERSON. They wear a red tracksuit and a large fake wooden camera box over their head, with the real camera positioned inside. They begin the show standing upstage left, in a row with other props, costumes and technical equipment, lined up along the far edge of The Red Backdrop. Throughout the show they move around, capturing 'behind the scenes' footage, unusual perspectives and extreme close ups. The DOCU CAM has a more grainy 'real' quality, and moves around zooming in and out, clearly being operated live by a person.

THE SCREEN hangs at the front of the stage. It is about 3 metres above the ground. Live feed from the onstage cameras, as well as some pre-recorded clips, and the captions, are projected onto this screen throughout the show. The audience watches the action happening live in the space from the perspective of their seat, whilst watching it from another angle on screen captured through the cameras.

Three large flatscreen TV monitors are positioned around The Red Backdrop – upstage centre, downstage centre and stage left centre behind the FANTASY CAM. These all point towards the centre of The Red Backdrop and show the image from the FANTASY CAM. The performers use these monitors when they are performing on the Red Backdrop to check they are in the right positions.

Downstage left is a second, smaller backdrop: the Wooden Backdrop, made of fake wood print material. This is 3 metres wide, 2.5 metres high, 2.5 metres long on the floor. This backdrop faces the audience on a slight angle. On the Wooden Backdrop are two director's chairs made with the same fake wood print material. This also matches the fake wood print material of the performers' tracksuits and caps. On one of the director's chairs there is a fake wooden microphone with a grey fluffy head.

During the show the small space behind the Wooden Backdrop, which is concealed from audience view, is used as an offstage area, and there are props and bits of costume hidden back here.

Visible props/equipment

Downstage Area

At the front of the stage, along the downstage edge of the Red Backdrop there are a number of props and pieces of technical equipment. At times, the performers enter this space to talk directly to the audience.

Here is a description of the Downstage Area from stage right to stage left. These props roughly form a straight line across the front of the stage.

The Cricket Stage A clear perspex box, 45 x 31 x 27.5 centimetres on four 80-centimetre wooden legs. Inside is a miniature red backdrop, mirroring the big one in the space and a cricket. The audience are unsure if it is a real cricket or not.

Tiny Wooden Camera on a wooden tripod, with legs made of thin dowels, and two special lights on stands, all focused on the CRICKET. Whenever the CRICKET talks ON SCREEN or in VOICE OVER, the lights come up on the Cricket Stage, and footage of a real live cricket is seen ON SCREEN.

Real Microphone (disguised as a wooden microphone) on a wooden stand with a red cable.

Two Wooden Panels on a red stand.

Pair of Wooden Clogs

Prop Table Downstage centre. A small wooden table with thick wooden dowel legs, and a variety of wooden props on top including dowels of various sizes, some with balls attached. Underneath the table are piles of wooden dowels.

Microscopic Camera Encased in a fake wooden camera with a long lens/nose and wooden reels/ears on top. Set on a spindly wooden tripod.

Upstage Area

Along the back of the stage, at the upstage edge of the Red Backdrop, is an evenly spaced line of costumes, props and equipment. Most of these are on spindly red tripod stands

Upstage area props from Stage Right to Stage Left.

Pinocchio Costume Stand A white ball holds a red pointy hat attached to a black lacquered short wig. A white flouncy ruff sits on a wooden chest plate. There is a pair of wooden clogs just in front of this stand.

Gepetto Costume Stand a white ball on top holding a dark blue apron. (Later in the show it holds the red Gepetto hat with grey fluffy beard and square wooden glasses and the other dark blue apron.)

Mic and Headphone Stand Holds a wooden fluffy fake mic and wooden fluffy fake headphones

Large Head A large white ball, 60 centimetres in diameter, with a large red pointy hat and large flouncy ruff. There is a large thick dowel which goes all the way through the ball horizontally, like a nose that is sticking out on both sides.

DOCU CAM This is where the **camera person** with the DOCU CAM on their head begins and returns to.

Giant Eye Balls A large Y-shaped object made of wooden dowels with big white balls on each end.

Performers / Characters

Rosana Cade (They/Them) – ROSANA plays themself in the performance. They are a white, non-binary person with a southern English accent with a very very slight Scottish twang. They are in their mid-thirties.

Ivor MacAskill (He/They) – IVOR plays himself in the performance. He is a white trans masculine person with a short gingery beard and a very soft Glaswegian accent. He is in his early forties.

Ivor and **Rosana** both wear matching fake wood print tracksuit tops and bottoms, with white socks and white turtleneck collars. There are red wooden sockets sticking out through their tracksuits; small wooden cubes with round holes in. Wooden dowels can be inserted into the holes and magnets hold them in place. The sockets are dotted around their bodies, at their nipples, thighs, bum, front genitals, arms, shoulders and sides.

Sometimes they wear baseball caps made of the same fake wood print material. Rosana wears a hat with one socket on top. Ivor sometimes wears a cap without a socket and sometimes with two sockets.

They both wear wooden clogs at certain points in the show. Rosana's clogs have a socket on. They wear real headset microphones which allows their voices to be amplified and manipulated throughout the performance.

Stagehand – Originally played by Tim Spooner. Also played by Ray Gammon. They act as an on-stage assistant and puppeteer The Blue Fairy and The Host. They wear a red tracksuit top and bottom with a red turtle neck sticking out of the top, red socks, and a red baseball cap. The tracksuit top has two red vinyl circles in the nipple position.

Camera Person – Originally played by Jo Hellier. Also played by Moa Johansson. This is the DOCU CAM operator and they also assist with various jobs on stage. They also wear a red tracksuit top and bottom with a red turtle neck, red socks and a red baseball cap.

Cricket – We see filmed footage of a real, live cricket. This is the narrator of the fantasy story of Pinocchio who returns throughout the show. It is voiced by **Ivor** in a pre-recorded VOICEOVER.

Pinocchio – Played by both **Ivor** and **Rosana**. The PINOCCHIO costume is a red felt pointy hat attached to a black lacquered short wig, and a white flouncy ruff.

Gepetto – Played by **Rosana** and voiced by **Ivor** in pre-recorded VOICEOVER. He wears a red baseball cap with a grey fluffy beard and square wooden glasses attached. He has a dark blue apron. In the opening scene his apron is full of dowels. In the mime scene the pocket on his apron is empty.

The Blue Fairy – Voiced by **Rosana** with special effects on the voice. A small blue glittery cube on a red string, puppeteered by STAGEHAND.

Later in the performance, **Rosana** plays **The Blue Fairy** by holding the giant eye balls.

Host – voiced by **Ivor** in pre-recorded VOICEOVER. A spindly wooden puppet with one moving arm, puppeteered by **Stagehand**.

Prelude: The Pre-Show Announcement

Scene 1: The Forest

Scene 2: The Blue Fairy

Scene 3: Intro Scene

Scene 4: Prop Table

Scene 5: Evolution of the Whale

Scene 6: Mime Scene – Gepetto's Workshop

Scene 7: Marionette

Scene 8: Theatre

Scene 9: The Artistic Director

Scene 10: Landscape

Scene 11: Pleasure Island

Scene 12: Inside the Whale at the Bottom of the Ocean

Scene 13: We're Not Ever Going to Finish This Show Are We?

Pre-Show Announcement

Pre-recorded and captioned ON SCREEN. This is the standard version that is edited for each venue depending on the access provisions available.

Ivor / Rosana (Together, Voiceover) Hello!

Ivor Welcome to The Making of Pinocchio.

Rosana I'm Rosana Cade,

Ivor And I'm Ivor MacAskill.
And we are really glad you're here.

Rosana This is a relaxed performance.

Ivor Ooh, lovely!

Rosana We hope you feel able to do what you need to do to be relaxed in this space.

Ivor You are welcome to tic and stim, move and make noise.
And you are also definitely allowed to laugh.

Rosana You can come and go as you need to, and there is a relaxed space in the foyer.

Ivor If you find that you have an overwhelming emotional response, be it positive or negative, and you would like to check in with somebody, there is a trained wellbeing practitioner in a dedicated quiet space nearby. They are available if you want to talk to someone at any point during the performance and for an hour after we have finished.

Rosana They are standing in the front waving now.

Ivor To find the relaxed space or the wellbeing practitioner ask anyone from the front of house team, and they will help you.

Rosana You may notice this speech is being captioned.
There are captions throughout the performance, including descriptions of all of the sounds like this:

Sfx ♪ BUBBLY SQUEAKS ♪

Rosana OK – anything else, darling?

Ivor Mmm . . . enjoy the performance!

Scene 1: Forest

THE SCREEN is bright red.

Performers enter.

Ivor *goes to the Cricket Stage downstage right. He has a small branch sticking out of his left side and one sticking out of his right shoulder from the red sockets in his costume.*

ON SCREEN video shows a bright red cloth. The camera slowly pans left revealing a real live **Cricket**, *that fills the left hand side of the image.*

Ivor *pans the tiny wooden camera copying the panning shot in the video.*

All sounds and text are captioned on the screen.

♪ ENCHANTED VIOLINS ♪
(GENTLE HIGH CHORD SWELLS)

♪ ENCHANTED VIOLINS ♪
(GENTLE LOW CHORD SWELLS)

♪ ENCHANTED VIOLINS CONTINUE ♪

Ivor *walks to his starting position on stage in the dark and picks up a small branch in each hand and raises them up to become* **Pinocchio** *in the form of a tree.*

Cricket (*voice over*) (*American Narrator Voice*) Hello. I'm the Cricket.

But enough about me.

I'm here to tell you a story.

A long, long, long, long, long time ago . . . and also yesterday . . .

And at the turn of every century . . .

And before the dawn of time . . .

And after the end of time!

There was,

and is,

and always will be . . .
a man!

Light comes up on stage revealing **Rosana** *as* **Geppetto** - *the man – standing downstage right, hands on hips, facing stage left.*

And the man lives here, in the real world.

ON SCREEN image fades to FANTASY CAM revealing a forest scene with **Ivor** *on the right of the image.* **Ivor** *is large as* **Pinocchio** *in tree-form, in amongst the other trees and* **Rosana** *in the left corner, is small as* **Geppetto**. *In this scene, using forced perspective* **Geppetto** *appears to stroke the trees with his hands and poke them with dowels from his apron.*

> The man is a carver, a creator. He wears square glasses made of wood. Through these box-shaped lenses, he always keeps his perspective. They help him see the trees for the wood.

The man spends most of his time in the woods, in communion with the trees. He strokes and pokes them with his specialized fingers, to discover the patterns of knobs and crevices.

Through these patterns, the man uncovers the wood's future. He reads what is written in its rings; what destiny is ingrained in its grain. What will this tree be?

Geppetto *shakes the dowel vigorously backwards and forwards in the tree, penetrating it, then pulls out and holds it above his head triumphantly.*

(*Deep, gravelly voice of* **Geppetto**)

'It's a set of colouring pencils!', he cries.
And so it shall be.

Geppetto *moves onto the next tree and repeats the stroking and shaking process.*

This ancient and intimate ritual between man and wood, through fingers and crevices, is what decides the fate of the wood.

What will this one be? When he knows, he knows!

(*Deep voice*) 'It's a church pew!'
And so it shall be!

♪ ENCHANTED VIOLINS CONTINUE ♪

Geppetto *walks jauntily through the forest towards* **Pinocchio***, and does an exaggerated double take on spotting it.*

Oh, Ho Ho! What have we here!?

The man spies a beautiful new tree in the wood, like nothing he has seen before. And the man has seen a lot of trees! He is immediately drawn to it.
Impressed by its girth, and the curvature of its trunk, he gets to work on it!

Geppetto *reaches his hand out slowly and starts rubbing* **Pinocchio** *on the bum.*

What could be in store for this fine tree?

Geppetto *gets his largest dowel and sticks it into* **Pinocchio***, shaking vigorously backwards and forwards.* **Pinocchio** *responds and shakes as if the dowel is going up his bum.*

A rocking horse? A chopping board? A set of toothpicks?!

Geppetto *triumphantly pulls out and holds the dowel above his head.*

(*Deep voice*) 'It is a puppet!', he cries. 'And I shall call it . . . Pinocchio!'
And so it shall be.

Geppetto *walks off.* **Pinocchio** *looks after* **Geppetto** *then looks quizzically at the FANTASY CAM.*

The tree listened to the man telling him his future. He had it all planned out for this little log. But something didn't feel quite right.

Scene 2: The Blue Fairy

Suddenly, a fairy appeared.

(TINY BUBBLY SQUEAKS)
♪ ENCHANTED VIOLINS BECOME EERIE ♪

The Blue Fairy *puppet is lowered into shot ON SCREEN close to FANTASY CAM and puppeteered by* **Stagehand** *as if it is flying around* **Pinocchio***, spinning about in a magical, jittery manner.*

Rosana *puts on wooden furry headphones and holds the wooden furry mic to voice* **The Blue Fairy** *upstage, not visible ON SCREEN.*

The Blue Fairy (*mysterious electric voice*) Oooh, hello, Pinocchio! It's me, the Blue Fairy!

Pinocchio (*high-pitched*) Oh! Hello, Blue Fairy! Maybe you can help me.
That man says he's going to make me into a puppet, but . . . I think I might be a real boy!

Fairy Yes Pinocchio, you are a real boy. And soooo much mooooore! But people of this world don't always understand the universe of multitudes that exists within you.

Pinocchio Well, I don't know about any universe. I just want to be myself!

Fairy Well, you're very lucky I was passing by.
Because I can cast a special spell, that will transform the way you look forever!

Pinocchio A spell?! What will happen to me?

Fairy (*dramatically*) Your wood will turn to flesh!

Your voice will deepen and command attention.

A forest of millimetre miracles will appear on your chin, and your chest, and your arse, as wiry hairs sprout forth.

Some things will get bigger and some things will get smaller.

And when all of these special signs and symbols are aligned,
then people will recognise . . . who . . . you . . . truly . . . are!

Pinocchio Wow! That sounds amazing! Yeah, OK, I'll do that!

Fairy (*angry and agitated – the blue block jumps wildly on the string as if it's flying at* **Pinocchio**) No, no no, no, no, Pinocchio! It is not so easy.

First, you must convince at least two people that you are a real boy! But believe me, people will doubt you. This is a suspicious world full of traps and liars!

Pinocchio So what do I have to do to prove myself to them?

Fairy You have to tell them your story, Pinocchio!

Tell them your truth again, and again, and again, until they believe you!

Pinocchio I don't know what my story is . . .

Fairy Well, make it up! But make it convincing. Give them the truth they want to hear.

Pinocchio Well, OK . . .
This all seems like an awful lot to ask of someone, just to be able to live the way they want!

Fairy It is! It's not fair!

But until the world changes its perspective, this is how it shall be!
But listen! You WILL transform! And it will be truly magical! And if those around you can open themselves up to it, then your transformation will be a gift to the world! A gift of possibility!

♪ MAGICAL GURGLING ♪

The Blue Fairy *puppet spins around the trees ON SCREEN before buzzing up above* **Pinocchio***'s head. He looks up in wonder and freezes.*

Rosana OK, I think we'll pause there.

♪ ENCHANTED VIOLINS CUT ♪

Scene 3: Intro Scene

Ivor *and* **Rosana** *drop their positions and shake off the previous scene.* **Ivor** *heads upstage to remove his branches and check in with* **Rosana**. **Rosana** *removes fluffy headphones and* **Geppetto***'s apron and hands it to* **Ivor**.

Rosana (*whispers to* **Ivor** *but can be heard by everyone through their microphone*) You alright, darling?

Ivor (*whispers back*) Yeah. How are you?

Rosana (*whispers*) Yeah, good.

Rosana *does an 'actor's jog' across The Red Backdrop to the Downstage Area and addresses the audience talking into a fake wooden microphone.*

ON SCREEN **Ivor** *starts removing the trees from in front of the FANTASY CAM to clear the shot.*

Hi everyone! Welcome. Thanks so much for coming. As you can see, we're right in the thick of it all! But we thought we'd begin this presentation by showing you a couple of scenes we're working on, to give you a sense of how we're creating this world of Pinocchio.

Obviously, what we're showing you this evening is in development. We might need you to use your imagination.

Anyway, let me introduce myself. My name is Rosana Cade. My pronouns are they/them. I'm a maker based in Glasgow. I'm thirty-six years old. And I'm one of the lead creators of this project. And somewhere over there . . . is my co-creator, real life partner, and, let's face it, the star of the show, Ivor MacAskill.

Can you say hi, darling?

Ivor *talks into the FANTASY CAM using a tiny wooden microphone – a miniature version of* **Rosana***'s microphone – and appears huge ON SCREEN.*

Ivor (*as if looking at* **Rosana** *in real life through the screen*) Hi, darling!

(*Smug and pleased with his joke*) Hi, everyone. I'm Ivor MacAskill. My pronouns are he/him or they/them. I'm also a maker based in Glasgow. And you might find this hard to believe . . . but I'm forty-three years old.

And as Rosana said, we are collaborators in both art and life. But I also make my own work.

Rosana Yes, you make work for children, don't you, darling?

Ivor Yes.

Rosana (*mocking*) Great!
So, obviously, people are here this evening because they want to know about the real story behind this project. So, Ivor, can you tell us about that?

Ivor Sure. We've been working on *Pinocchio* together since around 2018, which is also when I came out as trans.

Rosana Up until that point we'd had quite a solid lesbian identity in both our life and work.

Ivor Yes, but I was becoming more aware of a discomfort I had in my female identity, and I knew I needed to explore what possibilities there were to change.

So I began steps to socially transition. I changed my name, started using different pronouns, eventually I got a new passport. It's all a lot of admin, to be honest!
(*Both laugh sarcastically.*)

And I also began to medically transition. So first that meant being diagnosed as having gender dysphoria by two separate doctors. Then I was able to start taking the hormone testosterone, which I'll need to keep taking for the rest of my life.
That changes my shape, lowers my voice, and makes me much hairier. And I also had top surgery to remove my breasts.

Rosana Wow!

Ivor I should say . . .

Ivor *leaves SCREEN and moves to Downstage Area to address the audience directly. During* **Ivor***'s speech* **Rosana** *slowly creeps from their downstage right position and towards FANTASY CAM.*
(**Ivor***'s tone is now more 'real' – trying to be serious.*)

I should say that I'm incredibly lucky to have the funds to pay for this process. It's cost around £13,000 so far. If I hadn't been able to afford to go private, I would still be on the waiting list for my first appointment with the NHS.

And obviously, many trans people have no need or desire to change anything about themselves. But this is the journey I've been on. And even with its challenges, on the whole, it's been amazing! I feel so much better than I did before; so much more like myself. It's hard to comprehend what a massive difference it's made.

Rosana (*into FANTASY CAM. Appearing large ON SCREEN leaning on one elbow in a seductive position and appearing to look at* **Ivor** *in real life*) It is!
And, really interestingly, this change in Ivor inspired me to reflect on my own gender and sexual identity, and I started identifying as non-binary.
It took me a while to own this, because there are so many voices saying it isn't a real thing, that they don't believe in it.

The truth is, non-binary may be a relatively new way of describing it, but there have been people existing outside of the gender binary for as long as there have been people.

Being non-binary makes sense to me. It feels liberating. For me, it's about embracing fluidity, multiplicity, the potential for change. And I try to bring these ideas into all areas of my life.
You could say, Ivor changing has blown open the walls of my box.

Ivor (*looking pleased with himself and turning to the audience*) Mmm.

Ivor *crosses from downstage left to downstage right and picks up* **Rosana***'s fake microphone.*

During the next dialogue the DOCU CAM moves from its upstage left position diagonally across Red Backdrop towards a stage right position still on the Backdrop. They can be seen moving behind **Rosana** *ON SCREEN.*

Ivor (*back to smarmy director mode*) So obviously, being artists, we wanted to respond creatively to all these changes.

Rosana We know there's a real appetite out there for authentic stories at the moment.

Ivor So we thought, 'Hey! Let's make a trans version of *Pinocchio*!' (*Dramatically.*) Becoming a real boy . . .

Both . . . in a post truth world.

Ivor And I suppose, on one level, it's kind of a love story.

Rosana Oh, darling!

Ivor It's a love letter to (*dramatically and beholding the theatre around him*) The Theatre!

Ivor *picks up and puts on a wood effect cap and crosses downstage left to sit on one of the directors' chairs in front of The Wooden Backdrop.*

Rosana *speaks into the FANTASY CAM moving their face closer and closer creating an extreme close up.*

Rosana (*conspiratorially as if* **Ivor** *can't hear*) The truth is, when Ivor first came out as trans, I did have some concerns about how it might affect our relationship.
We were looking for other representations of queer couples in transition to help us, but we couldn't find much we could relate to. It's so often presented as a drama.
So we thought, why don't we make something to show what it's really like . . . for us?

ON SCREEN cuts to DOCU CAM filming from across the stage. The image shows **Rosana** *from behind lying on the floor with their face close up to FANTASY CAM, the backstage area behind The Wooden Backdrop, and* **Ivor** *in front sitting on a director's chair.*

DOCU CAM approaches **Ivor** *from the side, who is talking directly to the audience, speaking into his fake microphone.*

Ivor So, I will be taking on the role of Pinocchio, and I think I bring a nuance and complexity to this character who's often represented in quite basic terms. We all know him as the little wooden puppet who wants to be a real boy. But what does that really mean to him?

Ivor *turns and talks directly into the DOCU CAM, which is now close to his face.*

There's this amazing moment in the story, when Pinocchio finds his father in the belly of a whale at the bottom of the ocean.

♪ ENCHANTED VIOLINS RETURN ♪

And Pinocchio, he's done everything 'wrong'.

He hasn't taken the straight and narrow path, he's completely ignored his talking cricket friend, he's bunked off school to go to the theatre, he's told several lies, he's gone with the naughty boys to Pleasure Island to smash things up and drink beer and play pool. And he's halfway through transforming into a donkey, so he's got big ears and a tail.

But his father looks at him and welcomes him back with open arms.

And that's what we're interested in!

How can this boy, this hero, be accepted and celebrated by his family and by society as a hot, living, breathing puppet-donkey guy?
Let's tell that story.

Rosana *enters from behind The Wooden Backdrop stage left and forces their head into the shot, pulling the focus of the DOCU CAM. They sit on the other director's chair next to* **Ivor**. *During this speech the DOCU CAM zooms in for a close up on* **Rosana**.

Rosana Well, we are also interested in it not just being *his* story. Moving away from the solo hero narrative, and thinking, 'Who are the people around that puppet who have supported him? What's *their* story?'. Because no *one* person changes the world, do they? It's about connections!
A whole network of transformations stretching across time and space.
It's about how one person changing can change those around them. And over time, huge waves of change can sweep through society.

♪ VIOLINS FADE AWAY ♪

Ivor Have there been any challenges?

The following dialogue is spoken directly to the audience in 'real' mode, not using fake mics. DOCU CAM image frames both performers next to each other on director's chairs in front of the Wooden Backdrop.

Well, obviously when you're presenting this kind of work that's very personal, very sensitive, there is a risk. Because you don't know how it's going to be received and what impact that could have on you.
To be honest, being trans in the UK at the moment is difficult, because greater trans visibility has brought a backlash of transphobia, both in the media and in government. We're having a lot of our hard-won rights rolled back. It's very hard to access healthcare, for example.
So it's quite a toxic environment to be making this kind of work in.

Rosana It is.
And do we have a responsibility to represent that in *Pinocchio*? Is that what this is for? Or is this the place to imagine something different?

Pause as **Both** *look slowly around at their surroundings considering these questions.*

Their gazes end on each other at which point they shift modes and comedically shrug.

Ivor Soooooo . . .

Both *throw their fake microphones over their shoulders.*

Ivor There's still lots of questions!

Rosana Yes, lots of possibilities!

Both *walk in a synchronized side step out of shot and across the front of the stage to the prop table.*

Ivor But we're just trying stuff out.

Rosana Yes, nothing is fixed.

Ivor We're still dreaming up ideas.

Rosana Yes and this is where the magic happens.

Ivor Yes, here we are at the prop table!

Scene 4: Prop Table

Ivor *and* **Rosana** *deliver this scene behind the prop table, demonstrating as they speak with the various props on the table.*

ON SCREEN switches to FANTASY CAM with empty Red Backdrop. **Camera Person** *wearing DOCU CAM moves and sits on one of the director's chairs facing the audience.*

Rosana So this evening, we're going to be demonstrating some of the tricks and techniques that we use to bring the fantasy to life. *Pinocchio* is full of so many seemingly impossible things we need to make the audience believe are real.

Ivor *taps wooden panels together in the style of a magician proving something is real.*

Rosana For example, we've got to have a real fairy.

Ivor We've got to have real boys made of real wood. And then have them turning into real donkeys.

Rosana Yes and, of course, there's the iconic image of Pinocchio's nose growing. So we need to figure out how we're going to do that.

Rosana *extends a wooden dowel by adding smaller dowels in a row to form a long nose shape*

Ivor And we're currently working on ideas for the scene that happens inside the stomach of the whale.

Rosana Yes, the stomach of the whale. How will we make a whale?

Both *manipulate dowels to look as if they're puppeteering some sort of sea creature, undulating through the air*

Ivor Who is the whale?

Rosana What does the whale want?

Ivor Yes! And . . . however we make it, we want the whale to be real, to be believable. So we need to know what its motivation is.

Rosana Yes.

Ivor What can we give it to honour its story?

Rosana Yes.

Ivor What's its back story? Where does it come from? What's its ancestry?

Rosana Yes, yes, yes!

Ivor What's its evolution? Obviously the whale was once a land mammal, like us humans, before it entered the sea. So there's a biological connection we might use . . .

Rosana (*whispering*) Errrr, sorry, darling. What are you talking about?

Ivor You know, the fact that whales evolved from a kind of prehistoric deer.

Rosana No. I don't think – That's not true, darling.

Ivor Yes, that is true! (*To audience.*) That is true.

Rosana (*incredulous*) A whale was once a deer!?

Ivor Yes!
(*Scoffing*) Look, I haven't got the fossils here, but . . .

Scene 5: Evolution of the Whale

Ivor *jogs onto Red Backdrop and delivers the next text into FANTASY CAM gradually moving closer and becoming bigger.*

Rosana *moves upstage and puts on the* **Geppetto** *costume whilst watching* **Ivor** *in the upstage monitor.*

Ivor It's 50 million years ago. We're at the edge of a prehistoric lake in what will become Pakistan. I'm a creature, a bit like a deer, that lives on the land, but can sometimes go into the water.

Mimes being a creature a bit like a deer – in his hands he holds two of the wooden props and uses them as forelimbs.

Now, let's say it's two or three million years later, (*he takes two or three steps forward*) and I'm spending more and more time in the water. My legs have shortened, so I'm closer to the ground. My feet are webbed to propel me through the water. My tail's getting longer and thicker too. I've still got fur, but it's thicker. Maybe it traps air bubbles in it to keep me warm.
Then, say a few million years later . . .

Ivor *moves forward again, closer to the camera filling the frame. He lies on his belly and holds his back legs together to look like a tail*

I'm always in the water. I'm mostly using my tail for propulsion. My forelimbs have become flippers and my hind limbs and pelvis have got really small because I don't really use them any more. In fact, my pelvis has completely detached from my spine. I think I've probably lost most of my fur by now. I'm more rubbery and blubbery. I'm much bigger now. I'm about five metres long.
And so, in the course of around 10 million years, which is nothing in evolutionary terms, I've basically turned into a whale! And this is me, for now.

Ivor *continues being a whale, gently flicking his tail and flippers as the lights go down.*

Scene 6: Mime Scene – Geppetto's Workshop

♪ ENCHANTED VIOLINS RETURN,
GENTLE SWELLING HIGH/LOW CHORDS ♪

The video of the **Cricket** *reappears ON SCREEN*

Cricket (*voice over*) (*American Narrator Voice*) The man lived in a wooden hut at the edge of the forest. The hut was full of little creations he had carved out of wood, lined up neatly on shelves. And on the walls hung hundreds of wooden cuckoo clocks, which had all stopped ticking at a different minute of the day. Meaning it was always 'all the time'.

ON SCREEN fades to FANTASY CAM, revealing a silhouette of **Pinocchio** *small in the centre, with* **Geppetto** *large looming over him, hand on chin.*

The man felt safe here in this wooden world of his making. There was a truth to wood that he could understand, a solidity he could rely on. He knew hard wood from soft wood, and he always had the right tool for the job.
♪ VIOLINS FADE AWAY ♪

Using forced perspective ON SCREEN large **Geppetto** *uses various tools on smaller* **Pinocchio** *to turn him from a tree/log into a puppet in a stylized mime scene,* *performed in time to a musical score. He uses a saw, a hammer and chisel, a chainsaw, sand paper, and paint (all invisible). During the chainsaw section* **Pinocchio** *gets smaller and adds a hat and ruff to show that he has been transformed into a puppet. These are put on by* **Stagehand** *who then sidesteps off the SCREEN, trying not to be seen.*

♪ WOODEN XYLOPHONE CLINKS & CLUNKS ♪

Geppetto *looks at* **Pinocchio** *then turns to camera*

♪ WOODEN TWINKLE ♪
He has an idea

♪ CHEEKY WOODEN JANGLING ♪
He rummages in his apron pocket

♪ WOODEN NOTES RISE ♪
He pulls something long out of his pocket

♪ WOODEN TINKLES RISE & FALL ♪
He looks it up and down

♪ AFFIRMATIVE WOODEN CLINK ♪
Nods at camera

♪ HOLLOW RICKETY RATCHETING ♪
Shows us that it's a saw

♪ WOODEN NOTES FOLLOW GEPPETTO'S FEET ♪
He walks round to the other side of **Pinocchio**

♪ HOLLOW TAP ♪
Places the saw on **Pinocchio***'s arm/branch*

♪ COMEDIC WOODEN SAWING ♪
Saws back and forth

♪ WOODEN FRAGMENTS CLATTER ♪
The branch falls off

♪WOODEN TWINKLE ♪
Blows the dust off his saw

♪ WOODEN CLATTERING ♪
Chucks the saw away

♪ SCRATCHY SANDPAPER ♪
Scratches his chin looking at **Pinocchio**

♪ WOODEN TWINKLE ♪
He has an idea

♪ COMICAL WOODEN JANGLING ♪
Rummages in his apron pocket and pulls something out in each hand – a hammer and chisel

♪ HOLLOW TAPPING ♪
He chisels **Pinocchio***'s shoulder using a big hammer*

♪ LOPSIDED WOODEN CLANGING ♪
He walks round to the other side of **Pinocchio**

♪ HOLLOW TAPPING ♪
He chisels **Pinocchio***'s other shoulder using a big hammer*

♪ WOODEN PLODS ♪
He goes down on his knees

♪ WOODEN CLANGING ♪
He chisels **Pinocchio***'s genitals –* **Pinocchio** *looks shocked*

♪ WOODEN FRAGMENTS CLATTER ♪
He chucks away the hammer and chisel

♪ SUSPENSEFUL WOODEN TWINKLING ♪
He looks around for another tool, then sees something on the ground

♪ WHIMSICAL WOODEN PLODS ♪
He drags the heavy thing he was looking for across to the other side of **Pinocchio**

♪ SANDPAPER SCRAPE ♪
Looks at camera and wipes his brow

♪ WOODEN TWINKLING ♪
He lifts the heavy object off of the ground

(REAL CHAINSAW MOTOR POWERS UP)
He powers it up – it's a chainsaw!

(EXTREMELY LOUD CHAINSAWING)
He faces **Pinocchio** *with his back to the camera and chainsaws him*

(CHAINSAW SPLUTTERS OFF)
He moves away revealing **Pinocchio** *much smaller*

♪ WOODEN SPLATTER ♪
He throws away the chainsaw

♪ SANDPAPER SCRATCHES ♪
He scratches his chin looking at **Pinocchio**

♪ WOODEN TWINKLE ♪
He has an idea

♪ CHEEKY WOODEN JANGLING ♪
Rummages in the pocket in his apron and pulls something out

♪ SANDPAPER SCRAPES ♪
He shows us it's sandpaper by rubbing two bits together

♪ PLAYFUL WOODEN WADDLING ♪
He quickly plods to the other side of **Pinocchio** *and goes down on his knees*

♪ FAST SANDPAPER RUSTLES ♪
He uses the sandpaper all over **Pinocchio***'s body and* **Pinocchio** *visibly enjoys the sensation.* **Pinocchio** *cheekily turns round and bends over so that* **Geppetto** *is sanding his bum.*

♪ WOODEN DING ♪
He chucks away the sandpaper and puts his hands on his hips

♪ SUSPENSEFUL WOODEN TINKLING ♪
He looks at **Pinocchio** *again scratching his chin*

♪ WOODEN TWINKLE ♪
He has an idea

♪ CHEEKY WOODEN JANGLING ♪
Rummages in his apron pocket

♪ HOLLOW WOODEN BRUSHING ♪
He pulls out a paintbrush and palette and shows camera what they are

♪ HOLLOW WOODEN BRUSHING ♪
He carefully paints **Pinocchio***'s body*

♪ DELICATE BRUSHING ♪
He paints two eyes and a smiling mouth onto his face

♪ CLUMSY WOODEN TUMBLE ♪
He looks away and **Pinocchio** *falls down*

Pinocchio *finishes the scene lying on his back on the ground.*

♪ ENCHANTED VIOLINS GLIDE IN ♪

ON SCREEN fade to DOCU CAM held high on monopod with elevated perspective from the back of stage, showing the real distance between the two performers and breaking the illusion. ON SCREEN fades back to FANTASY CAM.

Geppetto *kneels and tenderly lifts* **Pinocchio***'s torso by the shoulder so that he is sitting up with legs outstretched.*

Geppetto (*voiceover, deep voice*) Look at you. You're my perfect puppet, Pinocchio! I wouldn't change a painted hair on your wooden head.

Pinocchio But I'm not a puppet, Father! I'm a real boy!

Geppetto (*voiceover, deep voice*) Hush now. That's impossible, little puppet. You're made of wood.

♪ ENCHANTED VIOLINS GLIDE AWAY ♪

Scene 7: Marionette

Geppetto *leaves the shot and re-enters holding wooden dowels in a cross like the top of a marionette puppet. He mimes tying* **Pinocchio** *to these sticks and then pulling him up.*

♪ WOODEN NOTES RISE ♪

♪ WOODEN NOTES TUMBLE ♪

Geppetto *puppeteers* **Pinocchio** *moving his limbs one by one then making him dance across the stage next to him.*
♪ PLINK ♪
♪ PLONK ♪
Pinocchio*'s left arm lifts*

♪ PLINK ♪
♪ PLONK ♪
Right arm lifts

♪ PLINK ♪
♪ PLONK ♪
Right leg lifts

♪ PLINK ♪
♪ PLONK ♪
Left leg lifts

♪ PLINK ♪
♪ PLONK ♪
Head nods

♪ PLAYFUL WOODEN PLONKING ♪
Short arm dance

Geppetto *continues to operate* **Pinocchio** *in the following monologue but isn't paying attention as he has turned to face the audience.* **Pinocchio** *dances away from his marionette sticks and gets bigger in the image and more free and fluid in his movements.*
♪ MELODIC PLAYFUL WOODEN PLONKING ♪

Rosana (*direct to audience as an aside, speaking into a fake microphone*) Hi, everyone. While we're working on this, I'm just thinking about what my role is in the story. At the moment I'm trying out being the father.

In my real life I don't want to have any actual children. But I remember after Ivor's first testosterone jab watching him really closely, and it felt a bit like how a parent might watch a new born baby – looking out for the slightest changes. Everything is magnified and miraculous. Fixating on his clitoris as it grows. Desperately trying to document everything. Part of you wants to hold onto the present form, but you're also willing and excited for what comes next.
And it is like a spell. The changes happen before your very eyes, but it's so slow that you can't really see it until you look back.
♪ REPETITIVE PLAYFUL WOODEN PLONKING CONTINUES ♪

It's funny, because Ivor is actually more than seven years older than me and was a lecturer on my degree programme, before we got together. So he was more like the daddy at the beginning of our relationship. And that age difference and power dynamic really turned me on.

But transitioning dislodges these roles. Ivor's age has been sliding around for the past few years. At times he's looked like a teenage twink, and I look like the older, more experienced one.
And actually, this turns me on as well.
♪ WOODEN PLONKING MUSIC INTENSIFIES ♪

But, if I'm being honest, recently I've been wondering whether I'm more suited to the role of the evil puppet master who steals Pinocchio and makes him perform for his own artistic and financial gain. There's times when we're working on this project and Ivor is actually struggling a bit. And I'm like, 'OK, great, how do we use this?'
And I've done things like filmed him when he's crying, and secretly recorded his family before he went into surgery.

Ivor *keeps dancing and moves towards FANTASY CAM getting bigger, before leaving the SCREEN and going behind the Wooden Backdrop.*

Sometimes it feels like I get so caught up in the conceptual art-making process, that it becomes a barrier to me really connecting emotionally and intimately with Ivor, and with what's happening.
♪ WOODEN PLONKING MUSIC FADES ♪

Rosana *looks around onto the empty stage behind them and realises* **Ivor** *is no longer there.*

Ivor?!

Rosana *spots* **Ivor** *hidden behind the Wooden Backdrop and runs over to see him as the lights fade and the* **Cricket** *reappears ON SCREEN.*

Scene 8: Theatre

♪ ENCHANTED VIOLINS GLIDE IN ♪

During the **Cricket** *narration,* **Stagehand** *is seen moving the Giant Eye Balls from their upstage position into the Downstage Area.*

Cricket (*voice over*) (*American Narrator Voice*) Unable to convince the man of his true nature, Pinocchio ventures out into the world and is enchanted by a building called 'The Theatre'. On entering, he is immediately hooked. There are puppets like him on stage, dancing and singing and being applauded. The painted hairs on his wooden arms stand on end, as his body tingles with a sense of belonging and possibility.
The puppet master spots him and invites him up.
'Why don't you make a show, little puppet? You look like you have a unique story to tell the world.'

♪ ENCHANTED VIOLINS CONTINUE ♪

The Wooden backdrop is lit from behind and we see the silhouettes of **Ivor** *and* **Rosana** *from the front.* **Rosana** *is helping* **Ivor** *to get undressed, taking off his pointy hat and ruff.*

ON SCREEN shows the DOCU CAM's view of them both from behind the Wooden Backdrop. We hear **Ivor** *grunting to take off different parts of his costume.*

Mid-undressing, **Ivor** *notices the DOCU CAM and delivers his text to it as he continues to change.*

Ivor (*conspiratorial whisper to the audience through the camera*) Hi!
I'm just practising what we like to call a 'quick change'.

Ivor *takes off his sweatshirt.*

Which is where you come off stage and you get changed really quickly, without the audience seeing. And then when you come back on, you look completely different.

He takes off the white collar and realises the DOCU CAM is still on him, so he continues.

Anyway, the reason I'm changing is because I'm going to try something out for the puppet theatre scene when Pinocchio puts on his own show.
And I was thinking that maybe you could help me, seeing as you're all here?
Maybe you could imagine that you're a real audience watching the show in the scene?

Ivor *turns away from the camera and pokes his head round the side of the Wooden Backdrop to speak directly to the audience.*

Do you think that would be possible?

Rosana *pokes their head round the other side of the backdrop.*

Rosana Yes, good idea, darling!

Ivor Maybe while I'm getting ready you can help them get into character?

Rosana Yes, good idea.

Ivor *goes back to getting changed behind the backdrop.*

Rosana *gets a fake microphone and a red stepladder which they place under the stage left corner of the screen and climb up to address the audience. During* **Rosana***'s monologue* **Ivor** *is ON SCREEN getting ready to be* **Pinocchio** *again, taking off his clothes, adding a ruff and pointy hat and being helped into a wood-print dressing gown.*

Rosana OK, everyone, this will be fun.

Let's get into character.

Let's imagine you're an audience, and you've come to a theatre to see a show.

Perhaps you've heard about this special puppet who can move without strings, and you've come to see it for yourself.

Who might you be?

Maybe you're also a puppet.

Or maybe you think you might be a puppet, and you want to be around other puppets.

Or maybe you're not a puppet, but you really support puppets' rights . . .

Or maybe you want to be seen to support puppets' rights, but deep down you're not really sure what you think about puppets.

Maybe you support puppets being on stage, but you wouldn't want one next to you in the toilet, or teaching your children.

Who might you be?

Who are you?

Who could you be . . . in this theatre?

OK. I'm going to close my eyes and count to three,

and when I open my eyes I want you to show me who you are.

Convince me, OK?
(*Whispers*) One, Two, Three . . .

Rosana *pauses to look out and assess different members of the audience.*

(*Pleased*) Yes.

Good.

Don't overdo it.

I want to believe you.
Keep it real.

Ivor *appears from behind the Wooden Backdrop, crosses the stage and waits for his moment.*

Rosana OK. I think we're ready.

We're a real audience, in a real theatre, watching a show.
Action.

♪ ENCHANTED VIOLINS GLIDE AWAY ♪

(THEATRE AUDIENCE CHATTERS)

ON SCREEN fades to FANTASY CAM. The image is framed by a wooden proscenium arch theatre, with wooden curtains pulled back at the side. An audience of simple wooden figures sits in front of the stage.

The **Host** *appears – a long wooden figure who slides in from the right of the screen, puppeteered by* **Stagehand***. The* **Host***'s right arm is articulated and manipulated by a string being pulled from above, out of shot, to make him gesticulate wildly as we hear his speech.*

While the **Host** *introduces him,* **Ivor** *prepares downstage, removing his dressing gown and being handed two flat wooden panels by* **Camera Person**.

Host (*voiceover, excitedly in the manner of a classic sideshow barker*) OK, OK, OK!

It's the moment you've all been waiting for!

Tonight, live on this stage, this is not an illusion! This is not a trick or a fake!

Lean in and feast your eyes on his miraculous body!

The magical, pitch shifting, metamorphosing wonder!
(*Dramatically and drawn out*) And heeeeeeeere he iiiiiis!

The **Host** *exits the screen as if leaving the fake stage on the right, and* **Ivor** *as* **Pinocchio** *enters from the left and appears to be the same size walking onto the same stage. He is naked apart from a pointy red hat with black wig, a small white ruff at his neck, white socks and wooden clogs. He crouches over as he walks using the two wooden panels to cover his body. When he reaches the centre of the shot a spotlight comes up on him and he stands up straight, placing the panels above one another to create a rectangle that covers his torso.*

Pinocchio *performs a strange striptease dance, slowly revealing different parts of his trans body from behind the panels to a soundtrack of drumroll crescendos and audience reactions.*

(AUDIENCE CHEER & CLAP)

♪ SUSPENSEFUL DRUMROLL ♪
♪ DRUMROLL CLIMAXES ♪
♪ CYMBAL CRASHES ♪

Pinocchio *lifts his right leg*
(AUDIENCE CLAP & HOLLER)

♪ DRUMROLL ♪
♪ DRUMROLL CLIMAXES ♪
He lifts his left leg and shakes it
(AUDIENCE LAUGH & WHOOP)

♪ DRUMROLL ♪
♪ DRUMROLL CLIMAXES ♪
He shoots out his right hand
(AUDIENCE LAUGH)

♪ DRUMROLL ♪
♪ DRUMROLL CLIMAXES ♪
He shoots out his left hand and moves it up and down
(AUDIENCE ENTHUSIASTIC SCREAMS)

♪ DRUMROLL ♪
♪ DRUMROLL CLIMAXES ♪
He squats down, balancing the wooden panels on the floor under his chin and revealing both hands
(AUDIENCE SCREAM & CLAP)

♪ DRUMROLL, ORCHESTRAL SURGES ♪
He slowly turns to his left then snaps his head back to look at FANTASY CAM
(AUDIENCE APPLAUSE)

♪ DRUMROLL ♪
♪ CYMBALS CRASH ♪
He slowly turns to his right then snaps his head back to look at FANTASY CAM
(AUDIENCE WHOOPS & HOLLERS)

♪ DRUMROLL ♪
♪ ORCHESTRAL CLIMAX ♪
He crouches down and turns the panels to cover his body
(AUDIENCE MEMBER EXCLAIMS)

♪ DRUMROLL , SUSPENSEFUL ORCHESTRA ♪
He shimmies the panels up to almost reveal his crotch
(ANTI-CLIMATIC ABSENCE OF CRASH)
(AUDIENCE DISAPPOINTED SIGHS)

♪ DRUMROLL ♪
He shimmies the panels down to almost reveal his chest
(AUDIENCE LAUGHS & CLAPS)

♪ DRUMROLL, DRAMATIC FANFARE ♪
He leans and slides the panels apart keeping chest and crotch hidden
(AUDIENCE JEERS)

♪ TWINKLING ORCHESTRAL FLOURISHES ♪
He reveals then hides his right nipple
(AUDIENCE CHEER & WHOOP)

♪ MYSTERIOUS WOODEN FLUTES ♪
He reveals then hides his crotch – the audience sees he has a triangle of ginger pubic hair and no penis
(AUDIENCE CHUCKLE QUIETLY)

♪ DRUMROLL & EUPHORIC VIOLINS SLOWLY ASCEND ♪
He moves both panels up his body slowly
♪ DRUMROLL INTENSIFIES ♪
He triumphantly hold panels out revealing his whole body
(AUDIENCE CHEERS & CLAPS)

♪ ENCHANTING ORCHESTRAL WOODWINDS ♪

♪ MUSIC DELICATELY PLODS ♪

Pinocchio *does a strange sidestepping dance where he alternates revealing part of his body from behind each of the wooden panels*
♪ WOOD PLINK-PLONKS ♪
He hits the panels against each other – as he did in the Prop Table scene

♪ WOOD CLINK-CLUNKS ♪

♪ HIGH PLINK-PLONK ♪
He hits the panels on his chest

♪ LOW CLINK-CLUNKS ♪
He hits the panels on his buttocks

♪ SUSPENSEFUL WOODEN TINKLES ♪
He moves the panels up his body

♪ DRUMROLL ♪
He holds the panels out to reveal his whole body

♪ CYMBAL CRASHES ♪

(AUDIENCE HEARTY APPLAUSE)
(AUDIENCE CHEERS)

Pinocchio *finishes his act to applause.*

A mobile phone with a wooden frame is lowered into the shot beside him and hung from the top of the wooden theatre set. The mobile phone screen shows a video of **Ivor** *from early 2019, standing in front of a wooden backdrop, strumming a ukulele and getting ready to sing a song. The video shows* **Ivor** *before he started taking testosterone or had chest masculinising top surgery. He is naked and we see his breasts. He has no facial hair and his voice is much higher pitched when he speaks and sings.*

In the video we hear **Rosana** *off-camera speaking to* **Ivor** *before he begins to sing.*
♪ FAINT UKULELE STRUM ♪

Rosana (*on video, offscreen*) OK.

Ivor (*on video*) Should I look at the camera?

Rosana Maybe not.

Maybe do it like you're singing it sort of to yourself?
But look at – whatever feels natural.

Ivor (*chuckles*)

Rosana (*jokingly*) Just be natural, yeah?
♪ LIGHTLY STRUMMED UKULELE CHORDS ♪

Ivor *in the video from the past begins singing 'When You Wish Upon A Star', the famous song that Jiminy Cricket sings at the beginning of the Walt Disney 1940 classic animated film,* Pinocchio. *He accompanies himself with his ukulele.*

The present **Ivor** *onstage has a microphone on a stand and harmonizes in a lower pitch, exaggerating how his voice has deepened since transitioning. He duets with his past self ON SCREEN.*

Ivor (*singing*)

#When you wish upon a star
Makes no difference who you are
Anything your heart desires
Will come to you

If your heart is in your dreams
No request is too extreme
When you wish upon a star
As dreamers do

Fate is kind
She brings to those who love
The sweet fulfilment of
their secret longings

Like a bolt out of the blue
Fate steps in and sees you through
When you wish upon a star
Your dreams come true

Ivor *finishes singing and the video on the phone stops. He walks towards the FANTASY CAM, becoming bigger in the frame, and unplugs and picks up the phone. He walks slowly back to the microphone stand, looking at the phone.*

Scene 9: The Artistic Director

Rosana *appears ON SCREEN, very large as they are close to the FANTASY CAM, poking their head inside the wooden theatre frame. They are also wearing a red pointy hat and white ruff that signify the character of* **Pinocchio**.

At first we see **Ivor** *still inside the frame with his phone, much smaller than* **Rosana**, *and* **Rosana** *looks at him when talking.*

Rosana Yeah. That was . . . I think that was really good, darling.

I think that could work for the theatre scene.

And I've actually had an idea for a scene that could happen after that.
I thought maybe I could take over playing Pinocchio.

Rosana *leans through the frame of the theatre and picks up two of the wooden figure audience members and puppeteers them as* **Pinocchio** *and* **The Artistic Director**. **Rosana** *addresses the rest of their monologue to the FANTASY CAM.* **Ivor** *leaves the image and slowly walks behind the Wooden Backdrop.*

And maybe he's gone to the bar . . .?

He's just finished his show, it went really well, and he's gone to the bar to have a drink. And the artistic director of The Theatre comes up to him.
So here we're at Tramway, so it would be LJ Finlay-Walsh.

Wherever the show is performed it should be the artistic director of the theatre or festival that we are in, using the appropriate pronouns.

She comes up to him and she's like,

'Wow, thank you, Pinocchio! That was really powerful and important. If you want to follow me, I've got something powerful and important to show you . . .
. . . downstairs.'
♪ ENCHANTED VIOLINS RETURN WARPED ♪

And Pinocchio's like, 'I didn't even know there was a downstairs at Tramway!'

And the artistic director is like, 'Ssshhh! It's a secret!'

So she takes Pinocchio's little wooden hand and leads him down a dark, damp staircase.

At the bottom of the stairs they reach a large metal door and the artistic director unzips her leather bumbag and pulls out an enormous key that has teeth as long as Pinocchio's fingers.

As she turns the key in the lock there is a deep satisfying clunk that sends a shudder of excitement rattling through Pinocchio's little wooden joints.
The door swings open, revealing a room that is covered in bright red shiny leather.

Rosana *removes the wooden audience members and the theatre set from ON SCREEN, handing them to* **Stagehand**.

Pinocchio cannot believe his eyes. The walls are leather, the ceiling is leather, and he notices that the floor is also like a padded leather. And as he steps through, he's a little bit unsteady on his feet.

And the artistic director turns to him and says, 'Don't worry, Pinocchio, it's all vegan! But it feels real, doesn't it?'

And Pinocchio doesn't know what to say. He's not had much experience with leather, real or fake.

She leads him to the middle of the room.

Rosana *shuffles on their knees into the centre of the Red Backdrop and delivers the rest of the monologue on their knees, gesturing with their arms, imagining the scene around them.*

♪ SQUEAKY ELECTRIC TREMBLES ♪

And she says, 'Kneel here and I'll get you fitted up.'

Then she goes to the far corner of the room, flips open a secret leather flap, and presses her fingers into some buttons on a keypad.

Suddenly there's a loud screeching sound from above Pinocchio's head.

He looks up, amazed to see the ceiling above him opening up and an intricate wooden cage being lowered down on a thick metal chain.

The artistic director comes back over to him. And as she fastens the cage around his head she says, 'I made this especially for you, Pinocchio. Tell me if it's too tight. I don't want to hurt you, but I don't want you to be able to move.'

'It's perfect!' he says, as his body rattles again with anticipation.

The artistic director disappears behind him and he can hear the clinking of chains, the zipping of zips, and the squelching of leather on hot flesh.
And he has this feeling that his life is about to be transformed . . . forever.

♪ ELECTRONIC BUBBLES & ZAPS ♪

And as he's sitting there, he notices a round hole in the cage, directly in front of his nose, (**Rosana** *turns their head right to deliver this directly to the audience rather than to the FANTASY CAM*) about the size of a one pound coin.

Suddenly, the artistic director appears in front of him and she is dressed head to toe in bright red, shiny, vegan leather, as if she's almost part of the room. She turns round and bends over, revealing a small hole in her outfit, directly over her anus, that's also (*delivered directly to the audience again, knowingly*) about the size of a one pound coin.

(*Seductively*) 'Tell me a lie, Pinocchio', she says gently under her breath.

(*High-pitched as* **Pinocchio**) 'I– I–I wanna be a real boy?!' he whimpers, as his body surges with pleasure, becoming hard and wet!

'Again, little puppet!', whispers the artistic director.

'I wanna be a real boy!', he gasps louder, as the pleasure intensifies in his face and he feels his nose bursting forwards out of him.

'Yes, faster!', the artistic director yells.

'I wanna be a real boy!', screams Pinocchio, as his nose almost reaches her.

But his body is branching out in all directions now, with wooden sticks erupting out of his chest and his legs.

'I wanna be just like all the other boys!'

And he sees little holes appearing in the walls of the room, with wooden sticks thrusting through, poking and piercing the leather, like the room itself is bursting with his desire.

'I wanna be a real boy!'

Then, in a moment of pure ecstasy he explodes out of the cage around his head.
And at the same moment, the little holes in the walls tear open and hundreds of trans masc and non-binary people pour through the leather gashes and flood the stage panting, 'I wanna be a real boy!'.

Ivor *crawls into the frame towards* **Rosana** *who climbs on top of him as they both moan and writhe*

Both I wanna be a real boy. (*Panting.*) Yeah, I wanna be a real boy. Oh I wanna be a real boy! Mmmm. I wanna be a real boy.

Rosana (*to* **Ivor**) OK, you take over as Pinocchio, darling.

Rosana *removes their black wig and red pointy hat and quickly plonks it on* **Ivor***'s head as they get up and leave him.*

Rosana Keep going.

Ivor (*high-pitched, repeating*) I wanna be a real boy!

Rosana *picks up the Giant Eye Balls prop. When* **Rosana** *holds this prop above their head it is to signify the eyes of the now giant* **Blue Fairy** *and indicates where* **Ivor** *should look to make eye-contact.*

Rosana Then an eight-foot creature dressed head to toe in bright blue latex with electric blue wings and a huge blue wand/paddle thing . . .

Rosana *picks up a long thin tube of wooden-printed material which they use to whip* **Ivor**.

She descends from above and starts saying, (*sinister, electric voice*) 'You'll never be a real boy! You're a liar! Evil, deceitful, double-crossing liar! You're a LIARRRRR!!!!'

On the word LIARRRRR, **Stagehand** *turns on a giant fan downstage left from behind the Wooden Backdrop that explosively inflates a large, floppy tree shape – one big long trunk reaches across the stage as its branches flail around on the floor and in the air. It is made of the same fake wood print fabric as the performers' tracksuits and is a bit like one of those inflatable air dancer figures you get outside car dealerships, but it stays horizontal, thrashing on the ground.*

ON SCREEN shows the DOCU CAM's view which is focusing on the details of **Ivor** *and* **Rosana***'s hands, bodies and faces as they interact with the tree, obviously gaining erotic pleasure from it and from each other. It is hard to distinguish between their limbs and the tree's branches as they writhe around, straddling and humping the tree, stroking its material, fondling each other around the trunk, pushing their faces through the branches, and fingering each other's sockets.*

♪ ROARING AND WHOOSHING FROM FAN ♪

Ivor (*repeating*) I wanna be a real boy!

Rosana (*repeating*) You're a liar!

♪ POUNDING BASS ♪

♪ WARPED VIOLINS SWELL AND SHUDDER ♪

♪ ECSTATIC SQUEAKY BURBLES ♪

♪ GLITCHY ELECTRIC WHIRLING ♪

After a while **Rosana** *crawls away upstage right leaving* **Ivor** *alone with the tree.*

Ivor Yes, yes, yes, I am a liar.

♪ ELECTRIC SOUNDS, BASS, AND FAN STOP ♪

Ivor *emerges from a mass of branches, breathing deeply and smiling into the DOCU CAM so his face fills the SCREEN.*

Ivor (*as himself*) Yes, yes, yes. I am a liar. I am a liar!

I don't want to be a real boy!

I don't want to be bound by your laws of legitimacy.

I am not your real and I am not your fantasy.

I am a boy and I am a puppet, and I am a donkey and I am a star, and I am a cricket and I am a fairy, and I am a tree and I am everything in between.

I have deep roots that stretch back in time.

And my branches reach out into our futures.
You may not understand the glorious revolutionary lives being lived at the horizon of your perception, but we have always been here, and we're not going anywhere.

IVOR *smiles and rolls out of the shot. The DOCU CAM focuses on the now deflated material of the tree which is slowly pulled away across the Red Backdrop.*
♪ WARPED ENCHANTED VIOLINS BREATHE & SWAY ♪

Scene 10: Landscape

♪ DISTORTED ENCHANTED VIOLINS REPEAT HIGH/LOW LOOP ♪

ON SCREEN switches to FANTASY CAM. **Ivor** *lies directly in front of the FANTASY CAM and as the lights come up we see him in profile – his head, torso and top of his legs filling the bottom third of the image and looking like a hilly landscape.*

On stage we see that **Rosana** *has put on a wooden cap with a socket on top, and in the socket is a large wooden dowel, about one metre long, pointing out of the top of their head. They are also wearing a socket over their nose, held in place by red elastic.*

They crawl onto the Red Backdrop with their head low, hidden from the FANTASY CAM by **Ivor***'s head. They slowly lift their head up positioning themself so that ON SCREEN the wooden dowel appears to come out of* **Ivor***'s nose, or to be* **Ivor***'s nose growing. Finally they pop up above his face, stand up, and look down at him.*

Rosana *then slowly moves downstage making it look ON SCREEN as if they are climbing across* **Ivor***'s body like a landscape. When they reach the point of* **Ivor***'s genital socket, they peer in, put their hand down into it and rummage around.*

By this point, **Stagehand** *has crawled onto the Red Backdrop with another wooden dowel that they hand up to* **Rosana.** *ON SCREEN* **Rosana** *then carefully pulls the* *wooden dowel out of* **Ivor***'s genital socket and holds it aloft, triumphantly, while* **Ivor** *looks on.*

Rosana *slowly moves downstage off the Red Backdrop into the Downstage Area, no longer in the shot. They pick up lots of wooden dowels from under the prop table and put on their clogs.*

♪ VIOLINS FADE AWAY ♪

Scene 11: Pleasure Island

Ivor *is still large ON SCREEN. He picks up a small wooden dowel and gently places it into his genital socket until it snaps into place. He fondles this wooden phallus and we see that he is looking at himself in the TV monitor above the FANTASY CAM.*

He then puts a dowel with a square block onto the end and fits it into the socket on his right thigh. He rubs his hand up and down the shaft of the dowel and also uses it to move his leg back and forth, like a rod puppet.

His body fills most of the screen as he watches himself rubbing his phallus with one hand and rubbing the dowel on his thigh with his other hand.

Rosana *walks onto the Red Backdrop and starts setting down the dowels they are carrying and looking towards* **Ivor.**

Rosana You alright, darling?

Ivor (*distractedly, still looking at himself on screen*) Yeah, I'm just trying out some ideas for the Pleasure Island scene.

Rosana Oh right!
I'm working on that scene as well.

Rosana *starts adding dowels to the sockets on their body and rubs them, while also using the dowels to move their body back and forth in a sensual manner.*

Ivor *turns onto his hands and knees so that his flat back is at the top of the SCREEN.* **Rosana** *appears much smaller under his belly, close to where he is thrusting his phallus up and down.* **Rosana** *has a dowel sticking out of their hat which looks like it's thrusting towards* **Ivor***'s pelvis as they sway forwards and backwards.*

Rosana I was thinking . . .

Ivor Mm-hmm?

Rosana . . . you know in the Disney 'Pinocchio', they were going to call Pleasure Island 'Booby Land', originally.

Ivor Oh right!?

Rosana Well, I thought maybe our Pleasure Island could be like an island that's just covered in enormous boobs! And we could just roll around and nestle in amongst the boobs.

Ivor *stops thrusting.*

Ivor Oh yeah!?

Eh – Is that because you miss my boobs?

Rosana *stops thrusting and puts a wooden dowel into their face socket, making it look like they have a wooden Pinocchio nose. They move towards the audience.*

Rosana No, I never miss them.

♪ MAGICAL WOODWINDS DELICATELY PLOD ♪

Ivor OK.

Ivor *picks up his own wooden nose, puts it on and begins to rub it.*

Well then, yeah, I think it's a really great idea.

Rosana Great.

♪ MAGICAL WOODWIND PLOD CONTINUES ♪

Both *continue to add wooden dowels of different lengths to their bodies by inserting them into the red wooden sockets all over their costumes.* **Ivor** *puts on his wooden clogs and a wooden cap with two sockets where he inserts two short dowels that look like animal ears.*

They seem to be experimenting, trying out different positions and movements. Sometimes appearing to puppeteer their bodies using the dowels, sometimes they shake and rub the dowels and move their bodies rhythmically, somehow simulating sexual thrusts.

Their attention is towards the screens around them rather than to each other or the audience. This gives the text and actions a slightly absent-minded quality. They seem more engrossed in exploring what they are doing and what it looks like and feels like, than what they are saying to each other.

Rosana I'll always love you, darling.

Ivor What?

Rosana (*louder and clearer*) I'll always love you.

Ivor Oh right.

Ivor *slowly moves towards* **Rosana** *centre stage as he looks for more dowels to put into his body.*

Rosana Every minute of every day.

From the moment I wake up, to the moment I go to sleep, I'm just completely in love with you.
And even sometimes when I'm asleep, or when I'm in bed and I'm trying to get to sleep, but you're making those noises . . .

Ivor You mean snoring?

Rosana Yeah!

Times like that, I just love you so much.
And I just know 100 per cent, for sure . . . that you're 'The One'.

Ivor Yeah, well . . .

I really love you.

And I just always feel like you're always going to be able to fulfil all my needs.
Always and forever, and I'll never want to be with anyone else.

Rosana Oh, that's good.

Ivor Yeah.

♪ ENCHANTED MUSIC BUILDS ♪

By now they have come together in the middle of the Red Backdrop. **Ivor** *is reclining and* **Rosana** *stands over him with a long wooden dowel phallus, which they try to insert into the wooden block on the end of* **Ivor***'s thigh dowel. They both try to get in the right position for the dowel to go in but have to use their hands to insert it.*

They sigh with relief once the dowel is in and gently move together.

Rosana It's so great that you're trans.

Because deep down, I've always wanted to be with a man.

Ivor Well I've always wanted to *be* a man.

So that's good.

♪ ENCHANTED WOODEN CLINKS ♪

They disconnect the dowels in the wooden cube and find a new position, connecting through dowels and sockets. **Ivor** *is on all fours facing away from* **Rosana***, who connects to a socket on his shoulder or arm.*

Rosana I don't miss being a lesbian.

Ivor No, me neither.

Rosana And it's so great now, when we're seen as just a nice, normal, heterosexual couple.

Ivor Yeah! It's nice to be normal, isn't it?

Ivor *stands up and they become connected by one short dowel coming out of a socket on top of* **Rosana***'s cap and going into the socket at* **Ivor***'s bum so that* **Rosana** *is bent over behind* **Ivor***. We see them in profile ON SCREEN. They are forming a strange, conjoined creature, like a pantomime horse, or rather, donkey.* **Both** *in clogs, they move their right feet backwards and forwards in unison.*

♪ SNEAKY ORCHESTRAL FLOURISHES ♪

Rosana (*lifting pitch on the word 'gay'*) We were gay, and now we're (*dropping pitch*) straight.

Ivor I was a (*high*) girl,

and now I'm a (*low*) boy.

(*Donkey-like alternating high/low pitch.*)

Rosana Girl, Boy. Girl, Boy.
(*High pitch*) We were weird, and now we're (*low pitch*) normal.

Ivor Weird, Normal

Rosana Weird, Normal

Both Eee aww, eee awww.

Both *slowly walk as one donkey towards the audience, exiting the SCREEN. Once downstage they split from each other and begin to interact with the set, shuddering and poking their dowels in any holes they can find as their voices become wilder and more like donkey brays.*

Rosana You were sad, and now you're happy.

Rosana *sticks their nose dowel through the hole in the wooden panel attached to a lighting stand and thrusts backwards and forwards.*

Ivor Sad, happy.

Rosana Sad, happy, ee aww.

Hee-haw! Ee-aw!

Both *improvise the high-low binaries and repeat what each other says, playing with their voices and movements.*

Ivor My voice was high, and now it's low.

Rosana High, low. High, looooowww. Eee-awwww.

Ivor *sticks his nose into a hole in the Wooden Backdrop. When he withdraws, a dowel covered in light-grey fur pokes out, which* **Ivor** *rubs and then takes for a tail in his bum socket before galloping over to the prop table.*

Rosana *is also on the Wooden Backdrop and begins penetrating a hole in the director's chair. Part of the Wooden Backdrop collapses in the excitement.*
♪ WOODEN KNOCKING ♪

Rosana (*high pitched*) This was your voice.
(*Low pitched*) This is your voice.

Ivor *gallops clumsily towards the prop table and* **Rosana** *takes the director's chair and trots upstage to the back, crossing in front of FANTASY CAM.*

♪ WOODEN TINKLES ♪

Ivor Eee-awwww.

I was broken, now I'm fixed.

Rosana Broken, Fixed. EEE-AWWW.

Ivor Eee – awww.

♪ WOODEN TAPPING ♪

Rosana That was then, and this is nowwww.

EEE-AWWW.

Ivor Then, now. Eeee awww.

Ivor *penetrates different holes in the prop table with dowels on his body and with a furry dowel he's picked up. He puts his phallus dowel into the top of the table and then lifts it up against his body so the legs stick out in front of him. The props go flying and roll around as he continues walking across the front of the stage towards the Cricket Stage.*

He removes one of the prop table legs and alternates hitting himself on the bum with it and banging it on the table on his belly.

♪ MUSIC PLODS ♪

Rosana Before, after.

Ivor Then, now.

♪ WOODEN RATTLING ♪

Rosana *has taken the director's chair upstage to the back of the space. They swap their wooden cap for a grey furry cone hat, and add a grey furry ball to their genital socket. A wooden half-table has been leant against the wall. They turn it over revealing its furry back and mount the front of it. It has two spindly, wobbly legs that walk behind, turning* **Rosana** *into another strange donkey creature.*

Rosana *starts moving back onto the Red Backdrop diagonally from upstage left.*

Ivor *starts walking onto the Red Backdrop towards* **Rosana** *from beside the Cricket Stage, downstage right.*

Rosana Girl, boyyyyyy.

Ivor Gayyyy, straigghhhttt.

♪ ENCHANTED ORCHESTRA MUSIC BUILDS ♪

Both Eee-aaw, eee-aww Eee-aaaaaaw

♪ TENSE ORCHESTRAL FLOURISHES ♪

Both *meet in the centre of the screen on the Red Backdrop. As they come closer their noses suddenly snap together magnetically, and they seem to have some kind of euphoric donkey climax.*

Rosana Eeeeeeooooooarrrrrwwwwwww

Ivor Eeeeeeeeeeeoooooarrrrrwwwwwww

Ivor *breaks the noses apart with his table leg before walking towards the Wooden Backdrop, collapsing and putting down the prop table.*

Rosana *moves slowly off The Red Backdrop downstage and out of shot where they drop their hind legs and wooden cone and put the microscopic camera on their head.*

Ivor *crawls back into the shot ON SCREEN as* **Rosana** *exits. He uses the two deer/ whale limb props from before to hold himself up. He lies down with his head downstage, just at the left edge of the shot, exhausted and removing his cap and some of the dowels.*

As the lights begin to fade, **Rosana** *moves towards* **Ivor**, *and appears ON SCREEN seemingly filming him with the microscopic camera.*

ON SCREEN switches to the microscopic camera footage as **Rosana** *gets closer and closer to* **Ivor***'s face with the camera. We see his eye and cheek before seeing a forest of his beard hairs sticking up at different angles.*

♪ ORCHESTRAL THEME DISTORTS AND FADES OUT ♪

Both (*donkey sounds transform into whale sounds*) Woooooaoaa.

♪ SEA WAVES GENTLY CRASH ♪
Stagehand *and* **Camera Person** *place the dowel mobiles on the floor of the Red Backdrop, clip them onto lines which have been lowered and raise them up using pulleys.*

♪ SEA WAVES ROLL & CRASH ♪

(MUFFLED WATERY ATMOSPHERE)

Scene 12: Inside the Whale at the Bottom of the Ocean

The stage is suddenly blue and watery. ON SCREEN the image fades from the microscopic camera footage to the FANTASY CAM. The image is filled with floating dowels similar in form to **Ivor***'s magnified beard hairs.*

Ivor *and* **Rosana** *sit up and look around them. They move with a floaty quality to suggest they are underwater. When they speak they quickly wobble their index finger over their lips to create a bubbling sound and they elongate all their words. Their voices echo in the cavernous space.*

Ivor (*bubbling voice*) Hellooooo

Rosana (*bubbling voice*) Daaaaarrrling?

Ivor (*continuing the bubbling voice*) Darling?

Rosana Is that you, darling?

Ivor I think so.

Where are we?

Both *slowly rise to their feet and gradually move diagonally across the Red Backcloth, upstage right, becoming smaller in the image.*

Rosana It's so big.

Ivor It's enormous.

Rosana And it's so slippy and slidy.

Ivor And wet.

Rosana *holds one of their clogs up in the air and lets go as it magically floats up with the other dowels. It is attached to the mobile via a magnet.*

Rosana Maybe we can slide around in here forever.

♪ FAINT DIGESTIVE BURBLES ♪

Both *have reached the upstage right corner now and float back down onto their knees as if sinking. In the next dialogue they slowly pull the remaining dowels and furry props out of each other's sockets and puppeteer each prop as if it is floating away.*

Rosana Hang on!

Are we being consumed?

Ivor I feel like I'm being digested.

Rosana I bet you would taste delicious.

Ivor I don't want to taste delicious.

I want to make them sick.

♪ ENCHANTED VIOLINS RETURN DRAMATICALLY♪

Stagehand *and* **Camera Person** *finish pulling up the mobiles so the wooden dowels are out of shot but can be seen suspended above the stage.*

Camera Person *starts shaking the cloth of the Red Backdrop on the floor, creating huge undulating waves in the FANTASY CAM, which conceal* **Ivor** *and* **Rosana**, *revealing them only in flashes between waves.*

Stagehand *shakes the upright section of the Red Backdrop.*

Rosana *and* **Ivor** *help each other to strip down to their bare torsos, taking off sweatshirts, white turtleneck tops, and peeling down their wetsuits.*

Stagehand *and* **Camera Person** *stop shaking the Red Backdrop cloth and as the waves die down we see* **Ivor** *and* **Rosana** *lying together in an embrace.*

Stagehand *and* **Camera Person** *enter the image ON SCREEN walking towards* **Ivor** *and* **Rosana**. **Stagehand** *carries the red ladder, and* **Camera Person** *has the DOCU*

CAM again. **Camera Person** *climbs the red ladder and gets into a position to film* **Ivor** *and* **Rosana** *from above.*
(WATERY SOUNDS FADE AWAY)

♪ ENCHANTED VIOLINS GENTLY BREATHE & SWAY ♪

Scene 13: We're Not Ever Going to Finish This Show, Are We?

ON SCREEN image crossfades to DOCU CAM, revealing a beautifully framed shot of **Ivor** *and* **Rosana** *in a loving embrace.* **Ivor** *is on his back.* **Rosana** *is on their side with their arm across* **Ivor***'s chest.* **Rosana** *is resting their head on* **Ivor***'s shoulder, who has his arm around them.*

♪ UPLIFTED VIOLINS ♪

Ivor Darling, we're not ever going to finish this show, are we?

Rosana No, darling.

But isn't that wonderful?

Because it means we can keep changing it.

Like, we could do that bit again, but you could be the whale and I could be the sea.

Or . . .

We could both be tiny fish and spend our lives swimming around in a whole shoal of fish.

Or . . .

I could be a donkey, and you could be the owner of the puppet theatre.

But one day you see me in a field and we fall in love and you decide to open a donkey theatre. And we tour the world with our unbelievable, gravity-defying tricks.
Or . . .

During this section, **Ivor** *begins to sing a gentle, repeated phrase that goes along with the chords of the uplifted strings. The refrain always begins with 'To Be Honest . . .' but then drifts off into humming or da-da-das. It sounds familiar but you can't quite put your finger on it. He looks dreamily off into the distance as* **Rosana** *continues describing possibilities.*

Rosana We could work on the box office at the puppet theatre . . .

Ivor (*sings tenderly*) To be honest . . .

Rosana . . . and maybe we fancy each other for ages

Ivor Da da da da da . . .

Rosana but we don't tell each other . . .

Ivor Da da da da da da daaa . . .

Rosana And then one day, you write me a note on the back of a ticket.

And the rest is history.

Ivor To be honest, Ba ba ba ba . . .

Rosana Or we could both be crickets . . .

Ivor (*continues singing until the end*) Hmm mmm mmm mm mm.

Rosana . . . and we could live with loads of other crickets and other bugs in a gigantic old tree, that's our whole world.

Or . . .

We could both be trees and stand side by side for centuries, gently caressing each other in the wind.

Or I could be the wind and you could be a leaf.

Or . . .
I could be a squirrel and you could be a nut.

Both *slowly move from their position on stage and get up and walk downstage towards the audience. However, ON SCREEN they don't move, remaining in the same position and talking as the video continues. The audience realises that what is ON SCREEN is pre-recorded.*

Once downstage **Both** *turn and look up to watch the screen, standing together with their backs to the audience and arms round each other.*

Stagehand *and* **Camera Person** *remain still in their positions, as if still filming* **Rosana** *and* **Ivor**.

Or you could be a fairy and I could be your wand.

Or you could be a carpenter and I could be your tool.

Or I could be a nail and you could be a piece of wood.

Or I could be a splinter in your finger.

Or . . .

We could both live on Pleasure Island,

but it's not a place that's settled, it's somewhere that we have to keep building together.
Or . . .

Ivor *and* **Rosana** *leave the space, whilst ON SCREEN the scene continues.*

You could be the sea and I could be the sky.

Or . . .

You could be a star and I could be the moon.

Or . . .

We could both be puppets and just live in a theatre somewhere.

Or . . .

We could be the curtains in the theatre and spend our life nestled up next to each other.

But then once a day, everyday, we move apart and something magical happens.
Or . . .

Image ON SCREEN fades to red.

♪ UPLIFTED VIOLINS TENDERLY RISE & FALL ♪

♪ UPLIFTED VIOLINS FADE ♪

Ends

Performance Documents

1 Scene 1: The Forest. Photograph taken at the UK premiere in the Grand Hall at Battersea Arts Centre. Photograph by Christa Holka. Courtesy of Rosana Cade and Ivor MacAskill.

2 Scene 3: Intro Scene. Left to right: Ivor MacAskill, Rosana Cade and Jo Hellier as Camera Person. Photograph by Christa Holka. Courtesy of Rosana Cade and Ivor MacAskill.

3 Scene 11: Pleasure Island. Ivor MacAskill and Rosana Cade. Taken in the digital production by Tiu Makkonen. Courtesy of Rosana Cade and Ivor MacAskill.

4 Early notes around the theatre scene and a sketch of a possible Pinocchio by designer Tim Spooner. Courtesy of Rosana Cade and Ivor MacAskill.

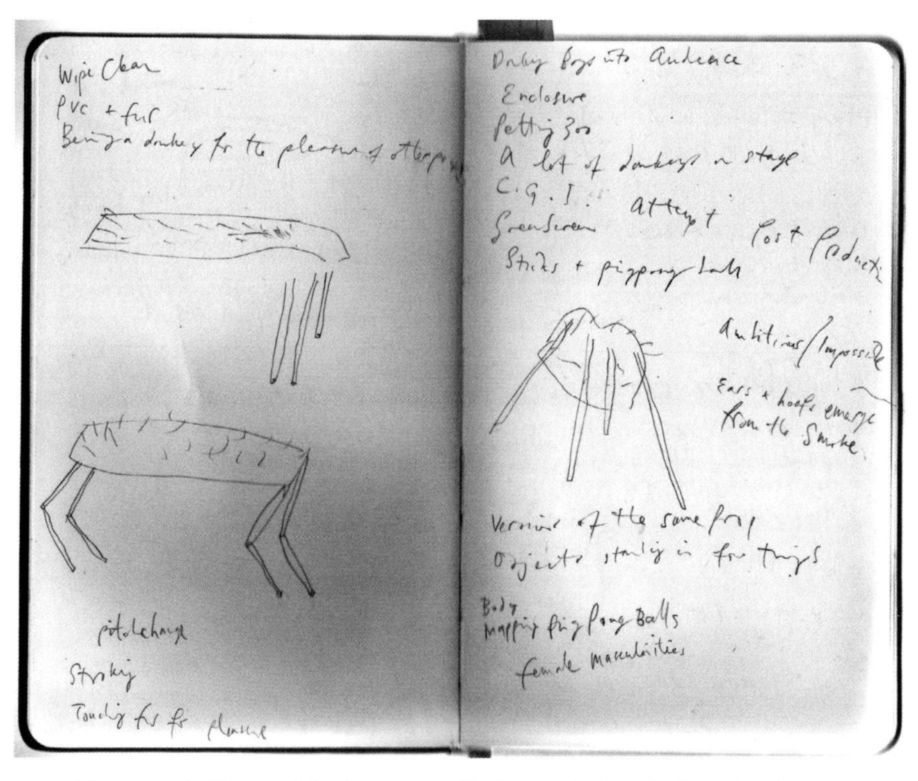

5 Notes on the Pleasure Island scene considering turning into donkeys for pleasure, by Tim Spooner. Courtesy of Rosana Cade and Ivor MacAskill.

Ten Commandments

Written and performed by David Hoyle

Created and written in collaboration with Jayne Compton and Mark Whitelaw

Credits

Director: Mark Whitelaw
Dramaturg and Producer: Jayne Compton
Sound Designer: Richard Torry
Costume Designer: John Krausa and Rick Owens
Videography: Lee Baxter

Premiere: The Lowry, Salford, 24 March 2022.

Scene Order

Welcome: Wide, Wide as the Ocean.

1. Thou Shalt Tolerate Living in a Rat-Infested Dystopia.
2. Thou Shalt Not Make Captain Mainwaring Out of Shirley Bassey.
3. Thou Must Stay Alive, Even if It's Just to Spite Others.
4. Thou Shalt Not Mistake Wealth for Success.
5. Thou Shalt Dip in and out of Cognitive Dissonance for Thy Own Convenience.
6. Thou Shalt Live in a Concrete Cube in the Metaverse.
7. Thou Shalt Honour People, Who Are Worthy of Honoring.
8. Thou Shalt Honour the Arms Trade as Thy Lord and Master.
9. Thou Shalt Input?
10. Thou Must Not Forget Thou Is Just a Grain of Sand in the Desert of Time.

Setting

The stage features a lectern upstage left, decorated with a purple cloth with David's initials, DH, embroidered above a golden love heart and a projection screen covering the back wall.

Video projection shows **David***'s head spinning on screen, singing:*

Wide, wide as the ocean, high as the heaven above;

Deep, deep as the deepest sea is my Saviour's love.

I, though so unworthy, still am a child of His care;

For His Word teaches me that His love reaches me everywhere.

David *makes his entrance.*

Welcome to this thermonuclear explosion of love and also hope for what may remain of the twenty-first century.

When I look back over my life, I've spent most of it tempted and yet undefiled. I went into the wilderness for way more than forty days and forty nights, so that you didn't have to.

On my return, into my housing association flat in Manchesterford, my attention was taken by a scuffling sound and I was drawn to a disturbance under my sink. I immediately thought the rats were back but it wasn't. It was these Commandments, a message from the Divine. There's Ten Commandments, but there are actually only nine.

Later on, in the spirit of democracy and inclusion, one of you will be revealing the missing Commandment.

I'm framing them as Commandments but see them as more helpful suggestions.

Believe it or not, I'm in no position to advise anyone else how they should live their own life.

After all, we are all on our own personal road to Calvary.

I was going to retire and die in poverty and obscurity but being in receipt of these Commandments has given me a new lease of life.

I feel that in these troubled times we need certainty, security, stability – that's what I'm offering you this evening song.

When you, the audience, follow these Commandments collectively, we will create a better world.

Without further ado, in the words of Dame Shirley Bassey, let's get this party started, let's see Commandment Number One.

Ends with **David** *walking to the lectern to read Commandment Number 1, which is projected on the screen.*

Commandment Number 1: Thou Shalt Tolerate Living in a Rat-Infested Dystopia.

Video projection shows scrambling rats while **David***'s voiceover says:*

Ain't they wonderful the way they burrow.

Sometimes I get lonely and these rats have now become friends.

Oh look there's Susan, I've got names for most of them.

Cheeky little things.

I've got a feeling that this Tory government want us to go the same way.

These rats aren't frightened of eating each other.

None of us need to starve.
Look at them chopping at the leg, nothing goes to waste.

Video ends.

Welcome to my world. I'm fast approaching sixty, and early in my career I had the belief that I wanted to change the world. I'm still waiting for a call from his holiness the Dalai Lama. I looked back over my life and took stock, I felt responsible for humankind, but I feel like I have failed in my mission.

Keep it light, keep it frothy.

Since I have been invaded by rats in my home I have become an expert on how to keep the rats out, and this involves the skilful use of wire wool, expanding foam and broken glass.

Projected image shows a rat sculpture.

Those of you like me who might have got a grade E at art A-level.

Being artistic I've made a sculpture. It is of course the Buddha.

The Buddha provides me with moments of calm in a sea of rats – but you can make anything.

Rather than the rats being a problem and invasion, see it as a ready food source.

We're on the run up to Christmas, what a lovely stocking filler *Cooking with Rats* by, say, Jamie Oliver is coming out, fifty tantalising dishes involving rats. He's generously showing the poor what they can do with dead or dying vermin.

As I say, I'm approaching sixty. How did I end up here with all my talents? After all, I'm still an underground artist and must live in grinding poverty. Even though I'm grateful for a roof over my head, I sometimes think where's the Tuscan villa, where's the infinity pool? Maybe I should have developed the instincts of a cornered starving rat. Which you need in showbiz. If only I was more rat-like.

People have said to me, David, if only you could visualize your life differently, if only you could visualize, then your problems would melt away and you'll soon have homes all over the world, all with infinity pools.

As I approach sixty I have an ambiguous attitude to life, as I look at society I can't see it turning into the freewheeling bohemian smorgasbord utopia that I was looking for.

Short audio clip of **David** *singing 'I'm so unworthy' on repeat.*

Ends with **David** *reading Commandment Number 2, which is projected on the screen.*

Commandment Number 2: Thou Shalt Not Make Captain Mainwaring Out of Shirley Bassey.

Video projection shows Captain Mainwaring in the British sitcom Dad's Army, *mixed with footage of Shirley Bassey on the* Morecambe and Wise Show *1971.* **David** *talks while the video is playing:*

It was assumed that I'd naturally become a Captain Mainwaring type figure; patriarchal, assertive, always in charge, life-sapping, no imagination, uptight with no feelings, dreary horrible people.

But all along it was more my natural inclination to be Shirley Bassey and you cannot make Captain Mainwaring out of Shirley Bassey. Self-expression rather than self-importance.

David *sings 'The minute you walked in the joint.' You get the idea.*

I'm a child of the 1960s but it could have been 1853. The year of the great exhibition. It was me versus the sea for my father's affection, who was in the merchant navy and the sea won.

Blackpool, believe it or not, was heteronormative. I found my space in Lucy's Bar, a queer space in Blackpool, that was just off Talbot Square.

When people are homophobic, they are normally obsessed by sex, particularly anal sex. Most of us are just looking for a companion to escort us around, a national trust property.

Going back to Lucy's Bar, once you had got through the National Front you could go downstairs into a windowless basement and meet people who knew that they were never going to turn into Captain Mainwaring but they might have an attempt at being with Shirley Bassey, so for me it was like being at home. I felt very protected by lesbians who weren't afraid of using a pool cue over somebody's head if they felt someone was being overtly predatory.

Yes, it was a safe space.

Towards the end of the evening we would form a circle and hold hands in unity before going back into the straight world patrolled by the National Front.

And we would always sing this song made famous by the Brotherhood of Man.

David *sings:*

'United We Stand, divided we fall, and if our backs should ever be against the wall, we'll be together, together you and I' . . . (*sings like Shirley Bassey towards the end.*)

At last I found my own safe place where other people related to the glamorous world of Shirley Bassey as opposed to Captain Mainwaring.

Ends with **David** *walking to the lectern and reading Commandment Number 3, which is projected on the screen.*

Commandment Number 3: Thou Must Stay Alive, Even If it's Just to Spite Others.

I've taken stock of my life, I'm sixty and I've got a new chat up line:

Hi, I'm David, you can call me Dave,

I have to glue in quite a large partial denture,

I'm no stranger to anxiety or depression, and sometimes both at the same time.

I haven't really looked after myself, so I may have a heart attack or a stroke at any second.

I'm offering you the opportunity to be my nurse, to look after me until the day I die.

What more could I offer anybody?

Please form an orderly queue after tonight's show.

When you take stock of your life you realise that not everything in life goes to plan, it can veer off.

People can let you down especially if you have expectations. A luxury of our age.

Let's go into the world of art.

An image of Théodore Géricault's The Raft of the Medusa *is projected on the screen.* **David** *moves towards the screen and points to the painting.*

David *asks the audience* – Does anyone know the painting?

It's *The Raft of the Medusa* painted in 1818 by Géricault.

It's a wonderful subject matter, as it ties into the times that we are living in.

The *Medusa* was a magnificent ship that ran aground on a sand bank and started to sink.

The elite on the ship were given lifeboats and people like us, the avant-garde were put onto a makeshift raft. This raft was tied to the lifeboats but the lifeboats weren't going away fast enough, so they cut the rope and cut the makeshift raft adrift. There were 147 people on board the raft. Some of the desperate souls got thrown into the water, others were eaten like rats and pieces of human flesh we nailed to the raft. Only fifteen survived as the ship, which is tiny in the painting, eventually came to rescue them.

I actually find hope in this picture.

Now in contemporary society we can't see a ship on the horizon. Yachts of the super wealthy would drive past and leave us to drown. They don't want us to unify and change the world we live in.

Let us unite and fight the real enemy, until I can say that capitalism is a wonderful, kind, all inclusive, genius invention. I can't because part of me thinks it's the most weird, satanic, evil, painful system that anyone could ever advocate.

That's why we are living in a rat-infested dystopia.

I'll leave you with that thought.

David *returns to the lectern.*

I don't know about you, it might be conditioning but when you meet somebody new you have the inclination to look at that the person and think, this new person, are they better than me or less than me.

And a kinda mantra forms in my mind:

Is this person Better than or Less than?

Better than, Less than?

We could all do it together –

Better than, Less than?

Better than, Less than?

Chants with audience.

Ends with **David** *repeating:* 'Thou must stay alive, even if it's to spite others.'

David *recites Commandment Number 4, which is projected on the screen.*

Commandment Number 4. Thou Must Not Mistake Wealth for Success.

This is probably how you imagine me.

Video projection shows **David** *living his glamorous, successful life.*

This is probably how you imagine me, and not living in a rat-infested dystopia.

Thou shalt not mistake wealth for success, that's what I keep telling myself. I'd rather be depressed in first class discussing my Tuscan villa rather than being depressed in economy discussing rats in my kitchen.

People say 'money can't buy happiness' – you're joking.

Jim Bowen from *Bullseye* had a phrase, 'This is what you could have won.'

I always think of this in terms of my own life.

It has resonance, I've plateaued in show business and real life – fingers crossed, it's a plateau – I am of course hoping for a lottery win.

However, let's shift the capitalist metrics – how are we measuring our success? How many of these multi-millionaires, oligarchs, walking talking parasites have had a cat named after them from some sort of obscure sanctuary in Blackpool?
Well I have. Meet David, our cover star –

The Catspaws Animal Sanctuary newsletter is projected on the screen which **David** *reads from centre stage.*

I don't think there was a more perfect cat that they could have named after me. Complex, challenging.

Short audio clip plays of **David** *singing 'I'm so unworthy' on repeat. Ends with* **David** *reading Commandment Number 5, which is projected on the screen.*

Commandment Number 5: Thou Shalt Dip in and out of Cognitive Dissonance for Thy Own Convenience.

David *walks centre stage.*

What is cognitive dissonance?

We turn a blind eye or pretend we have no knowledge.

We see the injustice but pretend it's not there.

For example, the banking crisis, who was saved? The bankers.

Who paid for the bill, the poor. we bailed out the massive, multibillion corporations.

An inconvenient truth, if we fail to see the problem, there isn't a problem.

I was in the hairdressers the other day and the hairdresser said of all the things to dream of, packing unwilling people on an aeroplane to fly them somewhere where they did not want to go, screaming, crying, feeling ultimately powerless and our current Home Secretary and that's her dream. And if we believe that we can't live without this from our Home Secretary that would be cognitive dissonance.

I mentioned Jim Bowen earlier. I've obviously got game shows in my mind.

Now let's spin the wheel of misfortune.

Where will the 'Wheel of Misfortune' land tonight?

Projected images of **David***'s painting rotating on the screen as in in a gameshow format. The paintings feature the slogans below written over the British flag:*

Fascist dystopia

AI and the surveillance society

Permanent child-poverty and food banks

Corrupt government and a complicit media

Money laundering and armaments sales

Where anti-racism campaigning is dismissed as mere gesture politics

David *reads from the lectern.*

And it's landed on Fascist dystopia – wooo wooo – Fascist dystopia.

Some of you in the auditorium tonight might say 'what Fascist dystopia'?

We're living in nirvana.

Some of you may feel that every morning or mid-afternoon when you wake up that you have to pinch yourself, because you're living in a dream.

Fascist dystopia – what Fascist dystopia?

Oligarchical money leads to the best democracy that money can buy.

Fascist dystopia – what Fascist dystopia?

To be patriotic is to support the class system. I had *Upstairs Downstairs*, now we've got *Downton Abbey*, which is charming to watch on a wet and windy Sunday but it shouldn't be used as a template for living in the so-called twenty-first century.

Fascist dystopia – what Fascist dystopia?

Children quite rightly going hungry in the foodbank.

Billionaires quite rightly buying super yachts

What Fascist dystopia? I don't see it.

A lot of the Cabinet was educated at Eton, it's just coincidence, are you mad?

What Fascist dystopia, there simply isn't – I wanted to tear an irreparable hole in the status quo, but it just repairs itself, now I want to get rid of it completely and live in a communist utopia. But I realise that communism can't be forced upon people. One has to want to be a communist.

Now let's spin the wheel of misfortune again.

Projected images of game shows appear on the screen again featuring **David***'s paintings.*

It lands on a corrupt government and a complicit media.

I want an egalitarian society but when you work out the press, television, radio, and all the rest has, for the last 100 years, exposed everyone in the auditorium to the most horrific propaganda, horrific assault on our senses, and brainwashing.

I'm going to leave it there.

David *returns to the lectern to recite Commandment Number 6, which is projected on the screen.*

Commandment Number 6: Thou Shalt Live in a Concrete Cube in the Metaverse.

Projected video of Karl-Marx-Platz, Berlin. **David** *is wearing a VR headset in front of concrete cubes, the British Royal Family on the balcony, miners strikes, South Korea, Ukraine flag, mixed with Torvill and Dean's Bolero performance from 1984.*

David *sits and watches stage left. Video ends and* **David** *gets up.*

Need I say more?

Let's romp ahead.

Ends with **David** *going to the lectern and reading Commandment Number 7, which is projected on the screen.*

Commandment Number 7: Thou Shalt Honour People, Who Are Worthy of Honoring.

In the Biblical Commandments, one is encouraged to honour our mother and father. Personally I find it difficult to honour anyone who does not honour me.

For each of us there are people who are worthy of honour, it's life affirming.

Honour someone who might be worth honoring. I would honour everyone who has come to this magnificent venue this evening, all of you are worthy of honour.

I'd like to honour the one and und only David Wojnarowicz.

Projected video of David Wojnarowic's Untitled (One Day This Kid...) *(1990) which features an image of the artist as a boy surrounded by text. The image is blown up big and slowly comes into focus.*

David *reads the Wojnarowicz text:*

> One day this kid will get larger. One day this kid will come to know something that causes a sensation equivalent to the separation of the earth from its axis.
>
> One day this kid will reach a point where he senses a division that isn't mathematical.
>
> One day this kid will feel something stir in his heart and throat and mouth.
>
> One day this kid will find something in his mind and body and soul that makes him hungry.

One day this kid will do something that causes men who wear the uniforms of priests and rabbis, men who inhabit certain stone buildings, to call for his death.

One day politicians will enact legislation against this kid.

One day families will give false information to their children and each child will pass that information down generationally to their families and that information will be designed to make existence intolerable for this kid.

One day this kid will begin to experience all this activity in his environment and that activity and information will compel him to commit suicide or submit to danger in hopes of being murdered or submit to silence and invisibility.

Or one day this kid will talk.

When he begins to talk, men who develop a fear of this kid will attempt to silence him with strangling, fists, prison, suffocation, rape, intimidation, drugging, ropes, guns, laws, menace, roving gangs, bottles, knives, religion, decapitation, and immolation by fire.

Doctors will pronounce this kid curable as if his brain were a virus.

This kid will lose his constitutional rights against the government's invasion of his privacy.

This kid will be faced with electro-shock, drugs, and conditioning therapies in laboratories tended by psychologists and research scientists.

He will be subject to loss of home, civil rights, jobs, and all conceivable freedoms.

All this will begin to happen in one or two years when he discovers he desires to place his naked body on the naked body of another boy.

Beat.

Short audio clip plays of **David** *singing 'I'm so unworthy' on repeat.*

Commandment Number 8: Thou Shalt Honour the Arms Trade as Thy Lord And Master.

Recently I did a painting for a group show, at a venue called HOME in Manchester.

Everybody was invited to send in a painting. I took a piece of paper and painted over it 'You are trapped on a planet of perpetual war'.

Down one side, I painted 'Your children and your children's children', and on the other side, 'ha ha ha'. I called that painting 'funnily enough'.

The painting is for sale.

As yet that painting hasn't sold.

But it made me think I need to open up other income streams.

I've launched my own shopping channel.

I'd like to introduce you to Dav£'s shopping chann£l.

Projected video of **David** *selling a domestic sized Nuclear Bomb in the style of a QVC shopping channel. A second video plays of* **David** *selling hazmat suits.*

Obviously, the armaments trade teaches us that you can make money out of destruction, it can also profit from protection.

Hazmat suits are £30 each and family packs for £100.

Commandment Number 9: Thou Shalt Input.

David *walks centre stage.*

I know a lot of you are living busy lives and are probably wondering how, and even if, you can pay for your bedsit, your night in the hostel, but I want you to open up your minds and think about your own commandment. Allow a commandment to form.

I understand I've kept your brains busy, so now I'm going to do rhythmic gymnastics, which may inspire you to come up with a commandment of your own.

David *goes stage left and warms up.*

Projected video of Minnie Ripperton's Les Fleurs *featuring a collage of flowers opening, mixed with bombs and destruction, plastic waste.*

David *does an expressive dance with ribbons during the chorus. Video ends and* **David** *walks among the audience.*

I can't help but make the observation about visualization, this is when you blame the person for being poor and you say to the poor person, it's your fault your poor. And that makes you an apologist for capitalism and fascism. If you don't believe that, the next time you see a homeless person sleeping in their own urine and living in a shop doorway, say to that person if only you could do a visualization and light a scented candle, you'll have homes all over the world.

Has anyone come up with a commandment?

David *gives out a prize of a scented candle to the best commandment.*

Ends with **David** *going to the lectern and reading Commandment Number 10, which is projected on the screen.*

Commandment Number 10. Thou Must Not Forget Thou Is Just a Grain of Sand in the Desert of Time.

You probably think of me as forever young.

I'm not going to live forever and what's the point of you honouring me once I'm dead. I'm very fortunate that I've had my eulogy written by a close friend from the underground, Gerry Potter Poet who, like myself, is dying in poverty and obscurity.

Who would like to read out my eulogy?

I'm being drawn to you – I need someone I can trust as I've got a special task for you – I'd like to reward one of you by reading my eulogy and the rest of you can imagine me dead.

David *selects an audience member to read aloud his eulogy.*

Please come and join me on stage, it's time for me to depart this world,

Before you read that, would you mind just unzipping me as I'm going to create an installation.

David *takes off his teddy bear dress and places it on the floor and then positions candles around the dress.*

I'm going to leave you now – in your best telephone voice please.

David *leaves the stage. An image of a headstone is projected upstage.* **David** *goes off stage and the selected audience member reads his obituary:*

After a long struggle with caring, David finally succumbed and died of empathy.

In the interests of the economy and saving electricity, it became patently clear he was no longer viable. So they had no alternative but to switch the life support off.

More than forty years of intolerable Hell . . . is this how you treat a supernova? Survived by a nest of rats and an avalanche of unpaid bills . . . is this how you honour a starburst?

Nameless, unremembered, abandoned, demeaned, devalued, diminished . . . is this where you place your oracles?

David gave his life to the vibrantly flaring multi-possibilities of humanity.
Laid bare his soul so our spirits may soar.

In those moments of universe empowered anarchy, the dance, the words, the fashion, the heels and of course the tights.

Oh that ethereal voice, to hear my friend sing was like listening to and tuning into the earth, sky, water, fire, air.

A shock opera of our scarred hopes, a Greek lament to our addictions, to our loves, longings and life.

Our Bible in human form, written in the Sanskrit of his soul.

His face, a million portraits, a series of unique artworks, a celebratory countenance of all our faces.

A blurring countercultural mask.

Our sacred clown, wise trickster. So many portraits, so little time.

Fly high my avant guardian angel and know from among the few you were cherished, understood and loved.

The End

Audience member has sat down. **David** *comes back on stage wearing a kaftan and encourages the audience to sing 'United We Stand' by Brotherhood of Man with him, as the lyrics are projected on the screen.*

He speaks:

We are now listening to the song that I listened to in Lucy's Bar, where we held hands in unity before going back into the straight world.

Please join me in singing the chorus

We are with each other in unity and strength.

Good night, I love you all.

David *takes a bow.*

Show plays out to Vera Lyn singing 'We'll Meet Again'.

Performance Documents

1 David Hoyle speaking from a pulpit in *Ten Commandments*, Soho Theatre, London, 2022. Photograph by Holly Revell. Courtesy of David Hoyle.

2 Théodore Géricault, *The Raft of the Medusa* (1818–19), Musée du Louvre, Paris, France.

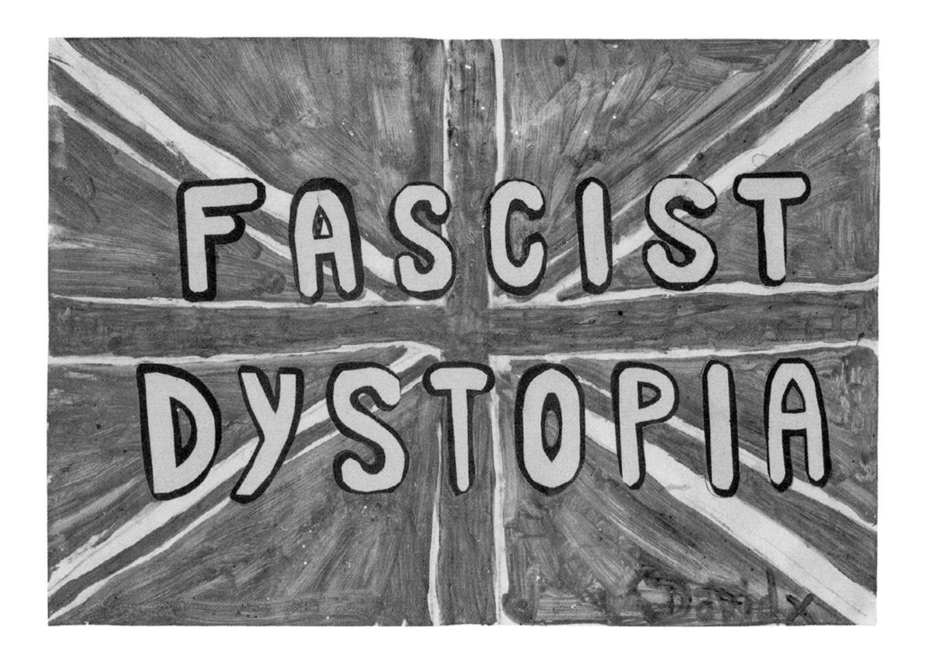

3 Hoyle's painting 'Fascist Dystopia' shown in the production. Courtesy of David Hoyle.

4 A video of Hoyle, used in the production, shows the performer wearing a VR set in front of clips of Jayne Torvill and Christopher Dean ice-skating. Screengrab from a recording of the production. Courtesy of David Hoyle.

5 Hoyle speaks in front of *a projected* image of David Wojnarowicz's *Untitled (One Day This Kid . . .)* (1990–1). Courtesy of David Hoyle.

6 Hoyle's painting 'You Are Trapped On A Planet of Perpetual War' shown in the production. Courtesy of David Hoyle.

Biographies

Artists

David Hoyle is a performance artist, avant-garde cabaret artist, actor and visual artist. For the last four decades, Hoyle has queered the boundaries between live art, performance, theatre and cabaret – conquering nightlife around the world and working extensively in film and TV. Hoyle's infamous alter-ego 'The Divine David' transported him from radical alternative settings in the 1980s to the studios of Channel 4 in the 1990s. Performing as The Divine David, an 'anti-drag queen' who combined 'lacerating social commentary' with 'breath-taking instances of self-recrimination and even self-harm', he appeared on the BBC's *Comedy Nation* (1998) and as a cameo in *Velvet Goldmine* (1998), and produced two shows for Channel 4: *The Divine David Presents* (1998) and *The Divine David Heals* (2000).

Hoyle killed the Divine David off during a spectacular show at the Streatham Ice Arena in 2000 and retreated to Manchester for 'a period of reflection'. He returned to TV screens in 2005 in Chris Morris's *Nathan Barley*, and then began performing live again, under his own name. This time round, the chances of serious injury in any given show seemed greatly reduced, but Hoyle's biting satire, bravura costumes, wicked comic timing and compelling charisma remained intact.

As well as the Royal Vauxhall Tavern (RVT), with which he is most closely associated, he's performed at the Soho Theatre, Chelsea Theatre, Battersea Arts Centre, National Portrait Gallery, Tate Britain and Victoria & Albert Museum.

In 2024 a major career retrospective called 'Please Feel Free to Ignore My Work' was held at Aviva Studios in Manchester.

Bourgeois & Maurice are the creation of writer-performers George Heyworth and Liv Morris. They met whilst studying theatre at Royal Holloway, before bursting onto London's alternative performance scene at Madame JoJo's in 2007. They've created 10 full-length theatre shows: *Social Work* (Soho Theatre, Edinburgh Fringe, 2009); *Shedding Skin* (Soho Theatre, 2010); *Can't Dance* (Sadler's Wells, 2010); *Started a Band* (Soho Theatre, UK tour, 2011); *Sugartits* (Edinburgh Fringe. Soho Theatre, UK tour, Adelaide Cabaret Festival, 2012/13); *How to Save the World Without Really Trying* (Edinburgh Fringe, Soho Theatre, UK tour, Adelaide Cabaret Festival, 2016/17). They've collaborated with artists including iconic LGBT+ club night Sink The Pink (*Santamental,* 2013) and avant-garde drag royalty David Hoyle (*Middle of the Road*, 2015). In 2017 they were commissioned by HOME, Manchester and created *Insane Animals*, an eerily prescient large-scale musical about humanity grappling with existential threats, which premiered in February 2020. In 2022 they premiered *Pleasure Seekers*, a high-octane homage to hedonism (Soho Theatre, UK tour, Adelaide Fringe, Offie Nomination).

Bourgeois & Maurice have performed at venues including Royal Opera House, Royal Academy of Arts, Southbank Centre, and toured internationally. They've released six albums, and been commissioned as songwriters by BBC Radio 3, Birmingham Rep, and Shakespeare's Globe where they created original songs for Jude Christian's innovative *Titus Andronicus* (January 2023). They earned special recognition at 2018 Raindance Film Festival for VR music video *Opinions*, and their web series *Youthanaisa* was nominated at the 2018 Stareable Awards. During lockdown they created the podcast *Curtain Twitchers*, interviewing performers from the alternative queer scene, including Justin Vivian Bond, Mawaan Rizwan, Travis Alabanza and Lucy McCormick.

Bourgeois & Maurice's work is a glittering explosion of glamour and social commentary. At the heart of all their shows is a playful fascination with the contradictions and banalities of human existence.

Dickie Beau (Richard Boyce), as a solo artist, may be best known for breathing new life into lip-synching through his distinctive playback performances. Described as 'Theatre's master of lip sync' (*The Guardian*), he has developed his solo work over nearly two decades and brought his performances to diverse contexts, including drag clubs, cabarets, nightclubs, mainstream and fringe theatres, dance spaces, cinemas, music festivals, opera houses, and art galleries.

Dickie has received multiple awards across the disciplines of theatre, dance and cabaret, including the Oxford Samuel Beckett Theatre Trust Award, London Cabaret Award for Best Alternative Performer, and Best Supporting Actor in the Off West End Theatre Awards. In Australia, he was nominated for a Helpmann Award for *Re-Member Me.*

Dickie has toured extensively with his repertoire of solo theatre shows, and has been presented at many international festivals, including: Melbourne Festival, Perth Festival, Fusebox Festival (Texas), Under the Radar Festival (New York), PUSH Festival (Vancouver), Progress Festival (Toronto), Crossing the Line Festival (New York), City of Women Festival (Ljubljana), Mayfest (Bristol), Outburst Festival (Belfast), Queer Notions (Dublin) and Brighton International Festival.

Dickie is an Artist Research Fellow at Birkbeck Centre for Contemporary Theatre and is a past recipient of a Harry Ransom Research Fellowship at the University of Texas. He has worked broadly across higher education as a visiting lecturer, workshop leader and mentor at institutions in the UK and abroad, including the Royal Academy of Arts, Royal College of Arts, University of Manchester, Chichester University, Rose Bruford College, LAMDA, QMUL and Bard College.

In theatre, Dickie has extensive experience as an actor in a range of contexts, from classical Shakespeare to pantomime to experimental physical theatre, and he has played leading roles on major stages, including London's National Theatre, Hampstead Theatre, and Salzburg Festival. Dickie's film and television work as an actor includes the BAFTA-nominated *AIDS: The Unheard Tapes* (BBC); *The Sandman* (Netflix); *The Gold* (BBC), *Bohemian Rhapsody* and *Colette.*

Ivor MacAskill (he/they) is a queer, trans, neurodivergent live artist and theatre-maker based in Glasgow, UK. They create award-winning performances and encounters for both children and adults, inspired by nature and driven by curiosity. His work is experimental, but through the use of absurdity and humour, is accessible and entertaining, aiming to make the familiar strange and the strange feel good.

With their long-term collaborator Fiona Manson, they have created several celebrated works for young children that have toured internationally since 2011, most notably the award-winning Polar Bears trilogy. As one half of Cade & MacAskill, his most recent and ambitious work to date, *The Making of Pinocchio*, has been surprising and moving audiences in Europe, Canada and Australia since its premiere in Hamburg in May 2022 and continues to tour.

They work as a dramaturg, mentor and consultant for a number of artists, particularly those live artists making a shift into creating work for children, or exploring complex themes with that audience such as gender and sexuality. He has previously been commissioned by Fierce Festival, National Theatre of Scotland, Creative Scotland, The Arches, Take Me Somewhere, The Unicorn, The Yard, Southbank Centre and Kampnagel and has toured to Lincoln Center, New York; A.S.K. in Shanghai and Beijing; Awesome Festival, Perth; FTA, Montreal; and Brisbane Festival.

www.ivormacaskill.com @ivormacaskill

Le Gateau Chocolat (he/they; George Ikediashi) is a performer and maker whose work spans drag, cabaret, opera, musical theatre, children's theatre and live art. His bewitching baritone has been heard in previous works *Le Gateau Chocolat* (2011), *I Chocolat* (2012), *In Drag* (2013 Royal Festival Hall commission) and *Black* (2014 Homotopia commission), which toured with music ensemble Psappha in 2017.

His children's show *Duckie* premiered at the Southbank Centre in 2016, and was included in the *Guardian*'s '6 of the Best Shows for Children' of the 2018 Edinburgh Fringe Festival. The show, which introduces young people to the ideas of otherness, tolerance and self-acceptance, has been presented at Theatre Royal Stratford East, Wales Millennium Centre, Roundhouse, Contact Theatre and across venues in the South East of England.

His recent production *ICONS* has toured to Sydney Festival, Wales Millennium Centre, Soho Theatre, Underbelly Southbank and more. *ICONS* has also been presented with accompaniment from the Little Coco Orchestra, a Le Gateau Chocolat initiative to support diverse musicians through the creation of an ensemble formed entirely of women of colour. This up-scaled production premiered at SPILL Festival in 2018, with a subsequent presentation at the Royal Birmingham Conservatoire as part of SHOUT Festival.

As a technically-gifted and celebrated baritone, Le Gateau Chocolat has been invited to perform at prestigious venues such as the Royal Albert Hall, Barbican Centre, Sydney Opera House, and as part of the Olivier-winning La Clique/La Soirée. He has worked with composers Julian Philips, Jonathan Dove, Jocelyn Pook and Orlando Gough. He has performed as Feste in *Twelfth Night* at Shakespeare's Globe (2017) and in the Gate Theatre and English National Opera co-production *Effigies of Wickedness – Songs Banned by the Nazis* (2018). He also appeared as part of Taylor Mac's *A 24-Decade History of Popular Music: The First Act* at London's Barbican Theatre (2019), and alongside Shaq Taylor, Adrian Lester, Beverley Knight and Clive Rowe in the guest role of Daddy Brubeck for the Donmar Warehouse's production of *Sweet Charity* (2019).

Le Gateau Chocolat most recently appeared in Wagner's *Tannhauser*, starring Stephen Gould, which opened the 108th Bayreuth Festival in 2019 and attracted headlines around the world for the reaction to his participation as a drag artist of colour.

Ray Young (they/them) is a transdisciplinary performance artist, experience maker, and writer, widely recognized for their ground-breaking work at the forefront of activism, queerness, race and neurodiversity. Their practice is centred around creating a safe space for those who exist at the intersection of multiple realities, through collaboration and resistance to traditional forms.

In recent years, Ray's work has been focused on exploring and shedding light on notions of rest, care and recovery in art, particularly as it pertains to the experiences of neurodivergent artists. Ray has been working towards creating a more holistic practice that draws together art, nature and technology, as they seek to challenge traditional capitalist ideologies of production that prioritize speed and productivity over creativity, care, and wellness.

For 2024 Ray is bringing back *OUT*, an interdisciplinary performance that defiantly challenges homophobia and transphobia across our communities. *OUT* is a duet – a conversation between two bodies, inspired by ongoing global struggles for LGBTQIA+ rights. It is a defiant challenge to the status quo, bravely embracing personal, political and cultural dissonance. Ray's other works include *BODIES*, an immersive water, light and soundscape installation that investigates the embodied experiences of our relationship to water. Through this work, Ray seeks to explore and understand the complex and multifaceted nature of our relationship with water, and to engage viewers in a transformative sensory experience that encourages reflection and introspection. Another recent work, *THIRST TRAP*, is a meditative sound piece that explores the correlation between social and climate justice, and how our actions and choices impact the world around us. Through this work, Ray invites viewers to reflect on the interconnectivity of our lives and the world we live in, and to recognise the importance of taking collective action towards building a more just and equitable future.

Ray's work has been presented widely across the UK, including in London, Cambridge, Brighton, Leeds and Edinburgh, as well as internationally including Portland, Mexico City and Venezuela. Their ground-breaking contributions to the field of performance art have earned them numerous awards and accolades, and their work continues to push boundaries and challenge conventional notions of what art can be and do.

Rosana Cade (they/them) is a renowned queer artist based in Glasgow. Their practice straddles experimental theatre, live art, cabaret, film, children's performance, site responsive and socially engaged practices. The form of their work is devised in relation to the context or inquiry they are responding to and they enjoy experimenting with audience perspective.

Rosana is known for some of their intimate performance work, such as *My Big Sister Taught Me This Lap Dance*, *Drag Mother* and their highly acclaimed participatory project *Walking:Holding*, which has been touring the world to over forty locations since 2011 and was made into a creative documentary in 2018 funded by the Jerwood Charitable Foundation.

They are one half of Cade & MacAskill with their life partner Ivor MacAskill, with whom they created *Moot Moot*, part of The British Council and Made in Scotland Showcase at the Edinburgh Fringe 2019; and their award-winning show, *The Making of Pinocchio*.

Rosana's work has been shown extensively across the UK and Europe, as well as touring to Asia, North America and Australia. They've worked with a range of venues and organizations including Gessnerrallee in Zurich, Kampnagel in Hamburg, Teatro Maria Matos in Lisbon, Frascati in Amsterdam, Tanzquartier in Vienna, Mousonturm in Frankfurt, Beursschouwburg in Brussels, Sophiensaele in Berlin, The National Theatre in London, LIFT, The National Theatre of Scotland, VierNulVier in Gent, Festival Trans Amérique in Montreal, The Bentway in Toronto and Arts Centre in Melbourne.

They have worked as co-devisor and performer in other artists' work such as *Cock & Bull* by Nic Green and *We Are Fucked* by Jo Bannon. They also support other artists in the role of dramaturg, director or mentor, most recently working with Tink Flaherty on *Benched*.

Rosana is the co-founder of Glasgow Buzzcut, an organization that supports live art and experimental performance in Scotland.

Sh!t Theatre is Rebecca Biscuit and Louise Mothersole. They make politically-engaged shows with a deliberately DIY aesthetic using a collage of live documentary, song, comedy and multimedia. They research, write and perform their own work, also taking on the roles of lighting designer, sound designer, video designer and musical director. Their awards and nominations include: Total Theatre Award for Best Emerging Company, Amnesty International's Freedom of Expression Award (nomination), Three Weeks Editor's Choice award, Off West End Award for Uncategorisable Work (nomination), Brighton Fringe Touring Award, Total Theatre Award for Experimentation in Form (nomination), a Lustrum Award, Off West End IDEA Award for best performance, The Holden St. Theatre Award, Adelaide Fringe Best Theatre Award and Critics Circle Award and two Fringe First Awards (2016 and 2019). Their background and training is in Live Art; their main influences are Taylor Mac, Split Britches and Bobby Baker, but they are equally inspired by *The Muppets*. Ultimately Sh!t Theatre is a queer performance art duo who make work that can fill a theatre and also be shouted over drunk people in a pub. Their last six award-winning shows have received four and five star reviews in the national press and three have been published by Oberon/Bloomsbury. Oh, and they f**king love Dolly Parton.

Vijay Patel (he/they) is a performance artist and access consultant/coordinator for theatre and TV industries. His work crosses live art, performance art and queer club/cabaret. The work they make predominantly surrounds cultural identity, making autobiographical/political work to shift perceptions and uplift marginalized, intersectional identities. Their debut solo show, *Pull the Trigger*, explored Indian corner shop culture, work, migration and queerness. It premiered at SPILL National Platform (2016), went on to Camden People's Theatre Sprint festival 2017 and an ACE-funded tour in autumn 2018 (Camden People's Theatre, Colchester Arts Centre, Norwich Arts Centre). The show went on a final ACE-funded UK tour in spring 2020 to Theatre in the Mill (Bradford), with further dates cancelled due to Covid-19. Their second solo show, *Sometimes I Leave*, explored their experience of autism, access and the need to sometimes leave difficult, often inaccessible situations. It was co-commissioned by Word of Warning, Contact and STUN for Works Ahead 2018 in Manchester. It then went on an ACE-funded UK tour in autumn 2019 to Ovalhouse, The Marlborough Theatre Brighton and Colchester Arts Centre. Other work includes: *The Weighting Game* (University of Chichester, Rich Mix and Latitude Festival 2015), *Walking the Line* (Duckie Family Legacy, Latitude Festival 2018, Aldgate Square Festival, Fierce Festival, Arcola Theatre, Dice Festival) and *I Died A Hundred Times* (Artsadmin, Toynbee Studios). Vijay has also worked alongside artists/companies including: Hunt and Darton, Sh!t Theatre, FK Alexander, Andy Field/Krista Burane, Greg Wohead and Scottee and Duckie. Vijay is currently Associate Director/Thinker in Residence at Colchester Arts Centre.

Editor

Fintan Walsh is Professor of Performing Arts and Humanities and Head of the School of Creative Arts, Culture and Communication at Birkbeck, University of London, where he is Director of Birkbeck Centre for Contemporary Theatre. Fintan's books include *Performing Grief in Pandemic Theatres* (2024), *Performing the Queer Past: Public Possessions* (Methuen Drama, 2023), *Queer Performance and Contemporary Ireland: Dissent and Disorientation* (2016), and *Theatre & Therapy* (Methuen Drama, 2013; revised and expanded 2024). Previous anthologies include *Queer Notions: New Plays and Performances from Ireland* (2010). Fintan is a former Senior Editor of *Theatre Research International* and is founding Senior Editor of the Cambridge University Press book series Elements in Contemporary Performance Texts.